Tassel Moss

A Fairly Scary Fairytale

Written By

Michelle Jordan Carpenter

Illustrated By

Austin Talynn Carpenter

COWGIRL COLORING COMPANY

This is a
work of fiction.
Names, characters, places, and
incidents are either the product of the
author's imagination or, if real, are used fictitiously.

ISBN-13: 978-615-61727-5
ISBN-10: 615-61727-1

Printed in the U.S.A.

First Edition
2012

For my family, and all the mothers on the bench...

Tassel Moss

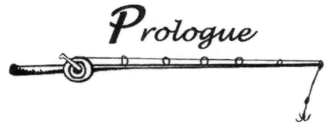

Summer 1933
Coastal North Carolina

Alone.
She preferred them alone.
Away from any hope of rescue...

The two boys didn't know they were being followed. Laughing, chasing each other—mashing more than wild-flowers under their dirty toes—they dodged and leapt over the soft forest floor. Shouts of pure happiness echoed through the trees as the youngsters were swept away by the joy of kid freedom. They loved exploring the woods. Seemed every time they played, they ventured deeper and deeper into the caverns of towering trunks, farther and farther from the security of their homes. Safety, a parting reminder from their loving mothers' lips, was the last thing on their minds.

The faster one flew ahead of the younger one as they raced amongst the trees. A marvel of nature, he was a redheaded, wild thing. His youthful body, amazing and strong, gave him an extraordinary physical advantage. He was never still—always careening down the path to dive on a find, then pouncing on the next curiosity. Preferably a toad.

The second boy—rosy cheeked with long, dark lashes—was an inspiration. Astoundingly bright and inquisitive, he too thrived outdoors. Discovery was his passion. He was apt to linger and investigate, holding up his find for inspection and wonder before carefully returning to its place. Calmer, slower, he stopped to study everything.

But their differences presented no bother. Their clever minds held the bonds of a forever friendship. "Friends for life!" That was their battle call. The way they figured it, in this solitary place—except for the super-duper multitudes of forest creatures and creepy crawlies—the only evidence of life were their hollering voices and the flattened trails left by their footprints. They'd have boldly bet their bug collection (chiefly their gargantuan hissing stink beetle) that this day's leisurely hours of tromping its woodsy depths was one more of oodles to come. That's what they thought.

They were wrong.

Off to dig up the fattest worms they could find with a dull pocketknife, the boys were bound for a great fishing expedition on the banks of the mighty Neuse River. The weather was plumb perfect. They knew a secret spot under a grove of Live Oaks where the earth was always soft. Worms there were legendary.

Within sight of the worming grounds, the swift one slowed to his languid walk. Bragging some, he claimed, "There's times I don't even need a knife. Just stomp my foot and a fat one shoots clear out of the ground into my hand. All you have to do is bang on the right spot and—"

A forceful blow whiplashed his head. He staggered to his knees and reached in his hair, feeling fleshy chunks. Examining the globs stuck on his fingers, he looked around confused. That's when he spotted his buddy eying him victoriously. A second mushroom was already loaded in the fist of his torqued right arm.

Both boys erupted with gleeful threats as another great war began. They peeled off in opposite directions, gathering armfuls of the abundant assault fungus. Like miniature soldiers, they rolled and darted and ducked behind trees, only to re-emerge pelting each other with the largest grenades they could plunder beneath the ferns. Twenty minutes later, exhausted and low on ammo, they called a ceasefire and sprawled out flat on their backs, showered in the guts of a hundred mushrooms. Their excitement— talking over one another, interrupting, describing in detail their precisely rocketed strikes—was euphoric. The accounts kept them laughing until they couldn't breathe.

Lying on the ground, they gazed up beyond the steeples of green canopy toward morsels of blue sky. Golden sunlight slid between the trees in rippling columns. Wisps of wind forced the Spanish moss, hanging thick as curtains from every limb, to dance in sudden poufs. It was eye-catching, almost pleading to be noticed—and one boy did notice.

"Tillandsia usneoides. Look at all that mossy stuff." The bookish one was acquainted with the botanical names of most the locals. "There's so much of it right here. Strange, ain't it?"

"Yep, strange," his friend agreed, taking in the frilly sight. "Lots more. Wonder why that is?"

"Such a swell plant, latchin on all over the place. Specially here close to the water. *Dagnabbit!* It's all over these trees. No roots. Just sucks water right outta the air." He blew an impressed whistle. "Wowee. Don't it remind ya of a scary picture show?"

"I wouldn't know. Reminds me of graveyards though," his friend said.

"Yeah, it's pretty and creepy at the same time. Looks all dead and crispy. Like the grey strands would turn to crumbles if ya squeezed a clump. But it's squishy with life. Really neato."

As he lay in the leaves scanning up and down an oak, something else caught his eye. An unfamiliar specimen was perched on a decaying log inches from his outstretched fingers. He thought they'd encountered every insect their forest sheltered. His rag-tag collection (in old jam jars punctured with lots of air holes) was filled with bunches of wigglies. But this new guy was nothing like the others. This caterpillar was extremely large. A vivid green stripe traveled the length of its tubular body. Blue tufts and black spines grew from its bristly back. A single antenna—flared at the tip with a flourish of fine gold hairs—sloped from the crown of its smooth bronze head.

As it sat motionless, the boy actually observed the bug inspecting him. His very reflection was mirrored in its dark eyes. He shifted position on the ground, rising to an elbow. The caterpillar's head rose as well. Its bulging eyes tracked and held his movement. The boy blinked. It blinked. He did it again. It did it again. He jumped up intrigued. It reared up ready to spar. Giggling, he dug his hands into the pockets of his grubby overalls.

"What do we got? What do we got?" His excitement was uncontainable.

"What do we got for what?"

"That hairy little booger." He pointed at the prickly critter.

Rolling over to see, his buddy scrambled to one knee, meaning to scoop it up.

"Stop! Don't touch it!" He flung his arms out to block him. "It could be poisonous. That color pattern's a warnin to predators. It might pack a wallop of a sting. We need somethin to pick it up safe. Ya got anythin to wrap it in?"

His friend stood up patting at his thighs, but finding nothing of use. "Hey, is it looking at me?" He leaned in cautiously. "Look at that. Now it's looking at you."

"I know! It is ain't it?" The boy was near to bursting. "It's been watchin us this whole time. What a wacky fella. Ever seen one like it?" He didn't wait for an answer. "I wanna take it home. Ya don't got nothin?"

"No, dern it. But I can get something." The last time they played shipwrecked pirates burying stolen treasure, they'd hauled their bag of pirate booty somewhere near this very thicket. He'd find it—dump the rocks and be back in a flash. "Wait here." He took off.

He didn't even say goodbye.

By himself in the hush of quiet, the eager boy knelt by the caterpillar. Again they tilted their heads in unison. The boy was delighted. This was a rare find.

In the trees there was movement. He spun around when he heard the twig snap. He didn't think to arm himself with a stick as a misty figure took shape and approached. His sharp mind prepared no defense. It was curious when it should have been wary. His mistake. He was an engaging child and appearances can be so deceiving. With one look at her angelic splendor—her flowing white gown, cascading hair framing a lovely face, her cloak of Spanish moss—he thought she was a woodland goddess.

"Jeepers," he muttered in awe. This would truly be his most amazing story, the one he was begged to tell and retell. He wished his friend would hurry back with the bag so he too could witness the miraculous sight. Together they could share this magical encounter.

But her treachery was absolute. Approaching gracefully, she spoke to him calmly—imitating kindness. Bewitched by the perfume of her wisteria-blossom crown, the boy listened enraptured, forgetting he was covered in the grime of dirt and mushrooms. By his captivated expression—unsuspicious and impressionable—she knew he would succumb to her enchanting offer. Every child did.

Glowing with charm, she circled him slowly. Here among the ghosts of the deceived, she unveiled her cunning. A sorrowful wind pulsed through the trees as the Spanish moss blew an ominous warning. If only he'd looked up, he certainly would have sensed it—would have heard the grieving memories of fear and run for his life. But he didn't look up. He noticed none of it. Forgot even the caterpillar. In his short lifetime, these woods had proven full of incredible surprises. He accepted them, certain that she was a divine revelation—a gentle spirit.

She was not.

A shimmering object rested in her hand. She extended a slim arm, holding the thing out for him to admire, swishing it merrily from curved and blackened fingertips. Softly she spoke to him—her laughter tinkling through the pines like music. Suddenly his face lit up. He looked happy as his head tipped back and his eyes closed in thought. Grinning, he opened them and began to speak—stepping forward with his small hand reaching for her sleek golden tassel.

Not until he touched it and felt the heart-stopping jolt did he hesitate. He tried to pull away. He couldn't. He tried to scream. He gagged. His tongue disintegrated into bitter ash—powdering his chin—as a ringing exploded in his ears, then extinguished, sparing him the sound of his own cells and blood vessels crackling to oblivion. His final act, as he gaped into her narrowing eyes, was to choke on his dying breath. Lifeless and withering, he collapsed to the ground. His warm body and soul were replaced by a grey, tangled tuft of stringy remains. It was quick.

Standing over her kill, she paused to survey the woods. Today was special. Hence, she would not linger to snare the friend. Instead she retrieved her caterpillar and returned it to her hip satchel. It crawled in over the others and squirmed to the bottom whilst she wound the tassel in her hair and sighed, well pleased. Soon enough she would return for the next, and the next, and the next.

As for this fresh clump of a lad, he would be fastened to her cloak alongside the other children she trickily ended. In time, this newest mossy lot would be flung to a branch—their forlorn eternity spent moaning in the breeze. Then she would begin anew, assembling her next cloak of slain loners—as she had done for centuries. After all, her endless debt must be paid. The powerful spell was ironclad.

With black-tipped fingers, she spiked up what was left of the boy. Humming softly, her filmy gown billowing around her ankles, she ascended on air. To the mist-caged treetops she soared with her mossy prize clasped to her breast.

Hoping that his friend was watching.

Standing over her kill, she paused to survey the woods.

PART I

Chapter 1

Summer

Coastal North Carolina

"Aye, aye, Skipper!"

They drove through the gates of Camp Seamist with the rental car windows all the way down. It was just that kind of fantastic—no air-conditioner needed—summer morning. A few yards up the road, another girl wearing cutoffs and a sailor cap hollered it.

"Aye, aye, Skipper!"

From the passenger seat, Nellie glanced at her dad with an incredulous you-gotta-be-kiddin-me grin. "Seriously?" She asked. But he was beaming.

As they rolled down the lane, a line of fist-pumping gals shouted the same cutesy greeting at them—one at a time. Nellie thought it was totally wacked and outright weird. Back home in Los Angeles, strangers rarely ever looked at each other in passing. Too annoyed they'd be bugged for a dollar.

Not like this state—where everyone made a point to be social. Eye-contact with a smile and a hello, that's the way they did it.

Nellie wasn't completely surprised by it. She'd been to North Carolina before, lots of grandmom visits. But this particular howdy was big doins even for the South. With that in mind, she stalled until they were halfway down the road before doing the unavoidable. Following her dad's lead, she chirped the showy, "Aye, aye, Skipper!" right back out the window at the welcoming brigade of teenage counselors. Hers just had a hint of sarcasm.

For a kid raised on movie sets (both her parents were actors) the whole exchange made cool-customer Nellie feel somewhat awkward. She knew her face had turned bright dork red, a face already marred by the absence of her customary thick, black eyeliner.

"Thirteen-year-olds don't wear that stuff, especially at camp," her sister had criticized. "You already have blue hair. Those southern girls are gonna think you're a mega oddball, which you are, but looking like a Goth groupie won't make you any friends. Give it a rest, piss-ant. Leave it home." Irritating advice from an older sister who routinely mistook Nellie for a pesky gnat she'd rather swat.

Based on that sisterly guidance, Nellie had caved. Robbed of her fashionable hipness, she sat slouched in the car with bald eyes and her beloved blue streak braided and hidden within her long, brown hair. The bland look was utterly regrettable and pretty tragic. But Nellie wasn't a total dweeb. Her contraband eyeliner was a stowaway—just in case Miss Pinch-Face-Know-It-All was wrong.

Much as Nellie was feeling like the blushing nerd of the west, her dad was having the exact opposite reaction. She could actually feel the pride pinging off him. As a past camper at this very camp, he was about to bust-a-gut watching her reaction to the down-home arrival ritual. Driving uncharacteristically slow, sitting with his good posture and that up tilt to his chin, he kept eye-balling her with his pleased grin.

"Knock it off, dad." Her belly was already brewed-up and giggly. He was just making it worse.

"What?" He said—all phony innocent.

"Stop." She punched an embarrassed love-slug on his arm to prove she was serious.

"Ouch!" Steering with his knee and rubbing his shoulder, he pretended it really hurt. But he didn't miss a beat waving at the next perkster greeter.

Nellie's butterflies actually started building the night before. The restaurants and hotels in the folksy town where they'd spent the night were swarming with families bringing their sons and daughters to sailing camp the next morning. Camp Stingray for boys. Camp Seamist for girls. Run by the same organization, but separate by gender. Purposely set apart by five miles of very dense, tick infested woodland. Her dad would be dumping her here and flying home alone. He was due back in Hollywood to start shooting a western.

In a month, when he flew back with cowboy whiskers, her butthead sister, and her mom for the Nellie pick-up, she'd have impressive skills as a sailor babe. She'd know how to sail a boat and tie a ton of nautical knots. She'd be able to navigate by the stars and understand the workings of an outboard engine. She'd have indulged in every water sport imaginable—from kayaks and canoes to water skiing and kneeboarding. Not to mention archery, golf, tennis, riflery, an equestrian stable stocked with horses and trainer girls in their black leather boots, a zip line with a lake splashdown, a giant rock wall, and literally a gazillion other outdoor activities. All under the watchful eyes of these bubbly summer job counselors and adult staff—including art teachers, fulltime photographers, a health clinic with a doctor and a nurse, and best of all, an off-the-hook cafeteria serving three square meals of lip-licking southern food, topped off by four-layer frosted cakes. Most definitely a new improved and highly skillful Nellie would be returning to California.

She owed her dad big. After all, he was the reason she was even on this adventure. Back when she started her begging campaign to go to camp, this was the only place he'd consider. The fact that it was on the opposite side of the country and required a round trip plane ticket didn't bother him one iota.

Her mom, however, needed some serious convincing. The first time it came up, she got her ditsy, preoccupied look, didn't ask a single question, and quietly left the room. When her dad started filling out the paperwork anyway, her mom figured it would never really happen. Nellie herself was a tad tweaked at the thought of going so far for so long. But then the Seamist video arrived in their e-mail. That there existed such incredible summer perfection, filled with the best of the best, and that her daughter was maybe going to experience it—well, that got her mom's happy tears flowing.

"Guess I can go, dad. Mom's crying." Nellie busted her.

"Am not," her mom lied, wiping her tattletale drops. She was the proud owner of a loving heart and a terrible actress at hiding it.

Two weeks later when her dad came home with an enormous rolling duffel bag, her mom actually led the charge packing the list of "Recommended Personal Items". Everything Nellie would wear—day and night—from nine swimsuits, to fifteen pairs of shorts and tees, to dresses for the Saturday night dances at the boy's camp, to a rain suit, a mismatch of pajamas, jeans and sweatshirts, countless pairs of socks and undies, tennis shoes, flip flops, lake shoes, hats, four sets of twin sheets, a pillow, a blanket, bath towels, beach towels, toiletries, stationary, her digital camera and a bucket. All of it crammed into her one allowed bag. Tackling that list and then closing that duffel was a Herculean feat. Nellie had to sit on it. When the heavy-duty zipper zipped without busting, her mom raised both arms like a ref signaling a fair kick through the goal posts.

Her dad called ahead, setting up an account at the camp store. For the forgottens. Or more lotion and shampoo or candy bars and gum. The deal was—what she didn't spend she could keep, money for school clothes when she got home. Incentive to budget her taste buds wisely.

So that was that, Nellie got her wish. She was a summer camper after all. Ecstatic, she found herself across the country in the Carolinas with her mother's blessing, her dad as short-term chaperon, and a sister who was outstandingly pea green jealous. It was awesomeness.

Hopping out of the rental after parking on the grass, Nellie's dad popped the trunk and heaved out her bag. With one fluid motion, he clicked up the handle and flipped it over on its wheels. It left twin roller ruts as they walked to the sign-in tent, manned by more smiling college girls. Since her dad was an early riser—meaning never late for nothin— she was in the first wave of arrivals. They checked in and found out she was assigned to Cabin 21, so they strolled over lugging her fifty pounds of stuff.

Four super personable counselors (wearing sailor caps and shorts) met them at the door. The girls showed them around the cozy bunk-filled cabin—where Nellie could unpack, where to stow her duffel, what hook to hang her towel on, which locker was hers, which bed. *Yes!* She was on top right by a window. Actually, more like a square hole in the wall. There was no glass, no lock, just a very fine screen. That got her attention.

But the view was something else. Before a wall of tall pines marked the wood's edge, it was all flat acres of fresh cut grass, spaciously arranged with cabins and camp buildings. As she looked to the right, the ground sloped and turned into the Neuse River. Near its banks, three huge swimming pools—complete with water slides, diving boards, racing lanes, and rope swings—sparkled in the sun. In front of the pools, a complex obstacle course rose from the grass, beckoning contenders to crawl, hurdle and climb. State-of-the-art athletic equipment was absolutely everywhere, just like in the video. It was pretty rad.

And that was just the beginning. Dozens and dozens of upside-down kayaks and canoes lined the shore. Various types of paddles leaned against a nearby cabin. Enough orange lifejackets to float an army hung from an outdoor rack. On a shelving unit next to all that, Nellie could see loads of water skis and wakeboards and kneeboards. And fishing stuff too, there was a huge bin of poles.

Beyond those goodies, a pier with a watchtower guarded the waterfront. Docked around it, all size sailboats, motorboats, and a yacht caught Nellie's eye—bobbing for attention. She could practically hear the boats calling her to sprint across the lawn and hoist the sails, lift the anchor and be whisked away by the wind. Any feelings she'd had about a teary goodbye were evaporating. It proved she really was the I-dare-ya type, not the couch-potato texting type.

"Nell Belle." Her dad had to say it twice before she snapped out of her ogling daze and turned from the window. She couldn't even attempt playing it cool anymore. She was way too mind-blown.

"So, what do you think? You too scared to be left alone? Should we go on home?" But of course he was smiling.

"Yep, grab my bag. Let's blow this dump."

"Yeah, right!" He laughed at her full-born glow. It wasn't lost on him that within ten minutes of arriving, she was already and officially one happy camper.

"Well, let's walk around, get a lay of the land, then grab some of that good-good cafeteria food. I gotta hit the road." He wrapped his arm around her as they went outside. For a guy who didn't live in the state anymore, his visiting schedule was mighty impressive. He was headed down the highway to surprise his own sweet mama and shoot skeet with some hometown buddies before his flight. Nellie was A-OK with him leaving. She was ready to fly solo.

After a buffet lunch of ambrosia salad, fried chicken, smoky collards, mac'n'cheese, maple syrup biscuits, coconut cream pie and icy sweet tea, her dad made the rounds saying his thank yous and goodbyes to the staff. Southern hospitality just rolled off his tongue—pleasant as melted milk chocolate. He was a real charmer, Nellie had to give him that. But she stayed on guard for any cracks he might make at her expense. Except for teasing a lunch lady—telling her that all she needed to feed Nellie was a plate of granulated sugar packets and a couple of coffee creamers—he pretty much behaved.

Soon they were back in front of her cabin, hugging goodbye with the universal pat, pat, pat. He told her not to sail off to Ocracoke Island and marry a pirate. She told him not to drive too fast. They both laughed at the boring advice. He turned to go but then turned back, reaching inside his shirt pocket like he'd forgotten something.

"Here, you want these cigarettes?" He asked all sneaky.

"Really dad? Gross." She looked around annoyed, hoping nobody heard. She knew he was only kidding. He didn't even smoke. Well not anymore. No doubt he was one of the Camp Stingray rascals sneaking smokes back in his day. Frowning, she shook her head in disapproval.

"Probably the right call." He winked. "All righty then. Don't get caught by the sheriff having too many beers."

"Dad…" She rolled her eyes and crossed her arms with one jutted hip. Her head was still going back and forth.

"Last offer." He patted his back pocket. "You want these stink bombs?"

"No way!" Her eyes lit up and she shot out a hand.

Stinkers were the worst things ever invented and perfection if she needed to whomp a prank on someone.

"You wish!" He whacked her hand away. Still, he was tickled that she'd inherited at least traces of hooligan. "That's my girl."

He gave her one last hug before walking away for real and loading into his SUV. She watched him back up off the grass and pull onto the paved road. A rockabilly accordion tune blared through his car speakers as his arm stuck out the window, waving. She could see him watching her in his rearview mirror so she waved back. The road dipped and his car disappeared behind the stables, headed toward the gate. The "Aye, aye, Skipper!" girls were long gone—off to meet up with their cabins full of eager young campers.

"Nellie, right?"

Nellie spun around. A blonde with a side braid was standing in the doorway—her head counselor, Kate.

"You the one from Hollywood?" She looked Nellie up and down.

"That'd be me." Nellie quit waving and did her best shy grin, complete with a cute little curtsy.

Kate strode right up, reached in Nellie's hair and grabbed the hidden braid. "Is this stuff permanent," she demanded, pulling it out and scrutinizing the turquoisey blue.

Nellie's body tensed. "Um…yeah… Is that a problem?"

"Only if you don't tell me what ya use and how to do it. It's way snazzy!"

Nellie's body relaxed. "Oh. Sure. It's like…totally easy."

"Goody." Kate let go of the braid but left it showing. "I love havin the smart girls in my cabin." She put her arm around Nellie and guided her toward the door. "Well...come on in then. We got some serious business to attend to."

By her animated lilt, Nellie knew exactly what she meant. Now that most everybody had arrived and the parents were leaving, the get-to-know-you fun and games were about to start. She walked inside calm as could be, set to check out her cabin mates. The sense of freedom welling-up in her felt tremendous. She was happy—not the slightest bit nervous. Here she was in summer camp paradise where the blue sky carried a warm breeze, the activities were endless and stocked with fun friends, the food was all-you-can-eat and pretty darn good, and nothing bad ever happens...

Chapter 2

A week later in the middle of a balmy night—whizzing down the zip line dressed in a furry rabbit costume—something woke Nellie from her dream.

"Nellie?" She heard her name and her eyes popped open. "You awake?" It was her new friend, Gwen, the next bunk over. "Ya hear that?" The girl sounded scared.

Before Nellie could moisten her mouth to answer, a faint scratching vibrated inches from her head. She froze and instinctively held her breath. The hairy spiders living in the rafters already gave her the willies. Now that flimsy screen window had her fully flipped-out. Lying on her back completely still, she cut her eyes over to look. A shadow *was* outlined in the framework. The pit of her stomach lurched when it moved ever so slightly. The sound came again— metallic scraping on wire mesh. Goosebumps rose between the damp hairs on her neck.

"Gwen…" She squeaked the girl's name in quiet panic. The scratching stopped. A swooshing noise, like heavy fabric, replaced it—then silence.

Gwen moved first. Whipping off her sheets, she crawled to her knees and stared out the window. Aside from a caterpillar on the screen, she couldn't see much. Thunderstorms had rolled in during the late afternoon and clouds were still hanging around, overpowering the stars. The moon was nowhere to be seen. Bolstered by Gwen's nerve, Nellie sat up. The caterpillar plopped in a puddle as they pressed their faces against the mesh, looking toward the woods. In the distance, right before disappearing into the trees, the girls thought they saw a hunched-over shape.

"What was that?" Nellie whispered shaky.

Gwen couldn't answer. Her face was petrified with eyes so huge they seemed stuck.

Intent on a non life-threatening explanation, Nellie recalled something promising. "Doesn't Mrs. Beauxleney have a dog?" The camp director did keep her Boykin Spaniel at her house on the grounds. Maybe it was on a nosey midnight stroll. That would make sense.

"Either that was Mrs. B's dog else we fixin to be black bear buffet," murmured Gwen. Now it was Nellie's turn at the scary-eyed face.

"And we're supposed to fall back asleep now," croaked Nellie. "Feel my heart." Her pajama top was jumping with every one of her banging beats.

"Mine too." Gwen was breathless. "Think I need me one of my daddy's itty-bitty heart pills."

Nellie was way too freaked to stay put and braved the five-foot drop, stretching from her top bunk over to Gwen's top bunk. "And here I thought all I had to worry about eating me were the mosquitoes and the crocodiles." Nellie was fans of neither.

Gwen slapped her pillow and put her head down giggling, all very quietly. "*Gurl*...there no crocodiles here."

"Really," whispered Nellie—looking seriously relieved. "I heard there were. Man, I can't tell you how much better that makes me feel."

"We got gators, honey. *Al-li-gators.*" Gwen elongated the word for dramatic punch. "But don't you worry none. Them scaly dudes won't be munchin your skinny legs. They can't afford no camp. You wanna dance with a gator you gonna have to go somewhere else."

"Thanks for clearing that up, Gwen-do-lyn." Nellie elongated her name with mock gratitude. "Now I'll be way more relaxed splashing around out there." Talking softly, she switched to a British accent. "Sorry for the inconvenience. No eating me today. You 'aven't paid the fee." Gwen grinned like she was pure silly. "I'm not kidding, Gwen. Every time I swim in that river I hear the theme from *Jaws* playing."

"That's cause you from Hollywierd, Nells. All y'all got hunky pool boys with jugs of chemicals. Here in the South, you gotta jump into nature. Let the fishies nibble your toes. Nothin better than that. I swum my whole life in lakes and rivers. Once you catch your first tadpole, you won't go for that city-girl livin no more."

Nellie was skeptical. Her house did have a big blue, chlorinated pool. She absolutely loved it. She was a goggle-wearing water-baby for sure. The kind that liked to know exactly what was underneath her in the depths—preferably rubber torpedoes and diving rings. This no-see-ums swimming required a leap of faith and a private pep-talk every time she jumped in. To hear Gwen talk, swimming in river water was just the best experience ever. But that was Gwen about absolutely everything.

"The cutest flip flops ever!"

"The yummiest body splash ever!"

"The cheesiest nachos ever!"

Gwen was the most positive person Nellie had ever met. This feisty southern belle—whose actual ancestors were plantation slaves and whose family now owned a chain of barbeque restaurants across the Carolinas—was one more reason Nellie was having a love affair with camp. Seemed Gwen's personal ambition was to brand everyone she came across with her infectious goodwill. Seven days in and already Nellie hoped they'd be friends for life.

Sitting shoulder to shoulder on Gwen's bed, the two chattered quietly for the next hour—looking through the window, waiting out the intervals until the clouds parted briefly, watching for the dogbear to come back—not tired one single bit.

Like all mornings at seven-thirty sharp, the rapid bugle call of "Reveille" blared over the camp loudspeakers. Rise and shine time. Nellie's groggy eyes opened to the sight of five prettily manicured brown toes nearly sticking up her nose. Rolling over, she shut her eyes and continued lying there—wondering just how long she could put off getting up—when a slap stung her fanny.

"Move it, Tootsie."

A squirming Gwen was trying to extract herself from twisted sheets, an epic struggle of girl vs. cotton. Nellie's slow-working brain finally figured out the problem. She was on the sheets, penning Gwen in. She didn't need a second booty-smack warning.

"Moving," she grumbled in compliance.

Lumbering over to her own top bunk, the first deafening song from Kate's iPod kicked in. The pounding rock beat and hip-hop vocals had the desired effect. Even the most stubborn sleepers began showing signs of life. Nellie indulged herself through the first chorus. After one more yawn into her cushy pillow and a lazy stretch, she sat up and jumped down.

Motivated by Lady Gaga, sixteen tousle-haired bedheads rose from their bunks and started their get-up-and-go routines. Nellie headed to the bathroom sink with her toothbrush and a generous squirt of minty paste. She had three songs to get everything done. In that amount of time, the girls were expected to dress for the day. A swimsuit under shorts and tees was the official outfit. Making beds was on that list too, as well as tidying the cabin—including a quick sweep. The tempo of moving bodies began picking up with the beat. By the end of song three, Cabin 21 was sun-screened, bug-sprayed and ready to go. Once the clean-up chores received checkmarks on the roster, the energetic group headed out the door. The morning flag-raising ceremony was next.

Like the start of a horse race, every other cabin had emptied at the exact same moment as a hungry herd of female adventurers crossed the dewy lawns and gathered at the amphitheater. Swaying arm-in-arm, they watched the camp colors rising up the poles. Three flags—the stars and stripes, the great state of North Carolina, and the official Camp Seamist pennant—hung limp in their folds, thanks to no breeze. Even at that early hour, the sun was a ball of hot as the a.m. sing-a-long (led by Mrs. B and her ever present guitar) got the blood flowing and the girls thirsty.

With the taste of cold orange juice on their minds, the crowd ambled over to the cafeteria for announcements served with a hearty breakfast. Bacon and eggs were already steaming on the plank tables—along with hash browns and toast, pastries and oatmeal, sliced fruit and yogurt, and those mini cereal boxes Nellie could never get her mother to buy. The choices of savory or sweet, either hot or cold, were deliciously numerous. And on this sultry Saturday a new excitement was in the air. Party dresses would be coming out later. The first dance at Camp Stingray was scheduled for that night.

Whoever started these camps had the right idea. The guys and gals were barely allowed to hangout. Just a pinch of socializing kept things interesting—once a week for three supervised hours did the trick. Plus the special occasions when boys were allowed in to perform their hammy skits. Other than that, they never saw each other, even out on the water. It was girls with girls and guys with guys. No distractions. No drama. It suited everybody just fine. In fact, Nellie couldn't recall ever feeling quite so pumped yet so at ease. She was surrounded by all-girl thrill seekers, doing whatever they wanted, from early-early until they dropped into bed each night. She didn't feel like she was missing out on anything. Well, almost anything. She did miss her family. Some. But she knew her parents. They'd be appalled if she wasted her time being homesick.

"Rip it up, Nellie. Have a ball. Just hang with your gang and don't go wandering off alone." That was her mom's advice. "And write to me about all the good gossip."

So she wasn't squandering a second. It was like she'd been exposed to the best disease a person could catch—an obsession for exhilaration mixed with the goal to outdo the day before. A dream existence crammed with hourly highlights. Life was good.

Leaving the breakfast table with full bellies, Nellie and Gwen deposited their dirty dishes in the k.p. bin. Faced with the first major decision of their day, the discussion to pick a morning activity heated up.

Choice 1: get on the water skiing list.
Choice 2: grab clubs and hit the golf course.
Choice 3: head to the art cabin.
Choice 4: sign up for motorboat class.
Choice 5: sail Sunfishes.
Choice 6: take the knot-tying test and get the badge.
Choice 7: go on a jeep ride through the mud.
Choice 8: report for softball.
Choice 9: fish from the dock.
Choice 10: hit the swim lake.
Choice 11: paint scenery for the skit.
Choice 12: climb the rock wall.
Choice 13: ride horses.

And that wasn't the half of it. The list was so endless, it was kind of maddening. No matter what they picked, there were ten other things they wanted to do as much. Days just weren't long enough to fit everything in.

But on this scorcher, the choice was a no-brainer. The river was calling and their afternoons were landlocked anyway. They had a set date at the rifle range and the archery field with Lee and Paige, two girls from their cabin. Lee could probably stroll out of camp and join any SWAT team—she had mad sharp-shooter skills. And Paige, though you wouldn't know it to look at her, she was tough. So far, Lee and Paige were the shoot-out winners; Nellie and Gwen hadn't beaten them once. But they weren't done trying by a long shot. A day without weapons was like a summer without popsicles. But no worries. Every whim was in abundance at this place, including one more piece of French toast stuffed with orange-zest cream cheese. Passing by a platter, Nellie nabbed a lone slice and licked her powder-sugar fingers all the way out the door.

Outside had turned brilliant. A slight breeze was stirring up light chop on the river. The girls grabbed two life vests and ran the length of the wooden dock. Luck was on their side. They were onboard with a boatload of skiers within ten minutes. Nellie had been hard at work tackling her ranks and marking them off in her little red book. Next on the list: the dreaded slalom ski. Gwen was a natural athlete and a pretty amazing skier. She'd grown up skiing with her family—brothers, parents, aunts, uncles, cousins, second cousins, and apparently half the state—since she was, as she called it, "a youngin". Water skiing was new to Nellie. With Gwen's expertise and very enthusiastic help, Nellie had managed to conquer two skis. Getting up on one was proving completely impossible.

"Today's the dang day! I can feel it! No givin up!" Gwen was like an angelic Drill Sergeant. "You make that ski do what you want it to do, not the other way around! Use your muscles, Nells. Keep the tip up and straight and keep leanin back when ya start. And don't get any slack in that rope. Let the boat pull you outta the water. Easy, right?" She slapped Nellie a high-five. "Now jump on in there, girl! Do it!"

With Sergeant Gwen's orders marching through her brain, Nellie dove in and swam to the enemy. She plunged the ski underneath the water while her lifejacket let her bob along on top. Holding the ski steady, she slipped her feet into the squeaky rubber bindings, one directly behind the other. Once snuggly in, she let go of the ski and wrapped her hands tightly around the tow bar—whereupon she immediately rolled onto her side like a dead shrimp. Mortified, she splashed and squirmed and shifted. She was rewarded by rolling all the way over on her other side. Swearing under her breath, she wiggled and maneuvered, finally centering herself over the stupid ski. Before rolling like a fool again, she quick gave the signal. The counselor revved the engine and the boat surged forward. Nellie's arms nearly yanked off, but she strangled that bar in fists of iron.

In the blur of spray and speed, she tried to keep the tip up and straight. Her legs and hands, even her abs were bearing down. She white-knuckle gripped the handle so it couldn't possibly get wrenched out of her fingers this time and made triple sure to keep the rope taut by leaning back. When her straining body stood up skiing on the one ski, she nearly wiped-out from her own excitement. The girls in the boat went nuts cheering. Yelling the loudest was Gwen. She was practically jumping right out of the back of the racing MasterCraft.

"Who's ready for their close-up now, Missy Hollywood! Roll that camera, baby! That sassy thang's a superstar!" Gwen did her own happy dance on Nellie's behalf, but she wasn't done with her new recruit just yet.

"Come on, Chicky Legs! Let's see ya fly!"

Nellie's beaming smile dissolved when she realized Sgt. Gwen was ordering her to jump the wakes. With froth misting her face at 35 mph, Nellie eyed the churning waves chasing the boat. She tried to convince herself to jump one. Since there was no refusing Gwen's command, she tightened her fingers on the wet foam rubber and decided, "What the heck." To Gwen's delight, Nellie pointed her ski to the right and angled her shoulders with a slight lean. She rocketed over the two-foot wave, going airborne for one whole second. The landing—if she could call it that—was insanely bobbly. The rope went slack. The jerk to straighten it almost made her face-plant. Only sheer determination kept her upright. She was elated. Until she realized she had to ski back—right through the teeth of the curling wake.

She lingered as long she could, bouncing over the white-caps. Long enough to work up the nerve to make a run for smoother water directly behind the boat. And long enough to get irritated—watching Gwen throwing her hands in the air, doing the what-the-heck-are-you-doin-get-on-with-it gesture. Nellie gathered her courage and faced the test. She thought it had the potential to get supremely ugly, so she sucked in as much air as her lungs would hold before aiming her body at the pint-size wave.

For the rest of the excursion, her disaster was the subject of a hysterical debate. The arguments were whether she'd overcompensated her body tilt. Whether she'd miscalculated the angle of her ski cutting through the wake. Or whether it was just the result of a bad attitude. That last one, she argued laughing, was completely false. She swore for a brief second that her confidence surfaced. The fact that the side of the ski—not the tip of the ski—met the inside of the wave was super unfortunate. Also unfortunate was the fact that she went under. Actually over and over and over.

Gwen said it looked like she'd traded skiing for gymnastics. Cartwheeling on top of the water, her ski flew off in one direction and she triple-flipped in the other. She was beyond amazed that she hadn't choked to death on a mouthful of briny water. The only real emergency—after her sensational spill—was getting her bikini bottoms back up. All in all, considering the g-forces her gangly crash generated, she knew she was lucky that swimsuit still clung to her ankles whatsoever.

The boat stayed out for a couple of hours while all the girls took turns rooting each other on. Gwen was the best of the bunch. With her jaw-dropping tricks—like skiing backward with the handlebar between her knees—she looked ready for the X-Games. Eventually the counselor sped up, accelerating in the hairpin turns and trying to dunk her. Daredevil Gwen never went down, though everyone else tasted salt. Even so, Nellie felt pretty fab about her day's achievements. Thanks to Gwen, she was getting up and staying up. And on her very last try, she skied over a wake and back—without stripping.

As the skiers headed for land, Nellie got wise to a potential problem. She was certain that by dinner time, news of her notorious spill would have spread throughout the camp. No doubt she'd be fending off dozens of jovial inquiries. She decided right then and there to condemn the story as a vicious rumor. One that she would deny, deny, deny. Especially once Gwen and the gleeful witnesses confessed, through uncontrollable shrieks of laughter, that her polka-dot bikini bottoms showed serious slippage after the first cartwheel. By the second and third, her shiny derrière was on display for all to admire. Seemed Nellie might be in for a hard time shaking credit as the inventor of a new water skiing trick. The girls in the boat already had a name for it. "A Cartwheelin Full Moon Nellie!"

By early afternoon, Gwen and Nellie were tethered to nylon ropes high above the ground. Reaching to find footholds and handholds, they were picking their way up and across the camp's colossal rock wall. It was extremely challenging—as tall as it was wide—and theirs to climb on until they ran out of strength. Gwen said it was, "The best full-body workout ever!" But after a big morning on the water, it didn't take long before Nellie's legs were done and her hands were getting tired. Gwen was slowing down too.

"What do ya say we call it," suggested Gwen. "I'm gettin plain wore out and I'm smellin me some french fries. My nose say it definitely lunchtime for the girlfriends."

Nellie was all for that. "Thank goodness. I have the total shivering quivers. Breakfast is way used up." She fiddled with her harness and started repelling from the top. "I. Need. Food." She spoke in perfect timing to her footsteps down the wall.

An earsplitting yell stopped their descent. They looked around just in time to see Lee jumping from a platform, attached to the 500-foot zip line. Her ripped body streaked over the lake in a karate-kicking Ninja pose. How she managed a war cry at peak volume for the entire length of the line was pretty radical. Lee routinely demonstrated a major case of the crazies as the most fearless female in their cabin, maybe even the whole camp. That's why she was picked first for every team. She was a lightning rod of energy and a phenom at every sport. Best of all, she was a total blast.

From the rock wall, Gwen and Nellie watched her splash-down. As she flew in for a wet landing, she purposefully aimed her heels to drench the counselor on duty. The girl knew spray was coming and dodged—unsuccessfully. Ever the class clown, Lee's high-kneed sprints out of the water were meant to be comical. Knowing that her stunt had attracted an audience, she turned and took a deep bow. Smatters of applause broke out as she unhooked the safety straps and took off her helmet. Her super-short haircut made her look like a boy. Addressing her onlookers, she struck a Miss America pose—one hand on her hip, the other robotically waving.

"World peas, baby!" She flashed a goofy grin. "My best friends are puppies!"

"Thank you, Miss Georgia," yelled Nellie. "Let's hear it for our peachy contestant!" She cupped her hands and whistled a catcall.

Lee—who only wore swim trunks and rashguards, never swimsuits—bellowed back, "I prefer the title, Madame President!"

"You got my vote, ya nut! You da man," shouted Gwen.

Lee dropped the beauty pageant routine and pumped her arms overhead, doing the double peace sign strut.

"Where's Paige?" Nellie hollered. "Let's go eat!"

"Save us seats! I'll round her up. I'm so hungry I'm fartin fresh air!" Heat didn't affect Lee. She took off jogging in the direction of the stables. Her buddy, Paige—a bona fide up and coming Charleston debutant—was a sucker for the ponies.

"Last one to the top pours the drinks." Gwen was headed up the rock wall as she said it. Nellie let out an exasperated groan, but even hunger couldn't stop her.

"Hey! Wait up, you cheater!"

"Hey! Hurry up, ya loser!"

Nellie had the pleasure of studying the soles of Gwen's shoes all the way to the top.

She had not meant to linger—
only pass through.
The sound of young voices stopped her.
Now the bleak reality of imminent danger
began
in earnest.
Invisible was the shift from safety to
peril.
For these were her fertile hunting grounds,
where the moss hung thick by her hand.
Concealed in the trees, she scouted prey—
swooping down, dispensing misery,
then vanishing,
only to return.
And she had
returned.

Chapter 3

Inside the mess hall, plates piled with grilled cheese sandwiches, brown bags of salted fries, bowls filled with watermelon wedges, and trays of cookies waited on the tables next to glistening pitchers of icy liquid. The red-faced girls collapsed across from each other—sweaty, starved and primed to chug.

"Bug juice, right?" Nellie was in order-taking mode, double checking. Bug juice was the girls' usual.

"That'll be finey-dandy, waitress. Fill 'em up quick with lots of ice in mine. I probably down a whole pitcher I such a thirsty champion. So be ready to hit me again." Gwen was making the most of her rock wall victory.

"Not happening. One drink, then my shift is over. So you be ready to give me my tip." Nellie wasn't pouring second rounds. She didn't lose by that much.

"A tip?" Gwen balked. "Short pencil be better than a long memory. There, how you like that nice tip? Now don't go blabbin it all around camp, slowpoke."

"Slowpoke! Who are you calling a slowpoke? You got the jump on me, remember?"

"Barely hardly a smidge. And I beat ya by a mile anyhow." Gwen defended herself. "Scouted new lands on the horizon waitin for you to haul your grouchy face to the top. As I recall, you was slow as a slug."

"Baloney! I was right on you the whole climb. I let you win." Nellie only said it to be a thorn. She'd never let anybody win anything. She just wanted to bug Gwen—a little payback appetizer.

"You so did not!" It worked. Gwen was bugged.

"I so did too." Nellie stuck to her story.

"Right on!" Lee applauded. "Bad blood on the opposin team. We love it."

"Oh, simmer down, Sniper. Me and my girl are tighter than ever. You shoulda seen her on the water today. She a doer. Ready for the *Cirque Du Soleil*. Make me all proud watchin her go at it. We still the team to beat."

Nellie instantly opened her mouth to stop Gwen from elaborating on her bottomless fall. Thankfully Paige interrupted before Gwen spilled the beans.

"You're the team to beat?" Paige laughed. "We'll see about that." She looked quite ethereal with white daisies in her blonde hair and sweat dotting her forehead like crystals. Jumping thoroughbreds all morning got her perspiring and smelling like hay.

"Sure enough we see about that. We be seein 'bout it right after lunch. But I tell ya now, Paige-A-Licious, gals with flowery hair usually can't shoot worth a hoot. This might be a first," teased Gwen.

"You're one to talk after havin electric-shock therapy to your hairdo, Gweny." Paige dished it back grinning. Gwen was sporting awfully bold hair due to the saltwater having its say.

"This is my *Afro*-dye-tee look. But you just go ahead and call me Goddess," quipped Gwen—acting all dignified.

"Goddess? More like Goofness," cracked Lee.

Zingers continued flying while Nellie filled glasses with the fruit punch, lemonade bug juice mix. She could hardly wait to latch her lips on a drink. She preferred the sweet tea herself, was pretty much hooked on the stuff. Sweet tea was the classic southern thirst quencher and she totally planned on perfecting her own sun-brewed recipe when she got home. Sloshing a brimming pitcher into the nearest glass, she poured and chugged without coming up for air, crunching shards of ice caught in the sugar flow, then clunking the glass on the table for an immediate refill.

"Hydration, ladies. That's how we keeps alive," proclaimed Gwen, downing seconds with the barest trace of red punch dying the corners of her mouth.

"And saves us from meltin in that gunk outside." Paige laughed between glubs but she wasn't kidding. Wiping her trickling crystals with a napkin, she dried her face and smoothed her hair. It was so unruly from the moist heat that her tangled locks practically swallowed every flower. The day was that sticky-thick, absolute hair massacre conditions.

Nellie wasn't immune. The weather wrought havoc on her hair too. She'd been fighting the good fight—brushing and brushing and brushing. It just looked worse. Tyrant fizzies were her new 'do. She was absolutely switching to tight braids the next day. Anything to stop the constant tickling around her face and keep her bangs from looking like some low-slung headband. In her opinion, Neanderthal hair was the ultimate fail.

And Gwen—regardless of the saltwater—she'd waved the white flag days ago, surrendering to her natural curly cues. She tamed her wild-woman hair with the contents of a zebra-striped case full of barrettes. Plastic bows, puffy poodles, double-scoop ice cream cones—you name it, she had it. "The baddest barrette collection ever!" The girl came prepared.

Despite their good-natured squabbling, the girls did agree on one thing. About all the heat and high humidity were good for was bad hair, slick skin and making everybody pant with the thirsties.

Revived by the bug juice, Paige cleared her throat. "Speakin of hair, me and Lee got to talkin on the way over here...and...well...we were kinda wonderin about a wager for tonight. Y'all interested?" Her smiling face—all freckles and plump cheekbones—could easily trick the gullible into thinking it was an innocent question.

Nellie and Gwen exchanged wily looks. The way Paige offhandedly worked in "tonight" probably meant something about the dance.

"What ya got for us?" Gwen asked, appointing herself spokeswoman. "And it better be hella good."

Nellie leaned forward and flopped an arm over Gwen's shoulder, doing her best to copy her friend's spunky attitude. It was high time for a team LePaige defeat.

"No big deal, just our usual. Me and Lee against you and Nell. Rifles and arrows. Team best wins." Paige presented it very nonchalant, like she'd offered them a jellybean.

"Wins what?" Gwen and Nellie knew that tone. They were fairly certain this was teaser-bait for a well thought out plan, something Lee and Paige had obviously discussed in detail on their walk from the barn. Nellie and Gwen would need more info before deciding whether or not to bite.

"Actually, we thought it'd be way more interestin if it was a punishment instead of a prize." Lee, the only one whose hair wasn't mangled by the weather, spoke with a complete poker face; she wasn't giving anything away.

"A punishment?" Nellie smiled. She liked the sound of that. "For reals?"

"What punishment you twins-of-trouble thinkin on?" Gwen sat up ready to negotiate—like a moth to a flame. And Nellie—discounting the whole thing could blow-up in her face—ignored her screaming voice of reason. Odds on it being a bad idea were shooed away by both, booted to a faint knocking. The truth was obvious: Lee was too good a shot. Playing against her was one thing. Betting against her was suicide. Looking across the table into her unblinking eyes was a reminder—just not a deterrent.

"Losers," began Paige. She stopped and caught a quickie look at Lee, exchanging teeny-tiny nods. Lee's expression remained blank, her face didn't move a muscle. Paige continued. "Losers have to blackout a front tooth with Nellie's eyeliner, tease and spray their hair *huge*-mongus, *and* wear bright red lipstick that we get to put on. And what I mean by that is…we get to put it on ya however we want, even way smeary." Snickering, Paige cut her eyes back over at Lee. This time Lee's lips were curling up. Paige leaned in and lowered the boom. "Now understand y'all, this would be to the dance. And it would be in dresses…without any shoes."

A silent stare down followed, sizing-up the competition's weakness. Neither team blinked.

"Let's see if I've got this straight." Nellie finally spoke. "For the dance, you guys are asking to borrow my eyeliner and use it on your teeth?" Her eyes were glinting as she performed a semi decent street-creed head-snap with a raised eyebrow.

Drumming her fingers lightly on the table, Lee answered, "Yeah, Nellie, that's right. You understand perfectly. We're askin that exact thing." Studying team GweNell, Lee tried her best to remain calm and hide her suppressed giggles. The sheer joy of taking them out under these circumstances was almost too much for her to contain. She needed them to hurry up and agree, commit with a handshake before they realized the moronic massiveness of their mistake.

"Are y'all in?" Lee slapped the tabletop. "As in let's go. Let's shake." She swiveled her legs over the bench seat and stood up extending her hand to Nellie. She was fighting hard not to blow it and laugh.

"You're so on. Let's go right now." Nellie smacked the tabletop and stood up mimicking her. She sealed the deal and shook, didn't even ask Gwen. She knew Gwen was in. No confirmation necessary. The instant she stood up with her hand out, Gwen stood up with her hand out—like they were the twins. And Paige, talking with a mouthful of grilled cheese, she stood up making the shakes official.

"Fun," said Paige, grinning at Lee. "This will be fun," she mumbled to her sandwich. She seemed real happy trying not to choke on her glee.

"No backin out." Lee was curt. Scooping up two grilled cheese halves, she smushed in a handful of fries and ate. The act of chewing helped her release some pent-up mirth.

Sifting through the tray, Nellie and Gwen selected perfect cheesy halves and answered in unison, "Fine."

"Fine." Lee smirked at Paige and Paige smirked back.

Biting into toasty crusts, the pregame psych-outs went full swing. Standing. Eating. No more talking. The four powered down food, not caring a lick about manners. They chomped sandwiches and gulped drinks, watching each other like Heavyweight Boxers at a Press Luncheon. Gearing up.

Stuffed on greasy carbs, they plowed into the trays of fresh-baked cookies. "Man," moaned Nellie with her mouth full, "that cafeteria lady with the false eyelashes has a gift." Before feasting on another, she checked her shorts for their pocket situation. She was swiping pecan sandies no matter what, even if it meant crumbs in her bikini top. She would absolutely defy the **No Food in the Cabin** rule for that late night sneak.

Looking up from the feeding frenzy, Gwen snipped, "And by the way...when we at that dance...don't y'all be standin near me and my wing-girl scarin off them cute fellas. That would not be cool." Her attention returned to dessert.

"Wrong!" Nellie disagreed. "We are so taking them around with us the entire night. It'll be a blast, I promise. You do Paige's make-up. I'll turn Lee into a hottie." Wrapping napkins around two highly ambitious stacks of cookies, Nellie talked like she thought they really had a chance. The comment broke Lee. Caught off guard by an explosive guffaw, she jerked her hand to cover her snot.

That's all it took to get Gwen laughing too. The out-landishness of Lee—all dolled up like girlie roadkill—would be beyond hysterical. Lee probably didn't even bring a dress, much less own one. She'd be forced to borrow. Gwen would make sure it was something extra fluffy and awful. Her imagination was on fire and she hadn't even started plotting the makeover disaster she'd slather on Paige.

Nellie's bring-it-on giggles were going volcanic. A sugar rush was turning her devilish as she looked from girl to girl. Clearly Lee and Paige didn't have a clue. They all knew about her beloved eyeliner stashed in her locker. (Though since arriving she hadn't bothered to wear it.) What they failed to realize was that it was waterproof. Spit wouldn't begin to budge it. It was practically permanent. And those lips and that rat's nest hair! Lee and Paige would be hillbilly sensations enduring three solid hours as side-show kooks. Nellie would be doubled-over laughing all night. For sure.

Scheming Paige, working her fourth sandwich half in between cookie bites, was equally delighted by the turn of events. Pleased they'd run into Mrs. Beauxleney out playing Frisbee golf with some counselors. Near speechless when the silver-haired camp director—a hugger with the toned legs of a former runner and tan, fit arms—offered up a tube of her very own fire-engine red lipstick for their plan. (The shade she wore to her Junior League meetings.) Ecstatic when Mrs. B volunteered to drop it off at their cabin. And overcome by one of her famous snicker-snort fits that a photog would be stationed at the dance, specifically sent to snap a picture for posterity—and the camp website. Yes ma'am, her mood was extremely upbeat.

Of course Lee wasn't laughing for any of those reasons. Lee cracked because Nellie and Gwen were such gung-ho scrappers, always coming back for more. She was wise to Nellie's wicked-tricky streak and Gwen's ballsy grit—loved that about them. Her new summer gang was crazy competitive, just like her. She had to be on her toes with this group. Even so, the afternoon—especially the dance—was primed to be epic. Those two were going down. She knew it and Paige knew it. Nellie and Gwen must have known it, but as usual they couldn't stop themselves. Lee's favorite kind of fun was about to begin, that's why she was spewing laughter. Damn straight she wouldn't be wearing a dress come seven o'clock.

Reaching for a chocolate chip, Lee muttered, "Must be nice livin in y'alls' fantasy lives." She ate the cookie after speaking, didn't talk with her mouth full. Lee preferred self-control when calculating shooting strategies.

"Lady LeeLee, you gonna wish you lived in my fantasy when you struttin your hips in a micro-mini floral. Them poor boys gonna get the shock of their lives tonight. You too, Paige. You gonna keep them dead daisies hangin off your head once we whip up on y'all?"

"Let's just get goin and see." Paige was feeling trigger happy and antsy to go. She wanted to make darn sure they had plenty of time back at the cabin. They wouldn't want to rush. Getting Gwen and Nellie ready would be a major event. "Why don't we quit yammerin and mosey on over to archery. Or do you and Nell need more cookies and warm milk first?"

"Milk was a *baaaad* choice!" Waving her arms and getting hyper, Nellie squealed a favorite movie line.

"Milk's the perfect choice for a wacko like you," chuckled Lee.

"Please don't correct me. It sickens me." Nellie kept them coming.

"What are you even talkin about," asked Paige, clueless. "You're not makin any sense."

"*Anchor Man* and *Mystery Men*," Gwen informed her. After a whole week of Nellie's movie-quoting, Gwen was getting used to it. "Duh, Paige, try and keep up." She took Nellie by the arm and proceeded to sashay from the cafeteria. "Anybody love shootin stuff best follow along. It time."

"Hasta la vista, babies!" Nellie bellowed leaving the lunch room. "Ve'll be back!"

"Yah, babies," Gwen chimed in. "Ve'll be back!" Both terminators were ready to duel. Their swagger said it all.

Lee and Paige fell in behind them whispering in each other's ear. Some of it was early celebration trash-talk, but mostly it was because Nellie—strutting with her cookie boobies—bore a serious resemblance to a Bactrian camel. And lanky Gwen with her slinky gait, she just looked like a diva goofball. At best, their intimidation factor verged on microscopic.

Anticipation made her tremble.
So many to choose from,
walking the wooded paths
from morning 'til night.
In groups they passed below,
laughter revealing an approach.
It would not always be so.
Soon, one would come
with no companion.
On a silent journey
to her silent
end.

Chapter 4

Nellie wrapped her fingers around the wood of her lucky bow. This recurve had a nice heft in her hands. Its draw weight was difficult but doable, well worth the extra effort it required for the arrow speed it generated. She looked halfway dangerous in her finger tab, her protective leather bracer strapped to her forearm, and the quiver of arrows clipped to her shorts. A side trip by the cabin had been necessary—to lighten her load. The pecan sandies were now safely stashed in her pillowcase. And everybody needed another round of sunscreen anyway.

Watching pensively, Nellie was trying to stay positive against mounting odds, but things were beginning to unravel. Paige was up. She'd already released two arrows. They were respectable—just inside the bull's-eye. Set to go again, Paige's left arm was braced straight out while her right was fully drawn back with the bowstring anchored at her cheek. She was looking down the arrow's carbon shaft, finessing her aim before freeing the nock from the taunt cord. Last shot.

Nellie was holding her breath. Not that it mattered. Predictably—like a magnet—Lee's arrows were in the heart of the yellow bull's-eye. Her best flirted with perfect, but was low by half an inch. Really irritating. The tire, covered by a target face printed with colored rings, was propped about thirty-five yards away. Nellie knew she had to put some serious muscle behind her draw. With scarcely any room left in the bull's-eye, her winning arrow had to penetrate.

She wasn't about to endure the ridicule that Gwen endured after firing a dud. Gwen's shot had flexed beautifully off the arrow rest and arced through the rippling heat, connecting with the middle of the target—the potential winner. Then tragedy struck. The arrow rebounded with a frisky backward bounce and fell to the ground like a tissue paper streamer. The chorus of heckling was ferocious.

Gwen's next two were stronger, though neither rivaled Lee's again. At least they'd stayed lodged. But they weren't contenders. Her aim was too erratic, too shaky. She kept giggling every time she pictured Lee come sundown. It was wrecking her concentration and Paige caught on quick. She was all for Gwen screwing-up, so she messed with Gwen's head by describing "glamour-girl" Lee at the dance. Gwen gobbled down every hilarious quip—and kept on missing.

Lee jumped on the bandwagon, fueling fire with gasoline. She behaved outrageously distracting—making faces, robot dancing, mouth-farting—every time Gwen anchored and tried to aim. She even got the whistle blown at her by a counselor for running onto the field and begging Gwen to put her out of her misery. She wailed about embarrassment: that the whole bet was a big mistake, that defeat would be personally unbearable, and that losing would stunt her growth from the humiliation.

Gwen reacted to everything, didn't realize she was being double-teamed until it was too late. She lost her killer instinct, forgetting that her night depended on it. Despite countless warnings, Nellie couldn't stop her friend from steering the challenge down the dusty road of regret. The agony of defeat was loitering on the sidelines, practically lounging in a chair and sipping on a Mint Julep. But Gwen didn't seem to notice. It was up to Nellie to rescue their team standing. Her sidetracked best bud had put them in a *baaaad* position. The sillies—wrapped up and special delivered by Lee and Paige—hadn't gotten the job near done.

Paige released her third arrow. Eight eyes locked on it—soaring across the field at an odd angle. All four heard the pingy clink when it hit one of Gwen's two and ricocheted sideways along the grass, burying itself. Nellie breathed a sigh of relief even though Gwen's arrow now barely stayed stuck. It hung straight down like a limp spaghetti noodle with tail feathers. Nellie suspected it could be some sort of insulting omen.

"Shoot," shouted Paige, irked. "I pinched it! Stupid, sweaty fingers!"

"Ain't that a bummer, cowgirl," chided Gwen. "Well you done now. Go sit your drippy self down in the shade." Rallying back from the sting of failure, Gwen was determined to protect Nellie from the double-barrel tactics of Lee and Paige.

"Thanks for the concern, Gweny. But I wouldn't miss out watchin your girl have at it, not for the world. I'm stayin right here. Good luck, Nellie." Paige said it with gooey encouragement—sincere as a crooked used car salesman.

"Ignore the freak in the bushy blonde wig, Nells." Gwen was getting testy. "She just some crazy lady come around lookin for cats. You just think about bringin home the gold and savin our hides. Get on up there and work that bow. Plenty room in that bull's-eye for your arrows. It's callin your name."

Easy for Gwen to say, thought Nellie. Her turn was over. But then Gwen added, "No pressure. Go for it like that full moon, Sweet Cheeks." And then she winked.

"Come on, Nellie, go." Lee had turned aggressive. "Thread the needle if ya got the balls. See how we left that big part right in the middle for ya?" Lee was done sugar-coating her plan to dominate and unleashing a different kind of mind game on Nellie, not the one she'd played with Gwen. Gone was the dumb and dumber act. Front and center was the wide planted feet, the one hand stroking her chin, and the bionic eyes. She was goading Nellie—deliberately standing too close. It was a little unnerving. And, as Nellie was about to discover, highly motivating.

"The contest is for fun. The contest is for fun." That's what Nellie kept telling herself—to calm down. But she felt her heart pump off a series of hard thumps anyway. Her rhythm of beats tripled. Nerves showed up. As she stepped to the line taking her stance, a thought came rocketing through her brain. She would absolutely make certain she didn't shoot fourth at the rifle range. Going last was the pits. Standing on her mark, flanked by anxiety and heat, it would be a total miracle if she didn't faint.

Oddly enough, something about Lee's hovering was starting to get her pumped. Lee's attempt to throw her was way over the top. Nellie was getting seriously ticked. Until she noticed the benefit. Anger was having a positive effect. It was overpowering her nerves. All the negative thoughts sucking the strength out of her arms, making her legs go rubbery and her fingers feel thick as anvils—were vanishing. Driven by a fierce resolve to prove her skill, teach Lee and Paige not to mess with her, she raised her bow. If she could beat them today in spite of Lee's jerky behavior, the dance would just be icing on the cupcake.

Nellie drew back hard—further than normal—and anchored on her ear instead of her cheekbone. (She needed the extra velocity.) Finding the bull's-eye, she sighted right on it—ignoring the sun on her shoulders and the perspiration on her upper lip and the nagging itch at her temple. A slight tremor still hummed in her forearms, so she strengthened her grip on the recurve's riser and stood up tall, flipping her bangs out of her eyes with a quick toss of her head. Feeling the brass nocking bead on the bowstring with her thumb, she adjusted the pads of her three fingers accordingly—making sure the hilt rested against the metal bump so that her arrow was squarely aligned. She felt tight contact and let go—too quick. Nellie's arrow lodged deep in the bottom of the tire. First ring. Worst ring. Gwen moaned. Lee and Paige pretended to.

Nellie stayed focused. Wasting no emotion, she withdrew her second arrow, jammed the string in the nock slit and stood at full draw. Again she took direct aim at the bull's-eye. This time she elevated her tip slightly above it, compensating for the curving trajectory. Adjusting the slant of her wrist, she got comfortable and released. But this one was a near disaster: the dreaded pluck. Her forearm received a nasty thwack as the bowstring slammed against her armguard. The angle of her drawback stunk—off to one side rather than straight back with the string. The result was like a slap in the face to the inside of her arm. If she hadn't been wearing the armguard, she'd have been nursing a painful bruise. Despite the mistake, her arrow found the target. But not the victory. Team LePaige high-fived. Gwen asked if she was hurt. She barely paid attention. She wasn't about to slow down. Silently thanking her protective equipment, Nellie strung her last chance. Her manner was so defiant that even Lee took a step back.

"Straight draw. Straight draw. Straight draw." Nellie's lips were moving as she talked herself through it. The girls' lips were moving too, but she blocked their voices out. It was only her and the target—the bow and arrow simply an extension of her arms. Sighting like a warrior brat, she glared down the thin shaft, waiting for her tip to sync up with the ideal mark: a tiny black smudge above the vital yellow sphere. When her tip locked on, she didn't hesitate. As her fingers rolled open—freeing the string—the arrow took off tracking perfectly, slicing through the air like a missile.

Gwen let out the first holler. "In your face!"

Nestled together like pigs-in-a-blanket, Nellie's final arrow now shared the same puncture hole with Lee's best. Her orange feathers were downright cuddling with Lee's blue ones. Even from thirty-five paces away, it was clearly visible. A tie.

"No way," shrieked Lee, verging on berserk. "Are you lucky or what!" Lee stared at the bag.

"Or good," screeched Gwen, jumping up and down—happy-dancing again. "Karma just slapped you in the face, Lippy Lee. Serves you right! All your blabberin an hulkin around, tryin so hard to mess us up. That's what happens when ya jump down the wrong side of a armed actress! Right, Nellie?"

"Geez, give it up for Nell." Paige was looking at the target, pretty surprised. "Thought you'd miss the whole bag today. Ya know with boys on the line."

"Y'all just keep on keepin on underestimatin. Seems like that's workin out real good." Gwen was yapping her wise-cracks to Lee's back. Lee was steamed, marching out to retrieve arrows.

Nobody noticed Nellie slide in a fourth and stand erect, fully drawn back and sighting. Lee was fifteen paces down-field when the arrow left the bow. She felt it whiz by her head with the suck of displaced air. Her hands flew up as she dropped to her knees panicked, hearing the thunk of impact. Cautiously, she lifted her head and saw an arrow lodged directly in the bull's-eye—dead center. She looked back stunned. The mouths of Gwen and Paige were hanging wide open. For once not a sound was coming out of Gwen's. Staring Lee down with hooded eyes, Nellie stood on the line, eerily calm. She didn't even attempt apologizing. She knew there wasn't a chance she'd miss that shot.

"Holy crap! Are you tryin to kill me?" Lee was shocked. The arrow just barely missed her head. She wasn't sure if she should be impressed or furious.

"Did I misunderstand? That invitation to shoot you was only for Gwen? My bad." Nellie dropped her bow and started walking out. "Thought you might look cool with one pierced ear." Striding by Lee, she added, "Not really. Just decided to show you how it's done. You're welcome."

Lee was astounded by the behavior. "Are you nuts?"

"No."

"Yeah, you are." Lee caught up, practically stepping on the back of Nellie's flip flops. "And that's your fourth shot, Nellie. Don't think for a minute it counts!"

"Don't wig out. I know it doesn't count." Nellie sounded defensive. "Fourth shot?" Then confused. She stopped and faced Lee. "I... I...shouldn't have taken it."

That's when Lee noticed her pupils. They were significantly dilated.

"But I... I knew it was my ace. I couldn't stop myself. I didn't... I didn't want to." Nellie stuttered. "But...but you were fine, Lee, really. I had a complete lock on it." She stopped talking and turned for the target. She didn't say another word—didn't know what more to say. The realization of what she'd just done made her stomach squeeze. It had been a complete out-of-body experience. Totally unlike her to behave so irresponsibly. She was naturally adamant about technique and procedure. Only idiots broke safety rules, never her. It was bizarre. Like something had numbed her and seeped inside, blocking out her good sense. She knew what she was doing when she was doing it. She just couldn't stop herself. Scary weird.

As far as Lee was concerned, one thing was crystal clear. Nellie's determination to win was a game changer. Lee's brows furrowed as she chewed on the fact that the walk in the park had just been cancelled. She and Paige had only managed a tie. That was an unexpected setback. If Nellie rallied at the rifle range and Gwen got it together, it could easily turn into the worst most hellish night of Lee's entire life.

"You're lucky the counselor didn't see that, Nellie." Lee said it glad the counselor hadn't seen it. She would have hated the girl blaring the whistle again and stopping everything to call them off the field and repeat what they already knew. "Do *NOT* shoot with a soul downrange!" Then the counselor might have banned Nellie permanently. Lee just figured Nellie went a touch ga-nuts because she'd behaved like a jerk. This was Nellie's way of calling her on it, making her back off. Like a pitcher throwing at the batter's head. So what. Lee understood.

"Good thing I'm so lucky twice now," said Nellie, recovering from her temporary onset of competitive insanity. But she decided to make the most of what had happened— join the cutthroat ranks of team LePaige. Team GweNell could start shoveling back obnoxious comments, same as them. Nellie was curious to see how team LePaige shot then. Maybe it would turn into the advantage that she needed. "Actually Lee, you're the one who's lucky it was a fourth shot. You'd be halfway to trying on cute dresses."

"Don't count on it," snorted Lee. "I'll just have to keep a closer eye on you, Hollywood. I think the heat's finally fried your brain. Else your good girl act is bull."

"It's bull," confessed Nellie. "Definitely keep a closer eye. I'm totally unpredictable. Wouldn't want you turning your back again and missing something. What's coming will be worth remembering."

"Fine then. I won't make that mistake twice." Lee was tugging out arrows. "Ya know though, you're absolutely right. I would look pretty legit with one earring."

"Ya think? Well...probably better not do it with an arrow. Unless you want to look like you work at Hot Topic," teased Nellie, grateful to be forgiven. She pulled Paige's arrow from the grass.

"Hey, gangsta!" Gwen had found her voice and was back to bellowing at her usual decibel. "Are y'all on a date out there? Can we go yet?" With their arms full of equipment, she and Paige were ready to move out.

"We're coming!" Nellie yanked her unofficial winner out of the target and offered it to Lee. "Here, a present. You have eight lives left." Nellie stuck it through Lee's waistband.

"I'll take it. Might use it tonight to fend off the boys." Lee smiled.

"Ha! Keep dreaming big, dreamer. No place on a dress to stick that thing. But maybe you can hold it between your teeth. For sure there'd be no kissing then." Nellie took off laughing, running back with the arrows in her quiver.

"Great idea." Lee caught up. "When you lose, you can borrow it. Hold it in your teeth, stick it in your hair, either way it'll look good on the Seamist website."

"The what? Oh, no you di'int!" Gwen heard her.

"Oh, yeah, y'all. Oh, we did," cooed Paige. "You bet paparazzi will be attendin. All the girls are gettin out their cameras. The picture lady might even come to our cabin to snap y'alls progress from ladies to losers. Did I not say this was gonna be fun?" She wanted to gush but she held it in.

"Sick in the head, that's what y'all are," squawked Gwen.

Truthfully, Gwen was up for the added bonus of party pics. However, parents had access to the camp's website, not to mention blackmailing big brothers. That's all the incentive Gwen needed to shoot straight. "A dope and a dumbbell, that's who we dealin with Nells." Gwen needled Lee and Paige, trying her best to burst their bubble. "Y'all gonna be sorry you ran your mouths when them cameras start flashin. Best get ready to meet your ugly, long-lost sistas."

"But Gwendolyn, how can ya possibly think you'll win," asked Lee, helping with the equipment. "You'd have to stop gigglin and get serious. Does baby really think she can handle that?" Lee was starting back up with Gwen. "Nod your head three times if ya do and I'll let ya hold a rifle."

Gwen unleashed her signature eye-roll. "I ain't talkin to you, Lee. I ain't even lookin at you no more. You know we done with that. Nellsy, why we hangin with such lowlifes? We gots to find us some classy dames. Put that on the top of our to-do list."

The bickering hardly let up as they dumped their arm-loads of gear in a pile on the counter and waited while it was checked back in. All of it was highly entertaining to the ears of the counselor on duty. And to the one she secretly phoned at the rifle range to spread the word. "The dance bet is just leavin. They tied. They're comin your way." She could still hear them going at it when she hung up the phone. She watched the girls sauntering along the curving path through the woods, deciding which team she thought would win and how outrageous they'd look at the dance. A fun night for all. She never noticed the treetops—gently rustling—directly above their heads.

Four attracted her attention.
Now she was closing in.
Captivated by all—particularly one.
Toying with that girl.
Infecting her actions with the bow,
coaxing that fourth arrow to fly.
Eager to harm the friendship.
Waiting for the golden opportunity
until that girl was hers.
Then the next.
Then the next.
Then the next.
Patient.
Anonymous.
Fatally treacherous.
For the moment—at a distance.
For the moment—just a breeze.
For the moment...

Chapter 5

The girls walked the blacktop path that led to the rifle range. It wound around the edge of the woods along the outskirts of camp. Underway in an adjacent field, a lively softball game got their attention. The batter had just cracked a line drive when the pitcher's efforts to catch the hit turned into slapstick athletics. She'd barely missed the ball on the fly—got enough glove on it to knock it down. She tried snatching the ball up and tossing it to first for an easy out, but the stupids got her. She used her glove hand. The leather nipped the ball and it scooted away, hiding at her heels no matter which way she spun. Squatting down to trap it, she searched with her bare hand but still found nothing. Her eyes followed the runner—not the ball—so the teaser kept rolling just out of reach. Turning in circles groping dirt, the pitcher churned up nothing but dust.

It was a fast-paced comedy of errors, performed with gusto and concentration. Nellie and her gang watched as the hitter, a big-boned gal, lumbered all the way to second base before the pitcher tore her eyes off the girl and spotted the ball between her feet. Seizing it, she stood up threatening to throw to third if the runner dared to continue. The girl came to a sliding stop and shuffled backward, elated to be safe on second. Shrugging, the pitcher trotted to her mound with the ball and a grin, repositioned her feet, windmilled her under-handed cannon, and threw a strike at the next chick with a stick.

"You show 'em, Slugger," shouted Lee, saluting. Nellie couldn't tell if Lee was razzing the runner, the pitcher, or the new up at bat. Consequently, the whole softball game turned to look and waves were exchanged.

"We got room! We need ya, Lee!" The invitation was from a girl playing first base, a popular counselor.

"Not today! I'm kinda up to my own no good," Lee called back.

"We heard! Can't wait to find out who wins! See you maniacs tonight!" Chuckling, the girl pounded her glove and put her attention back on home plate.

"Wow." Gwen couldn't believe her ears. "You really has put the word out on this deal, ain't ya? Remind me not to share any of my deepest, darkest secrets with y'all. Does about everybody know our business?"

"Just about. Word travels fast when it leaks from the top," blurted Paige, plenty spunky.

"And what top might that be?" Nellie asked, fakey polite.

"Mrs. B, I guess," answered Paige, cheerfully referring to the camp director—not fakey. "We ran into her on the way to the cafeteria. She thought the whole bet sounded like a real good idea." Paige held back the bit about her loaning the lipstick. She was saving that.

"Oh, Lordy," sighed Gwen.

"Hope you guys enjoy being celebs tonight." Nellie shook her head. "Sounds like you'll have a sold-out audience."

Rounding the corner of the art cabin, the hum of potter's wheels and conversation reached their ears. This was the place to get inspired, always filled with busy, budding artists. On the outside clothesline was the day's proof. Freshly dyed sarongs in vibrant patterns of azure and amber, periwinkle and fuchsia, and emerald with lavender were fluttering in the breeze.

Gwen grabbed Nellie by the arm and steered her up the walk, pulling her toward the door. "We need our good luck chokers," she whispered, a smidge superstitious. "Be right back," she hollered to Lee and Paige.

"That's not gonna help none. What are you bums up to?" Paige couldn't fathom what they were doing and she sure didn't want to stop. But Gwen and Nellie kept fast-walking away, ignoring her. "Whateve," she griped. "We were kinda hopin to stand around in the hot sun waitin on y'all. The longer we wait, the madder we get. And y'all know what they say about mad girls with guns, don't ya?"

"No, what do they say?" Nellie and Gwen said it together as they pushed through the screen door, into the refreshing breeze of ceiling fans—not waiting for the answer.

"They say duck!" Paige giggled out her punch line as the door slapped shut like one apathetic clap. She turned to see if at least Lee appreciated her little joke.

"Lame." Waving off a biting horsefly, annoyed by the sun in her eyes and the detour, Lee was not amused.

Inside, fans cooled the expansive room while girls worked quietly over all sorts of projects. Sable brushes swirled watercolors on rice paper. Gluey strips of newspaper dripped from a zoo of freshly made paper mache animals.

An altar of glass candles, decoupaged with pressed flowers and tissue paper, glowed with psychedelic light. One entire corner of the room was devoted to clay. Girls sat pinching pots, sculpting statuettes, and shaping beads on toothpicks. Others rolled out slabs like dough, cutting out tiles with wooden tools, then adding designs and poems. In the opposite corner, five potter's wheels were occupied by nimble hands, sponging and smoothing bowls. The artistic options in the room were as wondrous as they were numerous. Campers always left camp with cherished heirlooms packed in their duffels because of this cabin.

Monsieur Pitou—everyone called him Tou-tou for short—was presiding over a table of teenagers. They were listening to his every word as he taught the basics of batik. Speaking softly, he daubed his paintbrush in a skillet of melted wax, creating his own graceful example on a length of cloth. He looked up from his intricate strokes and deliberate drips to greet the newcomers.

"Hallo, ladies. Welcome." His distinctive accent carried precise phrasing. "Would you like a place at the table?" He smiled his dazzling smile, once again convincing Nellie that his were the whitest teeth on the planet. When he grinned— which was constantly—the lines that appeared, disappeared, and reappeared around his eyes and down the sides of his face looked like rays of sun. And his skin, the luscious hue of bittersweet chocolate, had the sheen of eggplants. Nellie always fought the urge to reach up and pinch his cheeks like she'd seen Mrs. Beauxleney do at orientation. Standing in his khaki slacks, his untucked Hawaiian shirt and leather sandals, he had the air of someone young at heart. The only clues to his real age were the flecks of silvery grey in his shoulder length dreadlocks and the tortoise shell glasses he wore when he worked. His manner was equal parts easygoing, open-minded and joyful. He was known around camp as an avid storyteller and art teacher with a favorite rhyming motto. "Please, let Tou-tou show you." By the time any girl left his art center after practicing what he'd taught her, she was pretty much an expert.

"Heya, Tou-tou." Gwen talked while Nellie did her usual gawking at the ongoing projects. "Nope, we can't stay. We in the middle of a shoot-out. Just grabbin our lucky necklaces. Don't tell 'em I said it, but today we need all the special help we can get."

"I see," he said, captivated by her flighty enthusiasm. "Am I to believe that you are enjoying your daily mêlée with Miss Paige and Miss Lee?"

"Don't know we much enjoyin it today," confided Gwen, walking over to a hook on the wall and removing two beaded necklaces with little plastic sunflowers, the ones she and Nellie had strung the day before.

"There happens to be a lot on the line this time. We kinda agreed to a bet involvin the dance…and…well…let's just say it won't be pretty if we lose. Me and Nells was hopin you'd rub some of your good luck on these. Please, please, please?" She held the colorful loops in front of him, swinging the things on her pointer fingers with an expectant look on her face. There was a slight pause while she elbowed Nellie to second her request. All Nellie could manage was a mumbled, "Uh huh, yeah…" Her attention was on a narrow-necked urn spinning on the closest potter's wheel.

"I see." With great reserve and friendly seriousness, he set his brush aside. Then, quite ceremoniously, he rubbed his hands together and blew into them. Shaking them out like a carnival showman, he revealed his palms for Gwen's inspection before carefully cupping the chokers. "You may have to rely on your own skillfulness, Miss Gwen, Miss Nellie. My magic is generally exclusive within these four walls."

To Gwen's delight, the necklaces slipped from her fingers as he rubbed them together briskly. Nellie could hear the plastic beads scuffing from the friction. She had to admit, if ever they needed a little oomph (corny spells or not) it was right then. He finished his make-believe ritual with a twirl of the chokers and presented them back to Gwen.

"Ta-da! I trust they will sufficiently aid in your endeavors." He bowed. Nellie noticed the sun rays shining by his eyes again.

"Whew, baby! I feels it!" Gwen, exaggerating her euphoria, stretched the elastic over her head. It snapped around her neck with a crisp, clattering click. "Catch." She tossed Nellie's into the air. If Nellie had been ready, she would have caught it. As it was, her eyes had wandered over to a cork bulletin board pinned with dozens of still-life paintings. Most were of bird's nests filled with speckled eggs, guarded by the outstretched wings of a red cardinal. But the painting she was straining to examine from afar was slightly different. It was a cowboy boot filled with golf balls, guarded by a cigar-smoking plucked chicken. So her reflexes were distracted. Seeing the necklace in midair, she made a herky-jerky move to catch it. But she missed, batting it away instead. It flew across the room and skittered under a table packed with lanyard makers.

"Girl, you gonna let your good luck escape? Get that thing and come on." Gwen turned to Monsieur Pitou. "We thank ya so much, Tou-tou. We'll be back tomorrow and tell ya if it worked out in our favor. Unless you chaperonin the dance? In that case you'll see for yourself. But we'll see ya tomorrow. Nells is gonna go off the deep-end if she don't get some clay under her fingernails and a seat at that spinney table." Gwen flounced away and yanked on the screen door. As she walked out to Lee and Paige, the whole cabin could hear her bragging, "Y'all in a heap a trouble now!"

"Let me get the long-handled broom to sweep it out," offered Monsieur Pitou, turning for the supply closet.

"Nah, that's OK. I can get it." Nellie stopped him. She didn't want to waste anymore of his valuable time. That table of teenagers was waiting on him.

Monsieur Pitou watched as she crawled on her hands and knees, weaving between shaved legs and bare feet to reclaim her lucky jewels. The necklace slid across the waxed floor further under the table than she realized. Once she re-emerged and stood up, she saw that her girls had begun meandering down the path, bound for the range.

"Nellie, we goin! Come on," shouted Gwen—not looking back, not stopping.

"Miss Nellie." Monsieur Pitou gestured to her from the batik table. She really wanted to catch up with the girls, but she didn't want to be impolite. Pulling on the necklace and untangling her hair from the cord, she left the window and walked over, flattered to be summoned.

"I could not help noticing your interest. I sense that you have exceptional talent. If you would like, I will keep the wax hot. Later today after your victory, perhaps you all would enjoy making something for yourselves."

"I've never tried batiking before."

"Please, let Tou-tou show you. It is my greatest pleasure to encourage creative expression. Tradition requires the passing of knowledge and skill from generation to generation and I am always eager for the new interpretations of my students. Communication through art bears the fruit of fulfillment. It is a conceptual invitation to shine."

"I don't know about that. I mean, maybe for some girls. I'm always afraid I'm gonna mess up."

"You know in art, Miss Nellie, there are no 'mess ups'. Only pathways defined with color and breathed to life. Albeit, some pathways are more spontaneous than others." He grinned. "Each work of art is an invaluable gift, the truest form of magic. Sometimes tranquil. Sometimes humorous. Sometimes emotional. It is entirely up to the artist to decide, as these first-time craftswomen have so adeptly proven." Motioning to a window, he proudly pointed at the sarongs clipped on the outside clothesline. Nellie was amazed that girls who'd just been taught the technique could actually create such beautiful pieces. Tacked to the wall directly behind him was the clincher—an intricate work splashed with the beauty of the lowcountry. Hunchback turkey vultures and windblown Spanish moss were clinging to the twisted limbs of a live oak. It was dyed with dark purple edges, staining over deep mossy greens, creeping onto fingers of burgundy and bleeding into bluish blacks.

Beautiful yet foreboding. A haunting masterpiece.

The thought of staying to make such a treasure was tugging at her hard. Inspired by him, she wanted to plop down and start right in. Tou-tou caught her staring and turned to the piece on the wall.

"That was done a very long time ago. It hangs as an aide-mémoire." He spoke the French phrase without joy. "A sinister legend is tied to this land." He paused, solemnly reflecting. When he continued, his manner was noticeably subdued. "One I prayed did not truly exist. Most regrettably, I myself have witnessed its undeniable reality. It happened at dusk as I walked a secluded trail. The black beast flew. Its shadow darkened my path." He gazed at the image on the wall with sad eyes. "I poured my sorrow into that cloth. Its creation was a cleansing of my soul."

Nellie thought she'd missed something. She knew he was a major storyteller, but she didn't get why he'd gone into scary-story mode out of the blue and she sure didn't buy his complete change of mood. "A turkey vulture legend," she squealed, going along. "I thought they were just famous for being totally ugly. You so have to fill me in." She was poking fun at his performance, certain he was pulling her leg.

"Turkey vulture?" He seemed genuinely puzzled. "No, no, my dear, those are not turkey vultures. Look closely at the tails."

She looked again. The tails were done like dragons; the ends bore spikes. She'd missed that.

"The monster has no given name. Nevertheless, it is feared as a brazen and unyielding thief. It steals children for its master, a tyrant who is as elusive as the mist."

Nellie nearly lost it and laughed. What a good actor, she thought. "And that creeper lives around here!" She shrieked, playing his game—and cutting him off. She knew he was trying his best to entertain her. Scary stories were the rage at camp. They even had "Scary Story Night" after Sunday dinner. But she really had to go.

"You must take care, Miss Nellie. This is a place of wondrous beauty and mystery. For the wise it is paradise. For the foolish there lurks unspeakable hell. Do not be a fool. That is my warning. I am, after all, your elder. It is my duty to protect and guide your wellbeing."

"Great advice." She tried not to act like he was off his rocker. "I'll keep on the lookout for any winged what-cha-ma-call-its. But if you really want to know, it's the water moccasins and the copperheads that scare me the most. I totally hate snakes."

"Snakes are a threat you can outrun, Miss Nellie. The beast is a foe you cannot. Please promise me that you will never ever walk the trails unaccompanied at nightfall."

His suddenly serious attitude reeked of uptight parental control. Then it dawned on Nellie. The whole point of his ridiculous bird fable? The dopey "moral of the story"? It was all just a clever lecture aimed at convincing her not to go off by herself. Tou-tou and her mom had plenty in common, that was for sure.

"Never." She offered her best street-smart smile with city-slicker sass. "Why would I want to be out there alone when I can be in here with my peeps, rockin-out with paints?"

The tension on his face disappeared. He laughed his rolling laugh. "Exactly!" He clasped a big hand lightly on her shoulder. "But after you win your gunslinger shoot-out. I am keen to hear the outcome and decide if I must place an order for another bag of lucky beads." The twinkle returned to his eyes.

"OK, that's a deal." She gave him a double thumbs-up, heading for the door. "I can't wait to try batiking. We'll come back later. But it might not be until tomorrow. But we'll totally come back. I'll totally come back. I'm totally psyched." She remembered one last thing before walking out.

"Thank you," she told him happily, sort of hating to leave.

Reaching into his breast pocket and withdrawing a mint leaf, he nodded a warm goodbye. Then he popped the leaf in his mouth and picked up where he'd left off with his table of teenagers.

Nellie set off, meaning to run. Heat pounded her in the face and expanded in her lungs, altering her plans. Running was vetoed. She thought about swinging by the cafeteria for an icy glass of anything to drink. She looked ahead and didn't see the girls. That changed her mind. No time to stop. They'd already disappeared down the trail through the woods. By now they were probably at the shooting range signing out guns, which meant she had to quit dawdling and hurry up. But the heat made her so lethargic that the best she could do was walk—very slowly.

From a cabin,
the chosen one emerged,
left on her own.
Alone.
Thinking
no one
had
waited.

Chapter 6

"Great," fumed Nellie, peeved at getting left. She took her frustration out on a rock. Maybe she could break her record and keep kicking it down the blacktop all the way to the end of the pavement. With her first kick, it shanked right, jumping off the path. She walked by scowling, leaving the stone where it hopped in the grass. Obviously her lucky necklace was a slow starter.

"Unbelievable," she muttered, looking ahead. This was the exact scenario she swore she wouldn't let happen. Actually, this was way worse. The girls were there without her, settling into a shooting bay and taking practice shots while she dragged up the rear. And where would this put her in the line-up? Only dead last, that's where. How could her one solid plan get totally turned upside-down. What a mistake to go in the art center. She should've known better—should've waited outside and let Gwen go grab the stupid necklaces. Every time she went in that building the same thing occurred. She forgot about everything else.

Paige and Lee knew that. As Nellie plodded along, a new thought cropped up. It was a total set-up. The route itself was probably another one of team LePaige's schemes to make sure they won. Walk by the art center hoping that

Nellie would find a reason to go inside and take her mind off the game. She wouldn't put it past them. It was just the kind of crafty thinking they were into. Nellie rolled her eyes at her own dumb pun. There were other paths they could've taken, ones that didn't go directly behind that particular cabin. The more she thought about it, the more she felt like a great big sucker.

Maybe if she started jogging she could get there in time and demand to go first, not even take practice shots. It's not like she needed them. She dug the air rifles. When she was loosey-goosey relaxed—just aim it and shoot it style—she was good, almost as good as Lee. She looked up from her feet and down the path, calling on her inner fortitude, willing herself to bite the bullet and run. But her fighter spirit, zapped by near heatstroke, gave her nothing back. It was far too hot for any kind of sustained physical exertion.

She had to man-up and accept it. Get there when she got there. Save her strength and hope for the best. No, Nellie, wrong! She scolded herself. At least she had the energy to revise her wimpy thinking. *MAKE* the best happen. *WIN.* Or better yet—she started giggling at the phrase that popped into her head—"*Win with Gwen!*" That's a good one, she thought, getting happied-up. Hanging with Tou-tou was contagious. Now she was thinking in rhymes too. *"Win with Gwen! Win with Gwen!"* She liked the ring of it. Especially since a new idea was forming: arrive at the range chanting it incessantly. Maybe onlookers would join in. After the tenth cheer, it would've driven Lee and Paige batty. Too bad, thought Nellie. By then it'd be stuck in their heads brainwashing them, getting them all agitated. They would literally beg her to knock it off, which she most certainly would not. Pay-back's a bee-yatch with sharp, pointy canines.

Perfecting the plan, she walked through the middle of camp absentmindedly yanking on her elastic cord, entertained by the hollow sound of clacking beads and liking the firm stretchiness. She stopped in her tracks when it slipped from her fingers and thunked on her windpipe. Rubbing her throat, she checked to see if anyone caught her moron move. Apparently this lucky necklace had a major defect.

Activities were in full swing all around her. In the waters of the camp lake, canoes were gliding toward a picturesque footbridge—a favorite apple-eating, foot-dangling rest spot. Turtles congregated on the boulders underneath the bridge, waiting for tossed cores. It was cute.

The river was still full of afternoon adventurer seekers too. Nellie saw the red MasterCraft speeding along the water, shooting up wakes. No skiers at this hour. Now it towed the yellow banana. The six girls straddling it were holding onto the handles, enjoying a bucking-bronco ride. Nellie hadn't mounted up yet, but it was on her mind. She wondered if she could do it like her dad *said* he did it on his honeymoon. Ride it backward. He claimed to have never been bucked. Nellie watched as the fat tube bounced through a swell, easily sending a girl flying into the river. He had to be lying.

Further out on the water, passed the second line of buoys, Nellie could see the striped sails of Flying Scots racing in a regatta. The lead boat was well in front—a shoe-in to win—but the chase for second and third was clogged with contenders. As was customary, a beaming Mrs. B would announce and congratulate the winners during dinner.

The trill of a whistle made Nellie look. At the sandy-bottom swimming pool, one of her favorite counselors—a redhead wearing a powder blue one piece—blew the all clear. She was pulling duty-watch in the tower overlooking the gigantic inflatable blob. Nellie guessed that the kid crawling out to be launched was only seven or eight. Her doll-sized body in a hot pink bathing suit was dwarfed by the floating bed. Standing on an overlooking platform was her significantly larger swim partner. At the sound of the whistle, that girl jumped, plowing into the oversize pillow. Upon impact, the little-little flew up squealing like a turbo-lobbed flamingo. Rotating backward, legs splayed over her head, she executed the perfect claw-the-air-in-panic back flop. Nellie couldn't help it. She laughed. The blob was adrenaline-rush fun, just like a rollercoaster—minus the safety bar.

For girls in the water, the day was perfection. For those who weren't, the temperature was downright unpleasant. Nellie picked up her pace. She wanted out of the sunshine. She wondered why there was always a breeze on the river but hardly ever one on land. A few more steps and it wouldn't matter. She was nearing the shade. The path through the woods was right in front of her and she could see that coolness awaited. The tippy-tops of the trees were swaying.

She entered the woods thankful to have the beating sun off her back. It was absolute tranquility, complete stillness, as if that breeze in the trees had been a mirage. It felt slightly cooler though. She slowed down, letting her eyes adjust to the dappled light. This was her favorite path, as long as she didn't see a snake—so green and lush, like something out of a fairytale. The live oaks and Spanish moss were especially amazing here. The hundreds of frayed grey clumps hanging from the branches reminded her of every witch story she'd ever read. It was spooky pretty. She loved it.

She stepped onto a wooden footbridge that crossed a shallow creek. A cluster of Venus Flytraps thrived near the soggy edge, so she stopped to have a look. She had the exact same plant back home in her room in a plastic container. But it was nothing compared to these. She was mesmerized by these fat green heads and fleshy pink insides and spines of interlocking spikes, poised to close without mercy if the plant sensed a victim—if the trigger hairs were touched. She squatted down, peering into the bouquet of gaping mouths. Half the traps were clamped shut. Poor bugs, she thought, dying inside, getting sucked dry. Hopefully it was mosquitoes. If these plants could eat all the bloodthirsty mosquitoes, that would be the bomb. Good thing she'd spritzed herself with bug spray. Without that pharmaceutical elixir, camp life would be tough and itchy. Not fun—being eaten to death.

Fanning skeeters away, she bent over the traps, examining them up close. As she lingered, a steady current of floral-scented air wrapped around the underside of her jaw, prickling the downy hairs at the base of her skull and seeping inside her eardrum, sounding like her name.

"Nellie..."

She wrenched her head around, almost choking on spit. Automatically her fist came up to slug the jerk who snuck up behind her. Turning that fast, she lost her footing and slipped off the bridge, splashing down into the creek. One flip flop suctioned to the mud, leaving her arch unprotected as she repeatedly stomped rocks, trying to regain her balance. Twisting her body and flailing her arms, she struggled to avoid the massacre of any flytraps. Once she steadied herself, hurting and smeared with crud, she stood up furious. She glanced around for the person responsible, figuring the idiot to be Lee. But standing in the creek with sludge to her knees, she discovered that she was still alone.

She whirled again—checking behind her, checking under the bridge. But the prankster shifted in perfect timing, sensing her movements. Abruptly she faked left, then spun right. It made this time—discovering no one—disturbing. Her esophagus went dry. She told herself to breathe, that it was just some practical joke she hadn't figured out yet. But she still felt the warmth in her ear and the shiver from her murmured name.

Kneeling down, using the bridge to hide behind, she watched for a head to peek out from around a tree trunk. She nearly fell backward in the water when the low hum began again.

"Nellie..."

Electric fear jolted her. Her heart clamped down and sped up. Palms chilled with the sting of panic. Thrashing her arms like she was under attack by killer bees, she splashed out of the water and onto the path, full-speed running, digging in as fast as she could dig—one shoe on, the other abandoned. It was fight or flight and she flew. She never looked back. Never saw the blackened fingers reaching for her hair. She didn't dare look, afraid that looking would slow her down or make her trip over roots and fall. She didn't even feel it when the meat of her heel landed on a protruding stone. Or when her ankle—unstable in the flip flop—nearly twisted in a rut. She hurtled down the path and burst onto the raised entrance of the rifle range with a silent scream jammed in her throat.

With her world moving in slow motion, she skidded to a halt, covered in gunk. Her equilibrium was off as she fought to get her bearings, searching for the girls. Spotting them, she tried making sense of what she saw—all three of them together in a middle shooting bay. How was that even possible? And everything else around her—the pop, pop, pop as pellets fired, the orderly racks of rifles, the rows of safety glasses and paper targets, the counselors chatting in their booth—all of it appeared so normal. No one even noticed her frantic arrival. Amazingly, she hadn't made any noise careening down the path. Not that she hadn't tried. She just couldn't get any sound out.

The arteries in her neck were still throbbing, but her heart rate was slowing and the fear was subsiding. After scanning the range, she forced herself to turn around and look down the path. She saw a Blue Jay swoop from branch to branch and heard its caw. She heard crickets and cicadas too. The sounds helped her regain some composure. Nothing was sinister, just a lovely forest trail lined with Spanish moss.

Thirsty, so thirsty. It hit her like a tossed sandbag. She stumbled to the faucet, rattling off question after question in her head. Was it her imagination? Did Tou-tou's story get her paranoid? Had she suffered a bout of heat exhaustion? Was that what jumbled her brain and made it go all haywire? Made her think things and hear things that weren't really there? She knew the dangers of extreme temperatures without drinking enough fluids. Was today that extreme? Rationalizing, she zeroed in on that as the culprit and turned the hose on full blast. She slipped off her flip flop and washed both legs, watching muck sinking between the planks until she had clean calves and ankles and feet. She turned the pressure down and angled the hose over her lips, sucking in cheek-bulging gulps of water. It slid down her throat like a savior. She didn't stop until her stomach felt heavy and her front teeth got cold. She ran it over her head and all through her hair. Cooling down. Calming down. Twisting the handle, she turned off the flow and dropped the hose in a puddle. She stood up ringing out her soaked hair, hoping she'd attracted no gawkers.

Her attention shifted to the girls. She'd expected at least one would be loitering in the woods, but there they all were. They didn't even seem to be watching for her. Standing in a semi-circle, they were busy talking and loading their weapons. She started toward them, limping on the sore foot.

Gwen saw her first. "Here she is! The star finally grace us with her grand entrance, barefoot and drippin wet?" Gwen noticed the stringy hair and the bib of drenched shirtfront. "That a different style. What happen to you? Why ya all wet?"

"You guys came straight here?" She asked in a rough-edged voice.

"No, we went to the mall first," snapped Lee. "Course we came straight here. Where else ya think we went, *Oh Great One* who keeps us waiting?" Her terse tone sounded convincing.

"You jump in the pool before ya decide to come on," teased Gwen.

"Not exactly. But just so you know, the necklace you threw flew way under a table. I had to crawl on my hands and knees to get it out. Then Tou-tou got massively excited to show me a project. I could hardly walk out while he was talking to me, could I? That's called rude. So thanks a lot for just leaving me." They could hear she was miffed.

"First of all, just so you know, the necklace was a perfect throw. Right at your head. Don't blame me you can't catch. And second, I know that man can talk once he gets goin. Between the two of you it's a miracle you got here before dark. And third, we walked slow. We was waitin while we was walkin. Can't expect us to fry in a griddle while you chit-chat. Didn't plan on you takin forever. Don't be mad." Gwen put her arm around Nellie in a side hug and instantly got wet. "And fourth, why you near drowned?"

"Yeah, Nellie," Paige jumped in, "you get in the middle of a water balloon fight?"

Nellie studied their faces for an ounce of unchecked deception. If she spied a hint of it she'd know it. But all she saw staring back at her were three guiltless friends. Taking a deep breath, she settled for the dehydration explanation and let go of her anger. With her next breath, she began filling them in on her starring role in *Terror in the Woods!*, blaming it all on the heat and her Oscar worthy imagination—starting with the gut-sucking Venus flytraps. She had them howling as she acted out her dramatic plunge from the bridge into the shoe-gobbling creek. How she spun in the water, this way and that, searching for someone to punch until the croak of a cicada flipped her switch and she tore off down the path of death running from ghosts and barely clinging to life, staggering to the safety of the range. She showed them how she stood her ground and turned to Jack-slap her pursuer, fending off nothing but a Blue Jay. Then how she leapt on the hose to wash away dirt and chug water before anyone saw her looking like an asylum escapee. She embellished every detail shaking with laughter.

Three minutes later, she made her next mistake. Brought back to life by the hose water and her girls, she signed her name for an air rifle, a tin of pellets, and a pair of safety glasses. The dance became her primary focus. Her determination not to be branded with boy repellant—the blacked-out front tooth, the gross red lipstick, and the Brillo pad hair—made shooting a hole through the center of a target her only concern. That strange heatstroke assault in the woods... She forgot all about it.

It had not been a failure,
merely a tease.
So the laughter did not vex her.
It was good that the girl was happy
and carefree.
Wary ones
were much harder
to
catch.

Chapter 7

Nellie got what she was hoping for. Walking back to the shooting bay, rifle pointing downrange and skyward, she saw that none of the girls had claimed the first spot on the mat. Flopping to her belly in the camp's mandatory shooting position, she adjusted her safety glasses and took aim—feeling James Bond cool. Before she could fire, she was stopped.

"Hold up, little lady. Skedaddle yourself to the back of the line. But nice try." Lee wasn't about to let 007 Nellie slip in first. She nudged her in the ribs with the toe of her shoe. "You got here last. You shoot last."

Nellie didn't budge. "You guys took practice shots, right? I get some too."

"No practice shots. We didn't take any," said Paige. "Decided that would make it more survival of the fittest."

"Ya mean survival of the nerve rackin," grumbled Gwen. "I ain't throwin no hissy fit but I ain't for the no practice shots, Nells. They just conveniently outvoted me since you weren't here yet."

"What are you, some namby-pamby? We all shot cold at archery. Should be the same for here," argued Lee. "I think that's fair and more fun. Don't you, Nellie?"

Nellie wasn't about to give Lee the impression that she needed any special prep. If Lee and Paige didn't want practice shots, Nellie didn't either. She reminded herself what was important. Loosey-goosey. If she kept things loose, kept her mind free-wheeling and didn't clench-up with doubts, she'd be totally fine.

"I have no problem with that." Nellie responded so confidently that Lee had second thoughts. "Right, Gwen?" She hinted to her teammate. "We don't care, right?" Gwen caught her leveled look and sighed in resigned agreement. "See," Nellie said. "It doesn't matter to us. Whatever floats your boat, Sparky." Smiling at Lee, she pushed her safety glasses to the top of her head.

"I guess," whined Gwen. "Whatever you say, I say. I'm just ready to quit jawin on it and get me a glass of bug juice lickety-split. I ain't drinkin from no moldy hose. If we gonna do this, let's do it!" Even with thirst wearing her down, Gwen was all about getting at the fun.

"Beat it then, Hollywood." Lee was anxious to shoot first, keep the pressure on. Her loitering patience was way used up.

Booted from the primo spot, Nellie played it like the seasoned actress that she was—getting up, stepping aside, making a sweeping gesture for Lee to take her place. She didn't broadcast her frustration. She kept her cool. But Paige was the one who didn't hesitate. Paige—plopping to her stomach with a grunt—lowered her glasses and aimed her gun at a target just 10 meters in front of their slot. To nobody in particular, she recited the rules of the challenge one more time.

"Two shots each. Best team shot wins." She never looked up, never took her eyes off the target. Watching her every move, the girls heard her complete the first task of a competent marksman. She clicked off her safety.

"Let the games continue." A second after Paige said it, her gun popped. Her well-aimed pellet left an off-center hole just inside the black of the bull's-eye. A sweet shot. The corners of Gwen's mouth went down.

"Sicky-gnar!" Lee shouted. "Now do us another, only better!"

Though Paige was clearly thrilled by the result, her expression remained very un-Paige like. It stayed serious. Rising to her knees, she broke open the stock, shoved the next pellet forward, and fell back on the mat clicking off the safety.

Pop.

Three heads swiveled again but this time they cocked to one side, confounded by two possibilities. Either Paige had just missed the target entirely or she'd shot clean through her first hole. Firing so fast, Nellie and Gwen were sure she'd missed. But Paige and Lee insisted that the second pellet traveled the identical path as the first. They swore she'd shot clean through the same hole twice. Either way, it hardly mattered. One great shot was all she needed, and her first shot was exactly that. It might just win the whole contest.

In all the hoopla, Lee called Gwen out, daring her to go next. Lee claimed that with Paige so close to perfect, she probably wouldn't shoot at all. "It's not lookin like I'll need to and I sure don't wanna rub it in." She was preening around, acting super cocky.

"We ain't worried 'bout you rubbin in nothin," sassed Gwen. "Just worry 'bout rubbin in your sunscreen, Rudolf."

Gwen wasn't intimidated by Paige's mediocre bull's-eye or Lee's dare to hit the mat and take her shots. Gwen was used to taking guff from her brothers and excellent at ignoring it.

"Back up a second. You're not gonna shoot, Lee?" Nellie loved the sound of that. Lee out of the competition was the best possible news.

"Just sayin I might not *need* to," shrugged Lee. "But let's not put anythin in writin. Prefer to keep my options open. If she needs me to bury team Sugar 'n' Spice, Paige knows I have her back."

"Sugar 'n' Spice? I like that," effused Gwen, approving of the new nicknames. "Nell's Sugar? I'm Spice?" She started cackling. "Cause ya know, Lee, sugar is Nellie's favorite food."

As if on cue, Nellie reached in her pocket and pulled out one of the raw sugar packets she'd filched from the cafeteria. Tearing a corner open, she emptied the contents into her mouth and crunched. "It boosts my brain and calms my nerves," she said between chomps. "I could balance a pearl on my fingertip once the sugar hits my bloodstream. Makes my eyesight go all x-ray visiony too. Great for target practice. Thanks for reminding me I had that." She crossed her eyes and wriggled, acting like a superhero tremor was shaking her entire body.

"And that a mild dose compared to her favorite," added Gwen. "She turn into Wonder Woman if she get her hands on a cherry Pixie-Stick. No lie." Gwen would have given anything to pull out one of those sweet and sour straws. She imagined ripping off the tip, presenting it to Nellie, and standing back to watch her friend pretend to transform from the sugar. If she knew Nellie, it would've been quite the show-stopping show—probably including a cartwheel. In the real world, all Gwen could do was step to the mat. Contrary to Lee's hopes, Gwen was perfectly fine with going next.

"Excuse me, ya bums. I feels me a winner comin on." She slid into place while Paige moved to a rickety railing.

"That's a major coincidence, Spicy G." Gwen's comment was just the reminder Nellie needed. "Cause you look like a winner. In fact, over the last week of being blown away by your skills, I decided to write an inspiring poem about you. Even memorized it."

"Oh, really?" Gwen started smiling. She knew Nellie was up to something. "Lay it on me, Sugar."

"Oh, I will, Spice. It's like totally simple but like totally profound. Once you hear it, bet you guys find it kind of sticks in your head permanently." With team LePaige looking suspicious and Gwen's grin growing bigger, Nellie cleared her Shakespearean pipes and started chanting.

"Win with Gwen!"

"Win with Gwen!"

"Win with Gwen!"

"Win with Gwen!"

The catchy cheer quickly attracted the attention of every girl at the range.

"Awe shucks, Sugar! Don't stop!" Gwen yelled over Nellie, arranging herself on the mat and loving it.

Lee and Paige yelled too—not loving it. Lee backhanded Nellie's arm but the whack did nothing to shush her. The only thing that shut Nellie up was Gwen disengaging her safety. Hoping that her teammate was about to fire the winner, Nellie gladly bit her tongue. Gwen knew more than your average girl about shooting a hole in a backyard can so Nellie crossed her fingers, praying that today was Gwen's day.

Gwen wasn't hot-headed like Paige. She settled in and took her time. Where guns were concerned, Gwen stuck with a tried and true routine, always going through a mental checklist before pulling the trigger. With the safety off, she did her thing, zeroing in. Then like a girl being kissed, her right leg levitated, bending at the knee. Nellie knew what came next.

Pop.

"Dang it," cursed Paige. Gwen's shot had stolen the lead, inside Paige's by a centimeter.

"Don't make me have to shoot," warned Lee.

"Too late. She just edged me out," said Paige, pouting at the target. "Ya have to shoot now."

"I doubt even the Leebot can improve on perfection," goaded Gwen from the mat. "And looky here, y'all. Round two's a-comin."

Quickly reloading, Gwen flicked off her safety and started aiming before Lee or Paige could think of a good comeback. Neither wanted do-overs because of distracting talk in mid-shot so they kept quiet. Only their eyes darted back and forth between the target, Gwen's trigger finger, and her foot. She made them wait until she'd gone through her checklist. Then her leg came up.

Pop. Even closer.

"Fan-tas-tic!" Nellie shrieked—feeling the pressure vice melting away.

"My gift to you, darlin," drawled Gwen with ample southern charm. She stood up brushing off her shirt.

Lee immediately stepped forward with the butt of her rifle resting on her hip. "So you twerps wanna play rough? No problemo, I can play rough. Just remember I told ya so. No cryin in your punch tonight." She tossed her tin of pellets to Paige. "Spicy G, those were two cute shots. Good job." She patted Gwen's back, genuinely meaning it. "Don't take this all personal cause I really do wanna keep enjoyin barbeque at your family's restaurants, but business is business. Step aside, Missy."

Lee withdrew the arrow from her shorts and handed it to Paige. Her blunt talk made the whites of Gwen's and Nellie's eyes slightly more visible. Nellie tried to rise above it, convinced they'd keep the lead. Gwen's last shot had to be the winner. Most likely Nellie was the one who wouldn't have to shoot. Lee was just throwing around her usual bull. She had to be a tad shook up over Gwen's accuracy, even if she wasn't showing it. Hopefully it was enough to throw her. Testing her theory, Nellie made a crack aimed at deflating Lee's ego. "Lee's gonna so embarrass herself." She stressed "so".

Lee chuckled. "Stick with the other one, Nell. It's way more factual. What was it? 'Nellie and Gwen will never win!' That was it, right?" Stressing "never", Lee started singing it and wiping dust specks off her barrel. Paige joined in doing back-up harmony, keeping the beat with the arrow like a conductor. After the first few verses, Gwen glanced at Nellie like their victory was about to be snatched away and stomped to death. The doomsday prediction was flashing its warning in her big brown eyes.

"Come to papa," called Lee, dropping to the mat and clicking off the safety. She repositioned her elbows a couple of times, getting her shoulders aligned, looking more and more like a sniper with every move. Lowering her head, she gauged her line of sight with premeditated precision. No girly leg came up in the three seconds that passed before she smoothly pulled the trigger.

Pop.

Three heads spun around to the inevitable. Nellie's body wilted. Gwen let out a long exhale. The whoops of team Le-Paige scattered the wildlife.

Lee didn't need a second shot. Jumping up, she exchanged a series of high-fives, low-fives, a hip-bump and a complicated handclap with Paige. Their celebration was off-the-charts monumental as her one and only shot said it all. Bull's-flippin-eyeball. Kill shot to the pupil.

"Nice shot." Nellie forced herself to say it—the toughest PC moment of her life. Her mood turned grim. The thought of going to the first dance looking like an extra from the set of a low budget horror movie was diabolically depressing.

"I'm gonna personally put a hairball in her pulled-pork sandwich when she comes eatin at our place," grumbled Gwen to Nellie. She was so dejected that she couldn't even acknowledge Lee or her ace.

"Now, Gwendolyn, let's not go there." Smirking, Lee leaned against the railing as Paige slapped the arrow in her hand. After Lee stuck it through her waistband like a saber, team LePaige grinned at team GweNell with their safety glasses pushing their bangs askew and their guns resting against their shoulders—pretty much the done-deal winners.

That loosey-goosey mindset Nellie was counting on began its ebb and flow out to sea. The feel of it leaving initiated her panic button. Fiddling with her gun, she started thinking things—like how they were about to be totally trounced, and why they'd ever agreed to the bet in the first place. Twenty-twenty hindsight had a way of illuminating her misfortune to occasionally pursue really bad choices. Her mind raced with ideas to get them out of the whole debacle. Before her mouth wrapped around some well chosen words and strung them into a persuasive sentence, she felt a forceful nudge pushing her toward the mat.

"You got us into this. You best get us out," ordered Gwen. "I don't do no brassy red lipstick. Makes my teeth look yella."

"I got us into this? But you...you..." stammered Nellie.

"Not the tooth in front, Gweny." Paige couldn't resist the easy set up. "Nellie's eyeliner will keep that one lookin jet black no matter what color lipstick you're wearin." Paige smiled sweetly, playing like it would bring Gwen peace of mind.

"Zip it, Blondie. Nells is gonna shove that smile right up your nose. Besides, I don't hear nobody singin a victory song yet." The second the words came out of her mouth, Gwen regretted them.

"Nellie and Gwen will never win!"
"Nellie and Gwen will never win!"
"Nellie and Gwen will never win!"
"Nellie and Gwen will never win!"

This time Lee sang it like a rapper while Paige slapped the beat on her thighs. The riffs were actually pretty funny, but neither Gwen nor Nellie was in any kind of laughing mood anymore. The reality of getting creamed made their spunk nosedive. They offered no exchange of barbs. Nellie, stiffening up by the second, was amazed at how her clever annoyance tactic backfired so viciously on its creator. Concealing a dejected groan, she placed the blame squarely on that unflappable female christened Lucille Ernestine Erhardt—Lee's real name—and total bum luck.

"Any day now," Nellie said pointedly at the rappers—for them to knock it off. They acted like they didn't hear, increased their volume instead. So, with the weight of defeat crushing her down, Nellie lowered herself to the mat, figuring out her options. But as the mind-numbing racket pummeled her brain, thinking proved difficult. Only desperation pulled her through.

As Nellie saw it, she had two potential rescue plans. Plan one: depend on her skill and pray for one incredible shot. Shooting a winner with two solid chances wasn't out of the question. It was doable. She'd hit the bull in the eye twice in a row yesterday. Plan two (and this idea she stole directly from team LePaige) would be tricky and totally dishonest, but with the perfect acting it just might work. She was still working out the kinks, but the gist of the idea went something like this: she'd take her first shot—maybe it'd be great, maybe not—it didn't matter. Then she'd take her second shot and miss the whole target intentionally. So there'd be no new hole. When the arguing broke out, she'd insist that her pellet passed clean through Lee's ace. End of argument. The bet would end in a harmless tie. Nellie was second generation showbiz trash. She was positive that she had the acting chops to pull off the most important role of her life.

Feigning interest in the rap duo, Nellie took her time getting comfortable on the mat, attempting to make the right crucial decision. Anxious Gwen stood in a motionless trance, hardly breathing or blinking. In fact, everyone at the range had stopped to watch. Even the counselors were standing on top of their counter for the best possible view.

Nellie lowered her glasses and tucked the rifle snuggly beneath her collarbone. Knowing she was preparing to fire, the girls abruptly curtailed their vocals. The flat quiet would have been unnerving had Nellie's mind not been zooming. She gripped the gun with sweaty palms and immediately let go for a double wiping off on the sides of her shorts. Feeling the hard boards under the thin mat, she repositioned her boney hips and dried the trigger housing as well, then gripped the gun again. Her heart went back to pounding as she sighted—picturing the word *BRASS*—just like Gwen had taught her. Slowly, she started applying each letter to her future.

B: *breathe*. She took a deep breath. Her acting teacher called them cleansing breaths. Gwen called them "centerin breaths". Their purpose was to clear Nellie's head, fill it with oxygen and refresh her body. It felt sort of good, so she took another.

R: *relax*. Relax, she told herself. Easier said than done when heartbeats were lifting her off the planks. *Relax!* She yelled inside her head. But berating herself was probably counter-productive. Fine. Pretend to relax. Visualize sandy beaches and swaying palms. The instant she thought up that boring cliché, she blocked it. No time for imagining tropical beaches. Tightly wound would have to sub for relaxed. There was no relaxing today. She gave up and moved to the next letter.

A: *aim*. The sight notch on the end of the barrel was rocking up and down like the bow of Nellie's sailboat. Not good. *Stop it!* She willed the movement to slow down by holding the gun tighter. The distance the tab traveled back and forth over the bull's-eye did shorten. Slightly. She tried timing when she should pull the trigger—the millisecond when the muzzle passed over target—but she couldn't get a steady count before it rose too high, then dropped too low. She gripped the rifle tighter, squeezing with hands that were back to slippery, and lay perfectly still holding her breath, seeing if that would help. She didn't detect much improvement, so she waited and waited…

"Breathe, girl!" Ten seconds had passed before Gwen unleashed the harsh critique.

Recognizing her elementary mistake, a somewhat startled Nellie took a deep breath. She didn't dare look up at her coach. She kept her head in the game and started over. *BRASS*. The letters re-formed in her head. *Breathe. Relax. Aim. Squeeze slack. Squeeze more*. She told herself that this time she'd go fast. When she got to the first S, the S to squeeze out trigger slack (assuming she made it to the first S this time), she'd just do it, just squeeze it. Fly through the whole procedure list and hope that speed helped her focus.

She attacked with a quickened tempo. The flow felt

better, not so nervy. The sight tip was still trolling the black bull's-eye when she got to the first S, but she was more in control. Steadying her hands, she kept breathing and concentrating, putting her faith in her go-for-it rhythm. She started squeezing the trigger, then squeezing it harder, then harder and harder—until the pad of her finger was pale and quivery from pressure.

Still no pop.

"Ya might consider clickin off the safety first." Paige said it deadpan for maximum impact. "Just a suggestion."

The tension, the embarrassment—all of it crashed over Nellie like a tidal wave. She was peeved. She cut her eyes up at Paige ready to spit out something ultra sarcastic, but she intercepted Gwen's dropped jaw before she could speak.

"There's a flaw in your system, Gwen," argued Nellie in self-defense. "It should be *SO BRASS*. *Safety Off*, then the rest!"

"Did you hear me say one thing?" squawked Gwen.

"I hear you thinking lots of things!" Nellie answered.

Gwen arched a brow and pursed her lips, staring down at Nellie like a disgruntled duck. Nellie turned away, looking back at the target and wiping her hands on the last dry place her shorts offered. Before doing anything else, she clicked off her safety. "There, OK?"

"That's a good girl. Now you can actually pull back on that widdle thinga-ma-jigga called the twigga." Lee enunciated every word like Nellie was a toddler.

Nellie dished it back. "Since you're being so helpful Lee, would you mind running out there and holding the target still. All your hot air is making it flap."

"Didn't we do that already?" Lee laughed. "Believe I'll stay right here in the safe zone watchin. Thinkin good thoughts." That last part she said with a cartoonish lisp.

Nellie knew when to end a conversation, especially one whose sole purpose was to bug her. She didn't give Lee the chance to keep talking. Not in a million years would the bouffant hair ever bother Lee; her cut was too short to be shocking. And the black tooth probably sounded fun to her. But if Nellie was terrified to wear smeared lipstick in front of a bunch of boys, Lee's dread must be quadruple. If the stuff came within inches of her face she'd probably implode, being so diehard tomboy. The only action that could lock Lee's lips was for Nellie to put her eye to the gun. That would hush the crowd.

Nellie lowered her head and it came true. Silence. She checked out her shot down the long neck of the barrel. What she saw definitely peaked her interest. The sight tab was miraculously leveled right on the bull's-eye; it wasn't even roving much. She tried not to get too excited. She maintained her steady breathing—feeling like her nerves had just been shown the door by a cerebral bouncer—and ripped through her checklist.

Breathe: she already was. *Relax*: she pressed the balls of her feet into the boards, stretching the tendons in her calves, never taking her eyes off the black circle. *Aim*: she couldn't do better. *Squeeze slack*: she started squeezing. *Squeeze more*: no need, the rifle fired and the target twitched. Nellie's head came up checking for the new hole.

"Baby girl," shouted Gwen. "Looky there, y'all! Baby girl's makin a stand!"

It was true. Nellie's shot was first-rate, barely a scootch off-center. Lee's hole now looked like a blimpy eight. Unfortunately Nellie saw, rising to her knees, hers was the outer hole. Not good enough to claim as another twin ace. So close.

In tune with the target, Nellie chambered her next pellet and flopped to the ground. Before anyone could say anything smart-alecky, she clicked off the safety.

Breathe. She was breathing.

Relax. She was relaxed.

Aim. Solid as a rock, right on target.

Squeeze. That's when the weirdness started again.

That same breeze from the woods blew across her face, dislodging a hank of bang and sending hairs under her safety glasses. The tips poked her in the eye—blurring her vision—while warm air passed over the perspiration on her top lip, fogging her lenses. Just in the distance beyond the target, she saw a flurry of white. Her gun popped right as the white pulsed and furled and vanished in the treetops.

"What the—" Snatching off her glasses, she wiped her watery eye with the back of her hand, knowing the shot stunk. She wasn't even looking at the target when the gun went off. The misfire should have had her screaming a series of expletives, but her attention was somewhere else, on something above the target. She stayed on the mat, craning her neck and scanning the trees. The shouts of Lee and Paige brought her back.

Examining the target and seeing nothing new, she thought maybe the miracle had happened—thought maybe she'd popped Lee's ace after all. But then, barely visible on the target's upper left hand corner, she spied her screw-up. A corner of the paper was missing. Unintentionally, she'd almost missed the target entirely—almost activated plan two. Instead, the glaring partial hole was the final word in defeat. She could practically hear it blurting the word, "Losers!"

"NO!" Gwen wailed. "Nellie, what happened? I thought you had this!"

Nellie started getting up, staring past the target line. "Nobody saw that?" She was pointing at the trees.

"You bet we saw that," howled Lee. "Why ya think we're celebratin?"

"Not the shot, I'm not talking about the shot," snapped Nellie. But Lee and Paige were only interested in their victory boogie. To them, Nellie just sounded like she was beginning to whine—which they'd fully expected.

"But there was a thing there! Right there! A white thing," she blathered away. "You guys didn't see that white thing?"

Nellie wouldn't drop it. Something was out there. The girls must have seen it. No way was she the only one. It was so blatant, right where they were looking. And that blast of air? They missed that too? How? They were standing right next to her. They should have felt it on their shins unless they were totally unconscious.

That paranoia from the bridge was fast returning. Something about these woods was creepy, even Tou-tou said so. But that was preposterous. He was joking, right? Just trying to get a rise out of her. She needed the weirdness to stop. She needed her girls to say that they'd seen it—an egret or something. That's what it was. Just bad luck it had to show up when she was shooting. But not only would none of them say it, they acted like they hadn't seen anything at all. And something else was wrong. But even to think of it… Those eyes—so human—staring at her… It gave her the chills. Kept her scouring the trees.

"Don't look so out of it, Nellsy. You almost wacked 'em with your first pop. You got in there closer than me." Gwen had switched to her soothing tone. Her buddy was acting embarrassingly thin-skinned. She reached over and shoved Nellie's muzzle so it wasn't aimed directly at her face.

"You really didn't see that white stuff right above the target?" Nellie heard the patheticness in her own voice. She didn't care. She kept staring at the trees.

Gwen made a show of searching the woods—to be nice. She saw nothing but leafy branches beyond the gently flapping targets. "Nope. Didn't see any white anythin."

Nellie didn't respond.

When Lee had fired the winner, Gwen had handled it badly, she knew it. But Nellie's behavior was taking the cake. "It's no biggy, Nellie," insisted Gwen. "Ain't the end of the world. We almost beat 'em today, thanks to you. Stop mopin. We done good."

"Something's out there, Gwen. I stared right at it and it stared back. When the gun fired, I wasn't even looking at the target. Something white and lacey was watching me." Nellie's voice was filling with desperation. "I could see right through it." A tingling tightness permeated her scalp, that same sensation she'd felt on the path. She did a full-body shiver to shake it off.

"See-through white?" Gwen repeated it doubtfully. "Well it coulda been a big egret. Maybe a albino pelican. We get both those 'round here." She stayed very calm. "They hang out in the trees. Probably one of those spooked right as you was aimin. Messed ya up."

Finally someone said it. Nellie shut her eyes to ease the pounding in her head. That it was a large egret made total sense. It really did. Except for that one other detail.

"Gwen," she whispered, "it had *eyes*."

Gwen's response was swift and matter-of-fact. "Birds in these parts has eyes, Nellie. Don't y'all have birds with eyes back in California?"

"No, Gwen." Nellie's volume rose. "I mean it had *human* eyes. Like a *person*. I looked right into them."

Gwen was taken aback by her friend's manic urgency— and her sudden paleness. It was time to take charge. "I'm gonna march you right back to that hose and douse your head if you keep talkin like that! It didn't have no *people eyes*, Nellie. It probably had two eyes wide as saucers cause you about to pop it! We need to get more sugar in you before that brain shuts down and you fall over." Gwen ranted like a mother. "Causa this heat, I bet. Probably sweated out all your lunch. You get a drink in you and somethin to munch, you be all right." Gwen searched Nellie's face for signs of life. "It's OK, Nells-A-Bub. We can handle this. Quit worry-wartin. We gonna make it the funnest dance ever. We still gonna be a big hit with the fellas." Gwen had Nellie by the shoulders.

"Dance?" In all the commotion, Nellie had forgotten about the dance.

"Yeah, the dance, Space Cadet. You get one look at Big Bird and forget the whole reason we out here? " Gwen was pretty dismayed at Nellie's low tolerance. Evidently, the heat and humidity took a lot more than a week to get used to.

Nellie finally sighed and gave in. "I think my wires short-circuited. This really isn't my day, Gwen. Too many oddball things happening." She rubbed her eyes. "Guess I totally choked wanting to beat those two so bad. I'm sorry." Her apology got a hug.

Nellie couldn't completely shake the image of the peculiar eyes staring at her, but she was ready to throw in the towel and accept that it was nothing more than frightened water-fowl. She was upset for jumping to conclusions, upset for losing her cool and blowing the match. She loathed the idea that she'd been beaten by the hot, muggy weather. It had turned her into a first-class ditz. Thank goodness for sensible Gwen.

"I'm tellin ya, it's dehydration," cautioned Gwen. "You's red in the cheeks but you's white as a sheet all around your mouth. That's a sure sign. You fill up on that tea ya like and you be good as new. But we better do it before you start tellin me how them squirrels is wearin high heels and those butterflies has on hats."

Put like that, Nellie's smile slipped out. Gwen had a comforting talent for making her feel like a total ding-a-ling. She was glad that Lee and Paige didn't overhear her driveling meltdown. At the height of their victory, they'd run off collecting congrats around the range, leaving team GweNell to what they thought was a moment of private commiseration.

"Oh, goody," grumbled Nellie. "We get to be the main attraction at the first dance. Can't wait."

"So much for romance tonight..." sighed Gwen.

There was no denying it, the dances were huge. All the girls got gussied-up before boarding the buses to see some boats—some dreamboats. Every assortment of male camper—from sunburned to suntanned—would be freshly showered and overly cologned, waiting for them on the tennis courts under twinkling white lights. Now one of those sacred nights of teenage bliss was headed for the dumper of public disgrace.

"I don't know about you, but my pick-up lines are pretty sharp." Nellie lied.

"That's good news." Gwen forced a smile, making the best of it. "You do all the talkin cause we sure to attract some looky-loos. I'll be right behind you. I just pray nobody recognize us next Saturday night."

"You don't get to stand behind her," scolded Paige, returning to stir the pot. "Side by side, that's the line-up."

"No hidin-out allowed" agreed Lee, popping out from behind Paige.

"Yep, no picture hoggies. Who knows, tonight might be y'alls' big showbiz break. Lookin how you're gonna look somethin funny's bound to happen, and when it does, I'll be right there with my phone takin videos." At first Paige meant it kidding, but the more she thought about it, the idea did give a whole new dimension to the night's amusements. Paige was the internet's number one fan, a computer whizkid. She wasted way too much time watching clips and posting links for her network of friends. Nellie and Gwen could practically see the smoke shooting out of her ears, imagining their debut on the World Wide Web.

"Forget it," barked Gwen, horrified.

"But if we got somethin hilarious, we could send it to one of those home video shows. Win ten grand and split the profits!" Lee was caught somewhere between reveling in triumph and directing their first YouTube clip.

"Easy money!" Paige concurred. "I say we go for it!" Her eyes were glazing over at the thought of all that mula.

"My future as a serious actress is *so* tanking," lamented Nellie with playful melodrama.

"But just think," crowed Paige, positively percolating with foresight, "tonight y'all might go viral!"

"See girls, losing isn't so bad. Life's still worth livin." Grinning from ear to ear, Lee spread her arms across Gwen's and Nellie's shoulders, pulling her feet up and intentionally weighing them down with her dead weight.

"If your plan makes us rich," grunted Gwen, straining under Lee, "I may consider participatin. I could find my way to forgiveness with a wad of bling in my purse." Gwen was shifting gears, fortifying herself for the night's unsightly transformation. Mainly she was relieved that Nellie was herself again. Regardless of the punishment for losing and all its impending awfulness, she knew the two of them could handle anything.

"You know what they say..." said Nellie, dumping Lee off. "When one door shuts—"

"Don't you dare say another door opens!" Gwen cut in, laughing and dumping Lee too.

"And what door would that be, Nellie?" Paige inquired.

"One that leads to a couple of seriously wrecked females," blurted Lee.

"It's gonna be great," exclaimed Paige, snicker-snorting up a storm. "We won't plan anythin. I got a sneaky suspicion when those boys get a look at y'all, their reactions will be plenty hysterical. It's a win-win."

"Most definitely!" Lee was in full agreement.

"Shall we, losers?" Paige motioned down the walkway to the exit, toward the path. "We wanna have loads of time at the bathroom mirror. Don't wanna be rushed. It's gonna be quite the process turnin y'all into supermodels."

"Feels like I'm being led to my execution," moaned Nellie, being a good sport.

"You are, Drama Queen," laughed Lee.

"Any last words," asked Paige.

"Lord have mercy!" Gwen yelled it to the treetops.

"Ditto Lord!" Nellie yelled it louder.

"The Good Lord don't have nothin to do with this. Or didn't y'all hear? He's not too keen on bettin. Y'all better talk to me and Paige if you're hopin for mercy."

"You mean *beg* us for mercy," corrected Paige. "But don't waste your time. We're not in a merciful frame of mind. Righto, Lee?"

"Righto, Paige. I'm not feelin it. Especially with Nellie almost shootin an arrow through my brain. But I don't care if I'm rushed. Bet rushed will make ya look even more amazin." Lee was closely inspecting the contours of Nellie's face. She wasn't one for make-up herself, but she couldn't wait to get her fingers in the stuff if it meant a good laugh.

"Winnin is everythin," shouted Lee, pumping her rifle overhead and leading the way from their slot.

Returning their gear to the booth, they underwent an

inquisition. Lee cut it short, clamping her hands over team GweNell's mouths and refusing to let anyone elaborate on the plans for the evening, telling the counselors they'd have to wait and see like everyone else.

Before leaving, Nellie reclaimed the lone flip flop she'd left by the hose. As she walked barefooted along the trail, the woods came abuzz with life. But song birds and frog croaks were quickly drowned out by lively girl talk. Even a pair of roosting turkey vultures went unnoticed. When they reached the infamous footbridge, Lee was the first to spot Nellie's shoe stuck in the mud. She jumped down to pluck it out, rinsing it off in the creek before tossing it up.

"So this is where the goblins attacked you," she jested.

"'Fraid so. Did I kill many flytraps?"

"Not sure how ya did this..." Lee was leaning over the plants, counting dozens of footprints. "Looks like ya managed to stomp all around them. I don't see a single smashed trap. That's some fancy footwork, Hollywood."

"They don't call me fleet-feet for nothing. I got super fast moves. Too quick for a goblin." Clowning around, Nellie gave a demonstration of her previous flailings.

You...can't...catch...me..." She sang it.

To her surprise, the silly re-enactment did ignite a spark of her earlier fear. She extinguished it, resisting the urge to protect her ears from the echo of her whispered name. Her girls were with her this time. There wasn't a single reason to be afraid.

"Nellie..."

Nellie's head jerked around so fast that she nearly cricked her neck. But it was just Gwen.

"Nellieeee..." gurgled Gwen, her arms slowly rising. Nellie screeched, performing a series of dainty, distancing leaps.

"Nellieeee...We're gonna get you..." Lurching after Nellie, Paige copied Gwen like a zombie. "Me want eyeballs! Chomp! Chomp! Me hungry for eyeballs!" Nellie squealed louder and backpedaled faster. With groping arms, Gwen and Paige began sprinting after her yelling, "Get chewy eyeballs!"

Screaming like a damsel in distress, Nellie skipped down the path, headed for the inviting splash of the crowded swimming pools. The zombies—with Lee joining the eyeball-eating chase—quickly closed the gap. Hot on her tail.

She floated
in the treetops,
blending with the breeze,
listening to the converging octaves
of their strong voices.
It was touching—she observed,
gazing down upon their antics—
watching someone so young
enjoying
the last day
of
her
life.

Chapter 8

Following dinner it began. Every girl in Cabin 21 had managed to squeeze inside the bathroom to observe the fashion slaughter. As a result, the temperature in the room heated up from sixteen bodies' worth of anticipation. At least they were freshly showered bodies dressed in party clothes, excited for a night of boys, boys, boys. It only made watching team LePaige and their attention to detail—Lee destroying Nellie, Paige annihilating Gwen—all the more entertaining.

A hot mess was the only way to describe the new team GweNell. The cabin—going hog-wild for the looks—had decided to dress exactly the same way for their upcoming skit. A few girls were even contemplating the outfits for Halloween. Nellie and Gwen considered neither as compliments. Subjecting themselves to humiliation once was bad enough. Going around fashionably dilapidated on purpose was nothing they intended to do twice. By dance time, the only thing recognizable about either girl was their matching beaded necklaces. Those had passed inspection due to their juvenile ridunculousness. Furthermore, Gwen and Nellie vowed to keep them on for the duration of camp. So hands off, else they got whacked.

When it came to the actual dresses, Nellie got off easy. Lee picked Nellie's cotton sundress from Tarjay. It was chosen purely for color: florescent lime to clash with the red lipstick, and its chiffony skirt printed with giant blue flowers was kind of hard to miss. Fashion wise, it was a real head-turner.

Gwen wasn't so lucky. Her dresses were deemed way too flattering. Bad news for Gwen. She was forced to wear a moth-eaten rag from the cabin's costume trunk: several sizes too big in iridescent mustard and really shimmery with geometric designs and frayed wiggers poking out from every seam. With its satin straps and short, puffy skirt, she looked like a ballerina bumpkin. Plus it was itchy.

As the festivities turned to hair design, Nellie and Gwen were impressed by the number of hairspray cans volunteered from lockers and thrust at Lee and Paige. For a few minutes the bathroom was seriously dangerous, steaming with an array of flammable scents. After the fog cleared and the coughing stopped, the two were brushed and fluffed and teased, then yanked and raked and tugged, then misted and fumigated anew—until their hair stood atop their heads defying gravity in hardening shells.

Lee had sculpted for sheer bulk: the classic *Bride of Frankenstein* 'do. She wouldn't stop pushing and pulling and pinning until Nellie's hair resembled a slanting skyscraper. Not a single painful wince convinced her to proceed more gently with Nellie's scalp.

Paige had a kinder hairdresser's touch. Gwen never once yelped. Twisting and molding, Paige shaped Gwen's hair into a landscape of furred-out cattails, creating as many tall spires as she could shellac into place with her borrowed can of cinnamon-smelling White Rain Extra Hold.

At some point Kate produced her own eyebrow pencil, suggesting that their eyebrows be darkened. Once Gwen and Nellie reluctantly agreed, Kate recommended that Paige and Lee pay particular attention to thickening and lengthening—right in the middle.

"A unibrow! I like that." Tickled to death, Lee didn't leave a slit of skin showing above the bridge of Nellie's nose.

"Oh. My. Gosh. Don't look in the mirror, Nells," snorted Gwen. "You look like a gladiator."

"You look like your grandfather!" Nellie shot back. She'd seen the grandpa's overgrown bushes in Gwen's photo album.

"Be still ya pretty thing. I need to get your lips perfectly crooked." Paige was closing in on Gwen with the special delivery from Mrs. B. She'd already twisted up the rocket-shaped tip from its gold tube.

"There it is. My favorite color," griped Gwen. "Dream about wearin that every day."

She was treated to a brief delay when Paige remembered that she should blackout Gwen's front tooth before doing her lips. The lipstick was stowed in her bra while she called for Nellie's eyeliner. A girl dressed in a navy romper with oversized white buttons, a red belt, matching red sandals, and white hoop earrings handed it over.

"Excuse me, Madison?" Everyone heard Nellie. "You

just went in my locker without asking?" She exaggerated sounding shocked.

"I got it." Lee grinned in Nellie's face. "I asked Madison to hold it. Thanks, Maddy."

"Nellie, ya know I wouldn't go snoopin in your locker without your permission," the girl said in her husky voice. Curly black hair framed her puppy-dog eyes. Madison had a habit of bobbing her head to the syllables of her words as she talked. Her dad—the mayor of her hometown—donated thousands of dollars to camp every year and her mom was a church pianist. Not the kind of girl Nellie would have pegged for the best dirty jokes. Madison bunked under Gwen and the three of them whispered together nightly, cracking each other up way later than curfew.

"Oh, come on, Maddy. Why didn't you hide it? I can't believe you turned on us. Be prepared for some late night retaliation."

"Oh, you come on your own self, Nellie. Ya know fresh-as-peaches I was pullin for my bunkmates. I can't help it if you're dumb as dirt, bettin on what you're wearin tonight of all nights! And bettin against Lee of all people! The super-shooter!" Her voice went up, emphasizing how boneheaded she thought that was. "That's just pure brainless. Y'all ain't beat her this whole last week. But I was pullin for y'all." She made a puppy-dog face to match her puppy-dog eyes. "That's gotta count for somethin."

"It counts for a cookie," Lee told Madison. "We're all pilin on Nellie's bunk when we get back. She stole a pillow-case full of pecan sandies that I'm sure she wants to share."

"I'll only forgive you for a dozen originals," bargained

Nellie, eying the girl. She wasn't talking cookies.

"Heck, that's easy." Madison beamed. "I'll call daddy tomorrow and tell him we need five dozen. He'll get Graydon to swing by the Krispy Kreme and drive 'em over. He likes checkin out the new girls anyway." She punctuated her offer by lifting her eyebrows a bunch. Graydon was Madison's six-foot two, green-eyed, good-looking older brother. He'd been a Camp Stingray counselor until he graduated from college. Now he was a suit and tie man working with the city planner across the street from their father's downtown offices. A visit from Graydon was fast-spreading news among the Seamist counselors.

When Nellie didn't answer right away, Madison sweetened the deal. "They'll be yummy heated up in the cafeteria microwave."

"You are forgiven." Nellie replied instantly.

"Toilet paper, please." The request was from Paige. Soon a lengthy strip fluttered over the heads, finding its way into her raised hand. Once Lee ripped off half, Gwen's and Nellie's lips were lifted like horses and their front teeth were scrubbed dry. The tiny white specks stuck to their gums were removed with fingernail flicks. When the TP was mostly out, the eyeliner was applied—dense and black. The toothless effect was killer. From a few feet away, Nellie and Gwen really did look like hee-haw hicks with falled out teefs.

Submitting to the horrifying makeovers, Gwen and Nellie watched their ruin in the giant mirror. The height of their low came when the red lipstick was slicked across their faces.

"Looks like they been suckin down Sloppy Joes with no

napkins," someone yelled. The tile bathroom reverberated from all the tittering.

Luckily the camera lady was a no-show. However, the combined wattage of digital camera flashes made her appearance unnecessary; the event was thoroughly well-documented without her. When Gwen and Nellie were medium rare and pronounced done, Lee and Paige stood aside like proud chefs in the kitchen, admiring their ghastly cuisine. Stepping in for the final blinding photographs, they dared to put their arms around their opponents. With team GweNell looking miserable, team LePaige posed smugly.

When the cameras finally stopped flashing, Gwen took a last look in the mirror. "What? Just brows and lips? No eye make-up?"

Lee and Paige nodded "no".

"Guys, my eyes look totally gross." Nellie studied herself as the shock set in. "At least let us do our eyes."

The negative nodding continued.

"You're really going to make us go like this?" Nellie stared at the catastrophe that used to be her face.

The nods eagerly changed to "yes".

"Ew, ew, ew." Examining herself in the mirror, Gwen switched to the perfect valley-girl accent. Gone was her southerness—replaced by a gum-chewing mouth-breather. "Like I don't care," she said. "I like still look smokin hot."

"There's an idea," muttered Nellie. Acting all valley could be a way to survive the night. They might as well try and have fun. "Like totally. Like we should totally be paid for our hotness." With the bathroom audience egging them on, Nellie matched Gwen's deviated-septum monotone.

"Like are you ready to like do this?"

"Like so ready. Like I can't wait to meet me some stud muffins. I like totally have my tweezers." Gwen was admiring herself up close, trying out a spastic head twitch, blink-blink with her feebleminded speech pattern. It was trés bizarre with her spiky headdress.

"Like I know, right! Like we need guys to understand that like manscaping is like a total must if they're serious about the ladies." Nellie spat out the first dullard thing she could think of as she analyzed her reflection, perfecting her character.

"Showtime, girlies. How about y'all tell those boys in person." Paige took Gwen by the arm, escorting her from the bathroom.

Lee clamped a hand around the back of Nellie's neck. "Just keep enjoyin yourself, punk. If you're havin fun, we're havin fun. Maybe we can get y'all a microphone while we're there and y'all can do your act on stage. That'd be a crowd pleaser."

"Like fer sure," chimed Nellie, allowing herself to be pushed into the warm evening. "Like my little black book is gonna be like massively filled with hot guys' numbers by like the end of tonight. Jealous?" She lifted her leg and let out a toot. Because of her timing and the way she clipped her words, the fart was fabtacular. But with the no tooth, the man brow and the clown lips, it almost made Lee pee. Good thing Nellie couldn't see herself anymore, thought Lee. She'd come to her senses and hightail it out of there.

"Somebody get this one an aspirin. I think all that hairspray made her delirious." Chuckling, Lee made good on her earlier offer and stuck the arrow through Nellie's hair. When Nellie called her a tool, Lee gave her beaded necklace a decent stretch. Nellie jumped when it delivered a sting to the side of her neck. Lee couldn't have been happier.

Pouring out of the cabin, the rambunctious girls headed for the buses. Gwen and Nellie—by terms of the bet—were not allowed to stop for shoes. Barefoot and eye-catching, they got their first taste of fame as they merged with other groups from other cabins. In no time flat, the teasing started up. They knew right then, if ever they were to live through the night, it would be on the wings of outrageous behavior. So they embraced their garish identities of Mimi and Fifee, a couple of toothless know-nothins straight from the bowels of the San Fernando Valley. Admittedly it was a one joke punch line, but they intended to repeat it endlessly. If any wisenheimer boys dared to cross their path and give them a hard time, they'd be in for some unforgettable slanguage.

Arriving at Camp Stingray, Lee and Paige stuck to them like grease. Any chance they got to blab the truth (that they were being punished for losing a bet) they blabbed. Mimi and Fifee acted as if that was news to them. They spread the word that they were two fashionistas out shopping for lip gloss. How they wound up at a dance in North Carolina was beyond them. They blamed it all on a wrong turn somewhere near Granada Hills. They kept wandering around asking startled guys if the bug juice was organic and if anyone remembered when and where the limo was picking them up. Just like she promised, Paige's phone (checked out of the office for this special occasion) was in video mode.

"Chad is like sending the Lear jet when I text him." Smacking her gum, Gwen blurted the comment for the benefit of some nearby curiosity seekers.

"Like that's so cool you like call your dad Chad," crooned Nellie, just as loud. "I like love the Lear. It's like different from a car. It like rides on air and like matches the clouds." Nellie's character motivation was a brown-headed dumb blonde. She was nailing it. The boys scooted further away.

For the next two hours, the comic genius of Fifee and Mimi cranked out their halfwit verbiage as they were led around by Lee and Paige, forced to mingle. The few courageous males who attempted closer looks changed their minds quick and disappeared quicker. When Lee and Paige were busy describing their big win to Mrs. B and Tou-tou, Gwen turned to Nellie asking, "So how you likin bein half a freak show?"

"Man, it blows. All this smiling and talking is making my cheeks burn. I need a break."

"Pull down your blue hairs and eat on 'em. Then you won't have to talk no more," suggested Gwen.

"I can't. They're glued in too good." She reached up and readjusted her arrow chapeau to a stylish angle. "You have any more bubble gum? I could just blow bubbles for the last hour. Not like the cute boys will talk to us anyway. They're way overwhelmed. Probably think we have the plague."

"I'd think so too," chuckled Gwen. "We look downright diseased. Probably think we're contagious. Bet some of 'em has nightmares." She hoped so.

"I'm beginning to think it's worse for them than it is for us. I see fear in their eyes when we start walking over."

Nellie giggled for the first time, feeling more comfortable than when they got off the bus. Nellie credited Gwen's brilliant valley-girl strategy. That idea actually turned the trauma into quirky fun.

"Are you kiddin me? Nothin could be worse than this. Don't feel sorry for them guys. We're the ones gettin stared at like stanky turds." But Gwen wasn't as outraged as she sounded. She was sort of enjoying their predicament. Sharing the experience with Nellie was the saving grace. "I left my gum on the bus. This baggy they hung on me doesn't have pockets. Let's go get a piece while they off braggin." Gwen took Nellie by the hand and headed to the far side of the tennis courts. She kept checking back, making sure that Lee and Paige didn't detect their departure. The sight of them holding hands only added to the spectacle. Groups of boys automatically separated, letting them pass by with plenty of room to spare. They never once had to say excuse me.

"Is it just me or are you noticing how everyone is watching us with the eyes in the back of their heads?"

"Indeedy," confirmed Gwen. "And here I thought my mama was the only one who had those. Know better now."

With such a cooperative crowd, they covered the length of the courts quick. In zip-time they were standing at the chain link gate. Gwen lifted the latch and pushed it open. Once they made their getaway, she let go and it clanged shut.

Just outside the fence, the lawn was brightly lit. Beyond that glow it was black as pitch. The buses, parked on the far side of the laundry building, were a good three hundred yards away—so off they went with Bermuda grass prickling their dirty feet.

As pop music faded behind them, the songs of the cicadas cranked up. Nellie kept a sharp eye squinting while her vision adjusted to the dark, making sure she didn't get the surprise of her life and step on a viper. She knew that some snakes were night hunters. She purposely adapted a stomp-step to improve her chances. She kept at it even when Gwen stabbed a finger in her ribs.

"You crack me up. Quit that."

"Don't!" Nellie sidestepped out of reach. "I don't want to get bit. You should do it too. The snakes feel the vibrations and think we're too big for their poison. They get out of our way so they don't waste venom."

"Where'd you come up with that," demanded Gwen, not at all convinced. She kept poking Nellie's sides.

"It's scientific. Ouch! All right, more like a personal hypothesis." Nellie rushed the explanation, dodging tickle digs. Her feet continued pounding.

"You mean a personal paranoia." Gwen was laughing at how stupid Nellie looked.

"Just do it, Gwen. Better safe than sorry," pestered Nellie, staying out of reach.

"Goodness gracious, Nellie," scoffed Gwen. "But seein how I'm such a big-time fan of old folks' sayins... 'Better safe than sorry!'" She mimicked Nellie with the perfect t's and r's of a cultured northerner. Then, not because she feared snakes but because she couldn't hold herself back, she joined Nellie and started up her own version of stomp-stepping. Hers had a tribal flair with air drums.

Hunkered over side by side, grunting and trampling the grass with their plastered hair, they looked like a foraging beast weaving across the lawn, silhouetted by the moon. Any unwitting loner with bad timing would have had a seizure and somersaulted in the opposite direction. Fat chance of that happening. Not a soul was around.

They reached the boy's laundry building and heard the clumpity-clump of a dryer. Whoever started the load left before it was finished. No lights were on inside. Only a single bulb burned over the screen door, illuminating clouds of gnats. It lit the surroundings enough that Nellie quit stamping. The coast was clear. No snakes. She stood back taking in the sight of her bff—still huffing, still clomping, elbows flying—spazing out purely for Nellie's benefit. Right in the middle of a spin-stomp-spin, Gwen froze. In the next instant she went ramrod straight.

"What was that?" She spun around looking at Nellie.

"Very funny." Nellie smirked her toothless grin. "The snakes aren't—"

"Shush!" Gwen held up a hand. "There it is again." She stared at Nellie with her cattails tipping and her smeared lips frowning. "You hear that?" She whispered big-eyed. Her ears caught a faint rustling and a twig snapping. Nellie's didn't. Gwen dropped to a crouch.

"You're so bogus." Nellie crossed her arms. "I'm not falling for—"

A thud came from the backside of the building. Blood drained from Nellie's cheeks just as Gwen's body came crashing into hers, nearly tripping them both.

"Don't tell me you didn't hear that." Gwen dug her fingernails into Nellie's arms.

With fear spiking, Nellie mouthed the words, "I heard it."

She nodded her head up and down in case Gwen couldn't read her lips in the low light. Gripped to one another, they turned in the direction of the thud.

Another twig—closer this time—told them they only had seconds before they were spotted. Nellie knees buckled. She forced herself to power through it, pulling Gwen away from light to where darkness would erase the shape of their bodies. But they were too late. Without looking, they knew it had rounded the building and had them in its sights. They felt its energy closing in and heard the distinct rhythm of pursuing footsteps bearing down on them at a run. With one great leap, she caught the girls from behind and sent them skidding to the ground on bleeding knees.

Nellie's face hit hard. Her teeth filled with dirt. The impact caused a meteor shower of stars behind her closed eyes. The hundred pounds of Gwen landed on top of her. Gold fabric and brown legs came crashing down next to her head. Nellie crawled like an animal, trying to get up, trying to run. Again she was slammed from behind and shoved back down. All she could see was Gwen crumpled on the grass with the queerest expression on her face, frantically pointing.

Nellie grabbed for Gwen, locking wrists before the attacker struck again. Yelling at her to get up, Nellie jerked Gwen and leaned back, straining to lift her. Wet slathered her cheekbone. It happened two more times before registering. Nellie's brain began rebooting even as she was knocked over for a third time. She let go of Gwen and lunged at their attacker—protecting her face and wrestling the squirming body, searching the curly-haired coat for the collar of Mrs. B's Boykin Spaniel.

The dog wheeled away, bounding free. A few yards out, it dropped low and spun in circles growling at their lumpy hair. It raced back barking, delivering more sloppy kisses, ecstatic over two new playmates. Nellie hardly had time to move before the leaper landed on her gut. Gwen had risen to her hands and knees, but her forehead still rested on the grass as she smacked the ground with open palms, downright prayerlike. Nellie stayed in ready position—arms spread wide—poised to fend off the overgrown puppy. Her instinct to escape their assailant was replaced by the command to tell her to sit.

Before obeying, the dog's ears pricked up. Three young boys were leaving the tennis courts. Without a goodbye, Precious took off, gaining speed as she streaked across the lawn. Two of the boys stopped to play with the incoming fur ball and were rewarded with grassy paw prints all over their clean shorts and button-down shirts. The third boy quickened his pace toward a cluster of secluded cabins. He walked off alone. Even from a distance, his need to find a bathroom was obvious.

"Nells, you a pistol." Each word took great effort. "Quite the sight watchin you in fightin form." Gwen remained on the ground with her head on the grass, recovering. "I doubt you need worry about them water moccasins. Those sorry snakes best worry about you. You probably so amped right now you'd grab one by the fangs and fling it in the river." Her head stayed down.

"How many times...do you think that dog...is gonna give us a heart attack?" Nellie was hyperventilating. "I didn't know what was coming...except it was big. Thought maybe that bear had us. Are you all right?" She put her head between her knees.

A moment passed before Gwen answered. "Bunged up here and there but I'll make it. Think I landed on my tail-bone." She stood up rubbing her lower back and examining her scrapes. "Out here riskin our lives for a stick of pink gum."

"Forget it. I'm over it. Let's go back." Nellie caught her breath and heaved herself off the ground, brushing grass from her chin. At some point during the skirmish, the dryer cycle had ended. The chorus of chirps had stopped too—the cicadas remaining undercover until it was safe to resume flirting. In the quiet, Nellie wiped her bloody kneecaps with the hem of her dress. "Great, now I'm an official wreck."

"Now you a wreck? You thinkin you was spiffy before?" Gwen chortled. "Nobody gonna notice any difference. All this dirt's a bonus. Like anybody's lookin that close in the first place. They afraid we gonna burn their eyes." She picked up Nellie's bent arrow from the ground.

"Geez Gwen, could this night go anymore downhill?"

"No ma'am. All I know is Paige done missed out on her billion dollar video. She gonna be real sad."

"She's gonna like totally flip her lid when we like tell her." Giving up on the dried blood, Nellie spoke the valley-speak with her hands on her hips, sliding back into character. She didn't bother stomp-stepping as she turned and headed for the safety of the music and the lights.

Gwen followed alongside. "Like yeah... She gonna be like in a total tizzy. She gonna have to like... Like she gonna be so totally like...like ah...she um... " Gwen shook her head.

"I got nothin. My brain still flustered. Give me a minute."

Finger combing her crunchy hairs back into place, Nellie helped her out. "Like she's gonna be in like such a total tizzy, she's gonna need like a venti iced Americano with like six pumps of toffee nut, extra whip and like ten cake pops."

"Listen to you, Miss Actress. Nothin flusters you. However you say it, Paige gonna be bum, bum, bummed." Gwen slashed the arrow through the air like a Zorro Senorita.

"You mean, 'Paige gonna be like bum, like bum, like bummed.'" Nellie rephrased it for her giggling.

"Yup," agreed Gwen, shoving the arrow into her own hair, not bothering with the valley-talk.

Glances came their way as they re-entered through the same squeaky gate, sketchier than before. "What you lookin at!" Gwen busted a boy red-handed as they sallied forth like derelicts, looking for Lee and Paige.

"OMG. Three o'clock! Three o'clock!" Nellie stopped short, tugging Gwen to a halt. They shuffled like bungling square dancers while Gwen tried to figure out which direction three o'clock was. Nellie spun her partner the right way. "Get a load of those dorks." Nellie pointed. Gwen's eyes followed her finger.

"Oh, Sissy! How the heck we miss that?"

Four boys—all with gelled cowlicks, highwater pants belted grandpa style, polo shirts buttoned to the neck, and black socks with grubby tennis shoes—were standing against the far fence. One even wore a rope bowtie. Worst of all, each sported his tighty-whities on the outside of his slacks. The boys, huddled close together, were actively checking out Gwen and Nellie.

"That Lord sure do work in mysterious ways," squealed Gwen with her fiery, lopsided mouth. "Let's go meet us some boyfriends!" With Nellie in tow, Gwen began plowing over people.

The instant the boys registered Gwen's and Nellie's approach, two of them stepped away mesmerized by the electrical system. The remaining two gamely waited, demonstrating their courage by bracing themselves. When the girls stopped in front of them, Gwen's opener was a valleyless, "Either y'all from the Little Rascals Orphanage else you done somethin terrible wrong today." She pointedly waited for one or the other to speak up.

The possibly cute one with the rope bowtie stepped forward, formally extending his hand to Gwen. Speaking with pronounced nasality and hunching over on purpose, he introduced himself while vigorously shaking her hand.

"Happy to make your acquaintance. I'm Dalton. Please excuse the humiliatin sight of our briefs in such polite company. Counselors' idea. You are correct! We're today's big losers. The winds weren't so favorable to our Flying Scot and Trevor here," he indicated his larger friend with a nod of his head, "he kinda capsized us." After elbowing the boy in his man-boob, Dalton continued. "Am I right to assume that you and that one..." he flicked his eyes up and down Nellie while continuing to pump Gwen's whole arm, "won the last place trophy as well?"

Gwen was about to snatch her hand back when he finally let go. Before she could answer, Nellie got all in his face and interjected, "It's like we just met and like you already think you like totally know all about us? I like totally think not."

The junk just flowed from her like a fluent foreign language.

"Don't make the poor boy wet his britches. He ain't even wearin his undies proper." Gwen had permanently jumped ship on the valley-talk and reverted to her southern self.

"Not to worry." The tubby one adjusted his glasses and joined the introductions. He was doing the stooped over, nasal thing too, just like his buddy. "You're perfectly safe. Skipper here is completely dependable with his bladder control long as he don't drink too much bug juice." After giving each other weakling high-fives, they turned to the girls doing the ultimate nerd move—jazz-hands with bucktooth smiles. Their heads even touched at the temples. It rendered Nellie speechless. As bad as she and Gwen looked, the prospect of standing with these two geeks was quickly losing its glam. She was torn between fascination for the boys and ditching them; though fascination was holding onto a slim lead.

"Come on now, y'all can tell us. How come a couple of fine fillies such as yourselves are attendin our social in such…high style," Bowtie-boy asked Nellie, staring at her plume of top hat hair.

Nellie wasn't as forthright as Gwen. She wasn't at all sure she needed these guys knowing their story. Without batting an eye, she recovered her abilities of speech. "Like our primo modeling agents sent us here for like a total fashion extravaganza but like this place doesn't seem totally trendy enough for us to like strut our sizzle looks and like I can't even find the catwalk so like I was gonna Tweet about it but then like my finger muscles got totally sore from like trying on designer dresses all day so like I was gonna massage my

feet and like do a quick mani-pedi and like... Like well...
Like I was gonna like... Like I mean I...um... Yeah..."

Effortlessly spewing her random gibberish, Nellie hit the
wall and drew a blank. She looked at Gwen, ready for her to
take over, but Gwen and the Rascals were hanging on her
every word with appreciation for her stamina. They kept
waiting for her to get a second wind, disappointed when she
stopped cold. The absurdity of the four of them—standing
in the awkward silence, trying to restart the bewildering
conversation—was being monitored by several groups.
Nellie even spotted Lee and Paige watching from a secure
distance. The cell phone was aimed right at them.

"Me and my girl lost a bet with those two hobos." Gwen,
deciding to set the record straight, pointed out the ducking
Lee and Paige. They waved. Gwen, Nellie and the boys
waved back.

"Like their prize was getting to dress us as their future
mother-in-laws." Nellie did a lovely spin.

"Nothin more dangerous than losin to friends," the cute
one said, non-hunched and non-nasal.

"We plan on makin our guys rue the day," the chunky
one added in his regular voice. "We got some tricks up our
sleeve they won't see comin. Them counselors ain't gonna
like it but everyone else will." He had a very pleasant smile.

"Oh, really," said Nellie as Nellie.

"Do tell," pried Gwen staying Gwen.

The Rascals—realizing they'd divulged *way* more than
they intended to—clammed up. "Let's just say we're armed
and non lethally dangerous." The cute boy answered with his
own humble-pie grin.

"Ya don't say..." Gwen nodded thoughtfully, like she knew exactly what he meant. "Y'all talkin fireworks? Roman candles? Bottle rockets? What ya got?"

The boys looked like deer caught in the headlights.

Abruptly, Nellie turned to Gwen. "Did I ever tell you, when my dad dropped me off he actually asked if I wanted stink bombs? Love to have one now and lock them in the bathroom." Nellie was looking at Lee and Paige.

"Sweet." The plump boy relaxed. "My good man Dalton, he specializes in black market goods." Trevor said it in his most confidential, manly voice. "For the sake of revenge, bet he could hook y'all up. Could we interest you in a complimentary tube of toe-curling pong? Seein how we're like like minds with like matchin objectives." He threw in the extra "likes" to validate their bond.

"Four-eyes say what?" Gwen asked, ignorant of the world of stink bomb lingo.

Dalton took over the explanation. "Just smash it on the floor when they're not lookin. It reaches maximum effectiveness in small enclosures. Say your pals were showerin and their towels and stuff went missin right as the door happened to lock shut. Bet the olfactory payback would be worth the scoldin y'all may or may not have to sit through, dependin on how quick y'all beat feet outta there." He summed it all up looking bashful and hazel-eyed.

Nellie was smitten before he even finished. She fell for him straightaway. Despite his geeked-out get-up and his Cloroxed underwear, she decided he was alright after all. Forgetting what she looked like to him, she began toothlessly smiling at him and introducing herself for real.

"I'm Nellie Landers, all the way from California. Hi." She shoved her hand out for a proper shake, shake, shake. "I'm like totally not really a model. Um…as tempting as your generous offer is…uh…we really shouldn't," she gushed, shaking hands with his buddy too. "Me and Gwen, if we'd won, we'd have dressed those two way worse than this!" She ran her hands down the front of her lime green dress and swished out the flowery skirt. "Amateurs," she scoffed. But she couldn't help sounding like she really wanted to pounce on Dalton's offer—and him.

"Well, take your time, take your time. You two think it on over. Nice meetin y'all too." Suddenly flustered, Dalton backed away. "If y'all change your minds…ah…come find me." But he didn't sound like he really meant it. The full impact of splat-mouth Nellie and her lone eyebrow was starting to unnerve him. And the way she kept staring at him—blatantly displaying that gnarly black tooth—was beginning to make him perspire. He even thought he saw dirt. Gulping and grinning, trying to act like everything was just fine, he tore his eyes away from her face. Switching his attention to Gwen didn't prove much better. He shot Trevor a time-to-bolt look.

Trevor misunderstood. "Oh, sure. Or come find me." Trevor didn't make a move to go, but he didn't say anything else either. It went totally silent again.

Nellie jumped right in resuscitating the conversation. "I mean, I guess in the spirit of good sportsmanship, we should let those doofusses enjoy their fifteen minutes of fame." She slapped at her hips with excessive excitement, laughing a semi-girly, semi-piercing laugh. "Actually, we're the famous ones tonight. Am I right?" She slapped at her hips again, thinking up her next witty remark.

"But me and Gwen, maybe you wouldn't know it, but we make a really twisted team. We're super tight!" She tried laughing the alluring laugh again, but a full-on cackle escaped instead. Gwen's chunk of eyebrow dipped in the middle and shot up at one end. She cut her eyes over and studied Nellie, immediately diagnosing crush-fever.

"I believe that. Y'all definitely look twisted." Dalton smiled in spite of wanting to cut and run.

"You got that right! Ask anybody. Yes, siree." Nellie nattered on, conspicuously rising up and down on her bare toes for no apparent reason. "We nearly totally slayed their butts!" She honked like a little kid.

"What was the bet?" Dalton asked.

"Just a friendly shoot-em-up with arrows and guns," answered Gwen, helping Nellie out.

"That explains your headgear." Trevor giggled.

"That short haired one must be part Cherokee sniper. We gonna bring an onion and stuff it up her sunburnt nose next time. Get her eyes stingin so she can't aim. Then we'll take her out."

"Now you're talkin," hooted Trevor. "Get after 'em!" He thought the girls were cool.

"That's what re-matches are for," allowed Dalton. He seemed to have gotten a grip on himself despite the girls' fierce appearance. Speaking valley, he leaned in and lowered his voice. "But like just in case y'all can't get that onion up her nose or like your nails aren't like totally manicured or whatever, like here, go ahead and take this." He reached underneath his briefs and dug around in his pants pocket before pulling something out and furtively placing it in Gwen's palm. "Insurance," he whispered.

"What the heck is this?" Gwen held up a thin glass vial, exposing it for all the world to see.

Nellie's hand struck like a tree frog tonguing a fly. How Gwen didn't know exactly what she was holding was unbelievable. Nellie tried covering Gwen's hand before anybody saw it. This was the real deal—the reeking sulfide variety that if traced back to them could set off angry phone calls to parents and big, big trouble. It needed to be kept totally hidden and super secret.

But Nellie's fingers didn't curl around the stink bomb. Instead, she right-hooked Gwen's thumb and sent the vial airborne—tail-over-tea-cups. Six arms shot out to grab it, but even with three determined people it was like trying to catch a pop fly blindfolded. And the twinkling night lights didn't help either. Trevor's beefy hand actually made contact. The forceful slap sent the bomb in a new direction—completely out of reach. They watched, knowing the end result, as the fragile torpedo sailed toward the middle of the dance floor. To predict it would explode at the feet of Lee and Paige in 2.2 seconds was 99.9 percent correct.

"Shall we, ladies?" Trevor took a millisecond assessing the situation before moving into action. Clamping both girls under his damp pits, he forcibly wheeled them in the opposite direction. "I suggest we clear the area pronto. Anyone for punch? I'm parched." It was plain as day by his swift gait that he wasn't interested in their answer.

Ducking their heads and laughing, they dashed from the tentacles of stench. They heard the result of the touchdown en route to the refreshment table—screaming revulsion. Looking back, they saw stampeding dancers experiencing mosh-pit mayhem; Lee, Paige, and her cell phone were leading the pack. Had anyone noticed the adorable foursome's hasty retreat, they could have busted the guilty perps.

Watching from the snack table, Trevor and Dalton busied themselves with paper cups while Nellie and Gwen fawned over a half filled bowl of broken potato chips. The girls dedicated themselves to scooping out handfuls as the boys splashed ladles of bug juice all over the tablecloth, paying no attention to filling drinks—hypnotized by the riot. As the four slunk away with their food alibi, the smelly survivors overtook the table.

From their sideline position, leaning against a fence and sipping punch, they tried to appear blameless. Their demeanor didn't fool one particular male counselor. In his navy blazer and pink bowtie, he strode directly up to the boys and bent down lecturing them quietly. Backing away, he kept pointing at Dalton with an accusatory finger.

"Good work, bro. We're impressed." He was grinning.

Dalton maintained complete innocence. His face—just a touch offended—registered no wrong doing. He wore a laidback, almost angelic expression. Even dressed as the biggest bore of all time in his knee socks and jockeys, Nellie felt the smile of smiles spreading across her Fifee face. Dalton glanced her way right as it plateaued. With one hand scratching the back of his head, he shrugged and stepped so close that their shoulders bumped.

"Do I really look like the go-to-guy for illegal booty?"

"You and my dad both," answered Nellie. "You guys think throwing off suspicion with schoolboy charm works, but I cracked that code a long time ago. There's a certain glint in the eye. You learn to recognize it when you live with it." She looked directly at him hoping he noticed just how perceptive she was. She kept forgetting about the tooth. And the eyebrow. And her lips.

Dalton wasn't put off by her this time. He didn't even flinch. "You really like stink bombs?" He grinned at that piece of info. If he so much as mentioned stink bombs around the girls he knew, they'd go all huffy. "That's mighty interestin."

"I respect a first-class prank. Especially if someone's deserving to the max. I should probably warn you, I'm kind of wired for shenanigans. I think it's a southern thing."

"How's that? Thought you were from California."

"Dude, my dad's name is Buddy. It doesn't get more southern than that. Just cause I don't have the accent don't mean I ain't got the 'tude, son." Dalton looked a tad perplexed. "My dad's from Winston-Salem," explained Nellie. "He went to this camp when he was a kid. Guess this is where you hoodlum trainees learn your trade."

Dalton's burst of laughter said that she was right. It gave her confidence. She didn't slow down bending his ear for the next ten minutes. She couldn't help studying his highly active dimples, or the way his nostrils flared every time she got him to laugh, or the lone freckle kissably perched above his top lip. She talked and talked and talked, deeply inhaling the stench of sulfur, far too giddy to care.

"Wow, like tell me to shut-up." She went valley again. But a calmer version this time. "Like I'm not letting you say anything. How like massively embarrassing." She threw her shoulders back, trying to look normal. It didn't work. "By the way, that's just eyeliner if you were wondering. I'm not really missing any teeth."

"Well, Nellie Landers, now that ya mention it, I was kinda wonderin." His dimples were getting a strenuous workout. "But don't feel like ya have to quit talkin on my account. Considerin how we're dressed, we sorta make the perfect couple, don't ya think?"

She knew it was just a rhetorical question, but the fact that he'd remembered her name made her cheeks heat up. She started talking faster. "I mean, I knew it was waterproof. It's my eyeliner. I just can't believe how good it stays on." She veered the subject in a neutral direction so she could get the upper hand on her pulse. "You should've seen it when we got here. Boys were actually crashing into each other and spilling drinks, trying to get out of our way. Back at Seamist, our cabin took about a million hideous pictures after Lee and Paige finished doing us. They're totally, totally heartless."

"And when they asleep tonight, they gonna see just how heartless we can be back." After giving Nellie sufficient alone-time with Dalton, Gwen stepped back over.

"Ah! The battle rages on," bellowed Trevor, coming with Gwen. "They gonna wake-up duck taped to their beds? Or better yet, wake-up wearing duck tape beanies?" It was obvious he had warfare experience and supported both ideas.

"Naw, duck tape tend to be too noisy unstickin from the roll. And that Paige, she's a light sleeper. But they might wake-up with green mustaches. Got a brand new felt-tip in my stationary box." Gwen was smiling about her evil plan, but it was Trevor—plum colored and jiggling with zest—who seemed the happiest about it.

"Geez, Trevor, wouldn't wanna get on your bad side," giggled Gwen.

"On it or under it. They're both bad," joked Dalton. "Trevor's been known to use his State Championship wrestler holds to win an argument. But if it's handy, duck tape is his weapon of choice."

"I'm what ya might call a duck tape connoisseur. Got a bunch of rolls stashed in my locker. Just let me know. I'll slip ya one."

The music stopped and was replaced by amplified static. Mrs. B's always smiling voice came through the speakers on the court poles. "And that concludes our lively visit for tonight. As for you rotten stink bombardiers... We will be puttin up Wanted Posters. Any campers with clues leadin to the identity of the sole stinker or stinker gang will receive a tasty reward." That got a big cheer. "As this is clearly an infraction of conduct outlined in our bylaws regardin rules and regulations, this *is* considered an act of aggression and *will* be dealt with accordingly. I'm thinkin off the top of my head, but seems to me a public sentence consistin of a cream pie facial could be a satisfactory penalty. I'm open to suggestions. Stinkers be warned! We're gunnin for ya! That said, would all Camp Seamist ladies please thank the kind gentlemen of Camp Stingray for hostin this fine evenin and finish up with your goodbyes. We'll be meetin at the buses in five minutes. Five minutes, ladies. 'Preciate it."

Mrs. B was known for adhering to a strict schedule. When she said five minutes, she really meant three. She got a kick out of watching girls running behind the buses in their good shoes. She would instruct Aubrey—her old-timer bus driver—to keep the pedal to the metal until they reached the entrance gate. That made for a full quarter mile before she'd allow him to stop. The good news was that it only had to happen once for all the girls to be converted into timely believers.

"I ain't scared," snarled Gwen like a career criminal.

"I ain't scart neither." Nellie guaranteed her thug status too.

"Dolls, dolls, y'all got nothin to worry about. We're home free long as we keep our traps shut." Trevor assured them.

"Couldn't wring a confession outta me no matter what kind of cake they bake for torture," promised Dalton.

"Y'all better hope they keep feedin us good. I know Nells might snitch for a slice of chocolate cake," warned Gwen.

"She wouldn't dare," cried Dalton, scandalized and betrayed, flagrantly overacting.

"Oh, wouldn't I?"

The distance between the four of them widened as Gwen pulled Nellie toward the buses. Both girls were pretty sure they heard Dalton yell, "How will we find y'all the next dance? I mean, how will we know y'all's y'all?"

"Guess you'll have to wear them same trippy outfits," shouted Trevor, jiggling again.

"Never! Look for the silver stars on our foreheads!"

Those were the last words out of Nellie's mouth before she and Gwen broke into a run.

The boys hollered, "Huh?" But no further explanation got screeched.

Trevor and Dalton stayed put, sipping the last of their lukewarm punch. Once the girls were out of sight around the far corner of the laundry building, they slam-dunked their cups in the trash and chased each other back to their cabin—weaving and dodging, boxing buddy-style.

It was Dalton who figured it out. "Bet they show up with duck tape stars on their foreheads." Trevor thought that was hilarious.

After diving onto their bunks and reliving every memorable moment, including rapid-fire questioning from the two Rascals who left them in the lurch, the boys zonked-out to the trombonal quality of Trevor's nightly snoring.

At 3 a.m. on that full moon night—after all signs of Fifee and Mimi were washed away, after all the girls had piled on Gwen's, Nellie's and Maddy's beds, after all the stories were told and exaggerated and told better, after all the cookies were devoured and the crumbs flung from the sheets, after Paige's videos got passed from hand to hand multitudes of times, and after the counselors begged and threatened the girls to please stop talking and go to sleep—Nellie woke up. Her eyes cracked opened and she licked her lips. By the stillness, by the steady breathing, she knew her whole cabin was in a deep, deep sleep.

From the safety of her bunk, her drowsy eyes checked the corners of the room. She rose up telling herself that she was just turning over, but really convincing herself that nothing was weird. Or creeping along the floor. Laying her head back down, she caught the far wall lighting up rosy and then going dark. And then going rosy and then going dark. She thought it was someone's electronics—Paige's cell phone plugged in and charging. Her springs squeaked when she shifted positions, looking again. Beyond the rows of beds, she noticed shadows outlined in the doorway. Her counselors. That finished waking her up. She scooched to her knees and peeked out her window, trying to see what they saw. She only saw woods. But that same red glow was lighting up the tree trunks.

"Nellie? What are you doin?" Her ancient bed had given her away. "Go back to sleep." Kate sounded scared.

"What are you looking at?" Nellie whispered as quietly as she could.

"Nothin. Go back to sleep." Kate's posture was rigid and her voice was clearly stressed. She went back to staring out the screen door.

"You guys, what's going on?" Nellie asked again—not about to lie back down.

"It's the police." Another counselor answered. "They're talkin to Mrs. B."

The police? Why?" Her heart sped up. "But I didn't think Mrs. B was mad about the stink bomb. She sounded like she thought it was funny. All that stuff about cream pie facials…" Nellie struggled to keep her voice hushed and the guilt out of it.

"It's not about that," said Kate. "Somethin…happened. A boy from Stingray's…missin."

"What! Who?" Nellie breathed in sharp. "Do you know who it is?" They didn't answer. "His name wasn't Dalton or Trevor was it?" Her whispering grew louder. Gwen's eyes opened.

"I don't know, Nellie. We don't know yet." Forced to tell, Kate got flustered. "They're just now speakin with Mrs. B. All we know is he's really little. Eight I think. He left the dance to go pee. His friends stopped to play with Precious but he walked off." She paused to wipe a tear. "He never came back."

The words hung in the air while Kate struggled to control her trembling. The warmth outside didn't stop her teeth from chattering. "They think he's lost in the woods," she said, extremely worried. "Now do me a favor and lay down. They plan on tellin everybody about it in the mornin. Hopefully by then…they'll have found the poor kid." She turned her back on Nellie, sucking in air through her mouth. Her teeth kept rattling as she stood shivering at the door. No one said another word.

Nellie put her head back down on her pillow. For the next forty-five minutes, she and Gwen watched the flashing lights splashing across their cabin walls. They didn't talk— just stared—until sleep overpowered them and forced their eyes shut.

In the hour before dawn,
her shadow crossed their window.
She watched them
sleeping,
clutching her newest
prize.
Lightly,
ever so lightly,
her fingertips caressed the screen
inches from their heads.
No one—
not Nellie,
not Gwen,
not the slumbering, worried counselors—
ever heard
a
thing.

Chapter 9

The day started with its usual fanfare, nothing seemed wrong. Like every other morning, the rat-tat-tat of "Reveille" sounded a brief and merry hello, followed by Katy Perry really loud. Gwen and Nellie got up looking for their head counselor, but Kate wasn't on her bed. They looked in the bathroom. She wasn't there either. They lingered over a sink, rinsing their bleary eyes and willing themselves to wake-up.

After the fitful night, Nellie took one look in the mirror and hated what she saw. Sick to death of frizzies, she manhandled her hair into two no-nonsense braids and secured them with four elastic bands. It was a brand new look for her. One that had her examining her reflection and mumbling, "Hey, pa, can I milk the cow?" The counselor at the next sink laughed, telling her they looked "darlin". That was surprising. After what had happened, Nellie couldn't believe the girl would comment on something as trivial as a hairstyle. In truth, had Nellie not woken up in the wee hours of the night, she and Gwen wouldn't have suspected a thing. For all the horsing around aimed at getting the pillow-huggers out of bed, they thought the boy must have been found.

At breakfast, no announcement was made—no mention of the incident at Camp Stingray. It gave Nellie the strange feeling she'd imagined the whole thing. She could've almost convinced herself that it was a bad dream, but on the walk from the cabin to the mess hall, Gwen noticed Mrs. B's car was absent from her driveway. That was unusual. She wasn't at breakfast either. But Kate was. At her first opportunity, Nellie reached for a second ham biscuit that she didn't really want and leaned in close, asking Kate the burning question.

"They find that boy?" She said it so only Kate could hear.

The teenager's eyes crinkled closed with fatigue. When she opened them, she gave the one word answer that Nellie was dreading. She didn't have to tell Nellie to keep it to herself. Her look of anguish did that for her. With a mouthful of grits, Gwen watched the exchange and deciphered its meaning. Nellie took a sip of juice to coat the lump in her throat.

"Shake it off, girlies. Y'all are lookin haggard." Paige plopped down next to Nellie. "You still broodin about last night? Chins up, right this minute. Y'all got killer new boy-friends out of the deal, thanks to Lee and me. Bet next Saturday y'all exchange promise rings." Looking like a gopher with puffed out cheeks, Paige was stuffing her face in preparation for another big day. "We got a great plan if you're up for it. Keep us busy 'til tonight. Y'all might get a chance to redeem yourselves." Working an oversized forkful of blueberry pancakes, her mouth—decorated by the sheen of Mrs. Butterworth's—chewed from side to side.

"You gonna wipe that mouth or you waitin to slurp that up later," asked Gwen, kind of low-key.

Lee slid down planting both elbows on the table, smiling with blueberry teeth and crumb covered lips. "Mornin." To further annoy Gwen, Lee didn't wipe her mouth either. Her unused napkin stayed peeking out from her collar.

Gwen managed a halfhearted eye-roll. "You ain't fit to eat indoors."

"Course not," agreed Lee, unfazed.

"Hey, Paige…when you're done storing nuts for the winter…take Lee and let her graze outside. I noticed Mrs. B's flowerbeds have lots of tasty weeds." Nellie attempted some breakfast humor to lift her mood. "Bet you could earn yourself that Billy Goat rank, Lee."

"Funny," said Lee. "But I'm good with pancakes." Then she bleated, "Pa-a-a-a-a-ss the syrup, ple-e-e-e-ase." She forked seconds from the plate and doused them.

"Eat up, y'all. You're gonna need your strength." Done with pancakes, Paige moved on to eggs and hash. Mid-bite, she shook her head at the lackluster slump of Gwen and Nellie. "I don't know, Lee. Looks like they've been rode hard and put away wet. Better take it easy on them today."

"Why does everybody keep comparing us to horses?" Nellie asked Gwen. Gwen just shrugged.

"Snap out of it then. 'Cept for those dorky necklaces, y'all look about like horse poop this mornin." Lee plucked the napkin from her shirt and finally used it. "Didn't you knuckleheads get enough beauty sleep?"

"They'll rally back once we get them outside. Amazin what a little sunshine can do." Paige figured fun in the sun for a sure-fire cure-all.

"I don't think so." Nellie was done with the chipper act. Deciding to fill them in, she rose from the table. "Let's go. Gwen and I have something to tell you." She wasn't worried that Kate would overhear. Kate and every other counselor had been called to the cafeteria office for a closed-door meeting. Through the plate glass window, Nellie could see a rep from Stingray talking to them—with a policeman.

They walked out of the mess hall and into a sweltering morning. It was even hotter than the day before, so they headed straight for the swim lake. Lee was already good to go in her trunks and rashguard. Stripping down to their bathing suits, Paige, Gwen and Nellie dropped their shorts and tees in a heap on the ground. Piles of clothes were steadily accumulating—strewn across the lawns. By day's end, the entire place would look like a yard sale of discarded summer apparel. Walking the perimeter of the lake and out onto the sunbathing platform, the girls dove into deep water and swam to the center. When their toes touched the sandy bottom, they stood in a tight circle with only their heads above water. Not a ripple creased the pool while they talked at length in total privacy.

The official announcement came at lunch. It had to. Rumors of the boy had spread through camp with menacing implications. Mrs. B called everyone to the cafeteria early and informed them of "a developin situation." She seemed calm enough, assuring the group that everything was being done to find the child. Police were, at that very moment, on the scene with blood hounds. The forest was undergoing a thorough scouring for any sign of him—footprints, broken branches, threads from his clothing. The department's finest were searching. An emergency call had even gone out for an experienced tracker. He'd driven over from a neighboring county and arrived before dawn to lead the Search and Rescue Operation. Mrs. B asked that the girls of Camp Seamist continue their activities with the missing boy in their prayers. She promised to let everyone know the instant they received the call that he'd been found safe. Of that outcome, she was certain. "It's only a matter of time."

While they waited for the good news, Mrs. B stressed that everyone should use common sense and stay with their friends. "Make the day count. Go out and accomplish your ranks, ladies!" She tried to smile with confidence, but the sparkle in her eyes was missing. Her smile struck Nellie as brave. And her voice, which was always motivating and powerful, sounded shaky. She excused herself and left without eating.

"I wonder if they've called his parents." Nellie mentioned quietly.

"You know it." Lee felt certain that they had. "Hope they're local so it's a short trip. My folks would be here in a heartbeat if they got that kind of call. Mom would be chuckin police out of her way, trompin through the woods in her slippers and curlers. Snakes or nor snakes."

"Ugh, the snakes! Why'd you have to go mention that?" Nothing could be worse in Nellie's mind. "It's bad enough thinking some little kid's lost out there. Wish you didn't remind me about the snakes."

"There's gators too, y'all. Depends how lost he is. Them woods over by the boy's camp ain't like ours. Gets swampy real quick over there," added Gwen bleakly.

"Stop!" Paige looked cross. "It's not gonna help sittin here awfulizin every terrible possibility. All the people that should be on it are on it. We have the best police of all the counties. Half their kids come here. Now we got dogs and a tracker. Sounds like serious manpower to me. They're gonna find him, just like Mrs. B says. Heck, he's probably already found, we just don't know it yet. Probably in some old lady's kitchen gobblin down a slice of apple pie and braggin on his big night out. Any minute now he'll be gettin his first ride in a police car, playin with the siren and orderin people to pull over. So let's quit predictin he's gator-bait and eat. It's time to visit Tou-tou and make somethin pretty." Her passionate conviction in his safe return was so adamant that before the girls could stop her, she'd loaded three plates with nothing but mayonnaisey tuna salad and pushed huge servings in front of each of them.

"Why, thank you, Officer Paige, for your dedication to civil service," quipped Nellie, glancing down at the milky liquid spreading across her plate. "And that looks absolutely disgusting."

As the girls stared at their lunch, the fishy smell hit. It forced them up from their seats, reeling away from the table with appalled laughter.

"What?" Paige attempted to ask, mildly confused, but since she'd just shoveled in an enormous bite, it came out, "Wa-wuh?"

"Make sure to brush your teeth and get a gum. I ain't

sittin next to no filet-o-fish the rest of the day. And Tou-tou will kick your hiney straight out his door if you show up smellin like that plate." Gwen grabbed peanut butter and jellies and handed them out. "We'll get four spots at batik while you pig-out on that nasty mush."

Scrunching her nose, Paige tried to detect a bad smell but she liked it. "Wait a minute," she said. But with the wad of tuna slowing down the dexterity of her tongue, it came out, "Waya wiyit."

"Didn't catch that, Missy Oink-Oink," grunted Nellie. "But don't rush. We'll beat the after-lunch crowd so we won't have to wait another day. When you're done eating slop, come over. But spray yourself with Fabreeze first. And no burping!"

Lee was wheezing so hard that she gagged on her first bite of pb and j.

"Very funny," yelled Paige as they hurried for the door. It came out, "Arhwee wawee" along with some projectiles of masticated tuna.

When Paige caught up with them twenty minutes later, it was obvious where she was supposed to sit. Fresh mint leaves were sprinkled over the empty seat next to Lee. Tou-tou, who'd generously supplied the mint and was in on the joke, greeted her with a bandana tied around his nose. Delighted by the attention—and in typical Paige fashion— she snarfed down every last leaf before taking her seat. When she'd finished, she placed both hands flat on the table and closed her eyes. Knowing that her girls were watching, she gulped down a huge breath of air. What followed was a most unladylike burp—blown straight across the table at Nellie.

"Ahhhhh, sweet minty revenge! With just a hint of chicken of the sea!" She had to out shout a roomful of highly offended protesters. "Can all y'all smell that!"

Once every camper in the cabin blasted Paige for her disgusting grossness, Tou-tou's imaginative world began consuming them. His guidance was friendly and simple. "Please, let Tou-tou show you." After fifteen minutes of instruction, he put down his brush saying, "Only paint what excites you. When an idea emerges, welcome it with open arms."

Lee's grumblings got the same response he was famous for. "You must not convince yourself that you cannot do it, Miss Lee. It is certain that you can. And by all means, do not be intimidated by mistakes. Mistakes are simply roadmaps leading to uncharted ideas. Enjoy the journey." His melodic accent made every word he said sound scholarly. Paige actually started clapping.

"Tou-tou, you're the gosh darn best, you really are. You know how to make me feel like a true artist. Every time ya teach, I just wanna stand up and applaud. Is that dumb?" The whole tuna episode had her excitable.

"It is 'dumb' not to have passion, Miss Paige. I am honored by your kind estimation. It is my greatest privilege to teach and your commitment truly inspires me. You realize of course that a work of art is merely a conduit to another. It represents a sequence of thought and humanity, a progression of mass and structure, a poetry of lightness and dark, an amalgamation of details that once blended and balanced can spark a revolution or quell the restless." He gathered himself to continue but then he smiled contritely.

"Perhaps one aspect of my dedication is dumb. I talk too much. I will stop. Please, begin." It was an order that needed no repeating.

"Did y'all hear how he said that?" Paige whispered all hoity-toity. "Even when he says 'dumb' it sounds elegant." The comment got her a triple eye-roll.

As they sat enjoying the cool air under the ceiling fans, the girls threw themselves into their work. Nellie's batik quickly emerged as insta-therapy for her number one fear. After outlining her cloth in decorative triangles, she used her brush to wax squiggly serpents over every inch. She filled in the background with watery green dye, then spent hours on the detailed patterns of her snakes—all different. Tou-tou predicted that once the sarong was finished and the garment touched her skin, her fear of snakes would disappear.

"That gal never gonna take to snakes. No matter how pretty they look in pictures." Gwen set him straight. "She'd rather stomp 'em. Believe me, I know."

"No, I can feel this actually helping. Long as I wear it with steel-toed boots, I won't be afraid of those ankle-biting shitheads ever again." Nellie's slip of the tongue surprised Monsieur Pitou. "Ooops, sorry..." She covered her mouth, embarrassed but giggling.

"Let's use our good manners, y'all." Paige was quick to reprimand Nellie. "Else somebody might find a bar of soap washin out their mouths. Wouldn't want that now, would ya?"

"Why no, Miss Foul-Mouth-Burp-Breath, we wouldn't want that now, would we?" Gwen reprimanded Paige right back. Grinning, they put their heads down, working intently.

Gwen's sarong was turning into a celebration of friends. She'd waxed three lines for double borders and crosshatched in between them. When that was done, she started in on an encore performance from the night before. Fifee and Mimi went smack dab in the middle of her fabric. She needed lots of room to do justice to their razzle-dazzle hair. The other smiling faces—including Lee, Paige and the rest of her cabin mates and counselors—all came to life on a background of purpley blues. Once it dried, the crazy circus of Cabin 21 would swing from her hips.

Paige planned on wearing her creation as a shawl to the next dance. Her horses were breathtaking. Everyone could tell that her favorite parts were their dramatic manes and tails. She didn't hold back waxing their swirling tresses ultra spectacular and bold. But the way she portrayed their muscular bodies was what impressed Monsieur Pitou. He praised her perspective as perfect. He watched approvingly as she chose earth tones for her stallions—black Friesians, chestnut Mustangs, and Appaloosas with spots of grey. She picked a yellowy dye to corral her herd, and, as an extra special touch in memory of the day, she lined her edges with mint leaves and tiny tuna fish.

"Touts!" Lee had called for assistance. "My map of uncharted ideas got me shipwrecked. Not too sure how to find my way back. Help." Two seconds later came, "Please."

Dutifully returning to the table, he took a look over her shoulder. Her white cloth had little wax and no color. A few willy-nilly lines were smeared in one corner, but nothing was recognizable.

"See," she said petulantly. "I don't know what to do."

"Miss Lee, that statement strikes me as uncharacteristic. I have seen with my very eyes that you consistently know how to make your way in this world." He paused. "This must happen." He took a patient breath—slowly in, slowly out. "You must permit your thoughts to flow artistically. I hereby grant you permission. Stop analyzing them. Do not judge. That only serves to delay your talent."

Looking at him like he was from Mars, Lee made a face—sticking out her tongue and crossing her eyes. "Ah, ha! There she is! You see?" He clapped his hands together. "Superlative! You naturally express yourself comically. I suggest you follow that impulse. Let your inner clown out." He was completely sincere in his encouragement.

"And all that hogwash means what?" She asked with the intelligence of a stump.

He smiled at her broadly, raising his palms to the heavens. "Surprise me."

"I already tried. I can't think of anything." Pushing away from the table like it was his fault, she gazed sullenly out the window. "Knew I should've just gone fishin."

"Fish are on your mind? Very good. Go fishing now. Right in front of you an ocean is waiting." Then he rhymed, "Fill it as you wish. Paint a swimming fish." When his face lit up, so did hers. He stepped back bowing and departing quickly, knowing he'd prompted her into action.

Her ideas went from zilch to zillions. As her partial lines were revamped into sea life, her sarong began swimming with a wacky school of fish—sharks wearing bowties, a one-eyed octopus, giant-lipped clown fish, and lightning bolt eels. Smiling starfish took up the blank spots. Lee painted no designs on her borders. She opted for phrases like "Gone fishing" and "Tuna Salad" and "Missy Oink-Oink" and "Ban Burping" and "Ahhhhh, minty!" and "Waya wiyit" and "Uncharted Art" and "Touts for President" and "Got soap?" and every other quotable quote from the afternoon that she could remember. And even though she'd been a pill—exasperated by the artsy-fartsy task, constantly leaving the table to talk, spilling a Dixie cup of red dye on her cloth (which she turned into a jellyfish), bugging Tou-tou about which colors to use, dropping her sarong on the floor and stepping on it, and dipping her whole hand in the melted wax—she was super stoked when it was finished. The compliments it received weren't half bad either.

After being cooped-up inside all afternoon, the girls thanked Tou-tou for his expertise and congratulated him on his saintly stamina. That got him chuckling. His friendly eyes did that sunsetty thing Nellie loved as he placed a mint leaf in his mouth and brought his hands together.

"We shall see one another at dinner. I look forward to it. I am bringing something special for tonight's story. I am certain all will find it enlightening." He was looking at Nellie.

"*Enlightenin?* Don't nobody wanna be enlightened on Scary Story Night," barked Gwen. "We wanna be *scared*."

"It is my understanding that this tale does both." He answered with a mysterious gleam in his eye.

"It better," grinned Lee. "Cracks me up when the little kids start cryin."

"In which case, Miss Lee, you will be the first to comfort them and ease their fears?"

"Sure!" Paige started howling. "Last year she comforted

that one little girl all the way back to her cabin just so she could put a rubber rat under her bed when—"

"Hey! Watch it, blabbermouth!" Lee cut her off. "I only did that once. And let's not forget who gave me the rat." Lee laid the blame right back on Paige. Tou-tou's easy laugh rolled out.

"Don't worry. We'll frisk them both. Make sure they're rodent-free before they're allowed in tonight," Nellie assured him.

"I would appreciate that, Miss Nellie. You and Miss Gwen have your work cut out for you, indeed."

"Just leave Runtness and Rat Girl to us," giggled Gwen. "We'll keep a lid on 'em."

"Please do. And where may I ask are the four of you going now? Off to wash-up for the evening's festivities, I hope?" It was more of a suggestion than a question.

"What are you sayin, Touts? We stinkin up the place?" Lee took a whiff of her underarms, making sure that she wasn't too fragrant with lake water and sweat.

"Far be it from me to imply such a thing, Miss Lee. Your hygiene is not the issue. I do think it prudent that you check-in with your cabin and let your counselors know your whereabouts. Certainly they would appreciate that."

He didn't come right out and say he was worried, but Nellie sensed that something was bothering him. The Stingray boy was probably on his mind. Suddenly, she knew he was gearing up to launch into his bird story for the girls. She could just tell. The lecture about the perils of the trails was on the tip of his tongue. No way was she down for that. They'd be stuck inside listening to him for another hour.

"We'll go over there now," she offered quickly, grabbing her sarong and making a break for the door. "See you later." The girls did the same and followed behind her.

"Now ya learnin," whispered Gwen. "Get the heck outta Dodge before he traps us with more of his talk, right?"

"Uhg! You don't even know how right," answered Nellie.

"Bye!" They hollered heading out. Tou-tou waved and was called over by a table of youngsters making potholders.

The girls took their wearable art outside to dry. Their four new sarongs joined a collage of others on the clothesline—a gallery of color-stained banners. In the morning when the dye was set, they'd come back and toss them in Tou-tou's paint-splattered washing machine for the finishing touch. But for now they needed action, not cabins and counselors. Their rumps were sore from all that sitting and the dinner bell wouldn't start clanging for awhile. There was plenty of time to wash-up later. Fortunately, the cruelest heat of the day was over. Ideas were tossed around. None cared to head for water; the boats were docking for the night anyway. But one activity sounded good and was quickly agreed upon. The timing was perfect.

"Go! Go! Go!" Paige urged the three to take off running. She would stay right there and count for a full five minutes. No cheating, she promised. Then the searching would begin for the game of the hour. Hide-n-Seek.

Alone.
She preferred them alone.
Away from any hope of rescue...

Chapter 10

The three friends immediately separated, focused on spots where they would not be found first. Nellie kicked off her flip flops, running as fast as her bare feet and tanned legs would go. In the background, she heard Paige counting down. The five minute mark would give her ample time to disappear into a secluded place. The one she had in mind was by archery, so she was haulin it.

Lee and Gwen took off in different directions across the lawn, but wound up doubling back and slinging it out for the same hiding place, elbowing each other to get ahead. Neither gave in. Only fifty yards from Paige, they didn't make a sound either. Compromising, they paired up and ducked under some stairs. Not too original, but close. Paige would not look close. She'd set her sights further away—jog right on past their watchful eyes before she seriously started searching.

Second thoughts flashed by as Nellie dashed for the woods. "Stay together girls" went through her head. She ignored it. You couldn't stay together playing this game, even Mrs. B would agree with that. And after yesterday, she needed a win. The giant ferns she was headed to would mean absolute victory. This particular clump was on steroids—as in gynormous. She'd have to grab a stick for swatting out webs from underneath the umbrella sized leaves, but she could handle that. Only one thing was important now: that Paige—that none of them for that matter—knew anything about her hiding place. With a widening grin, she tucked her chin and ran hard. No way could she lose.

When she reached the wooded section with live oaks, she veered off the path. Quickly performing her stomp-stomp-stomps, she threw a handful of pebbles to scare off the copperheads. She waited—listening for movement—before deciding it was safe and entering the thicket. Supple leaves slapped her waist as she slid between the chartreuse frills. Grey clumps of Spanish moss hung so low that she had to duck. One rubbed against her cheek and latched onto a braid. Stopping to untangle herself, she brushed the stringy stuff aside, breaking free.

Satisfied with the location, she walked around looking for the perfect spot. A rotten stick broke under her foot. Picking up the longer end, she heard the faint call, "Ready or not! Here I come!" A glance down the path assured her that Lee and Gwen had not followed. Concentrating on quieting her breaths, she surveyed her fern choices. Fifteen paces to the right, the hulkiest fern of the pack sat like a snoozing ogre. "And I pick you." She pointed with the stick and made her way to its concealing fronds. After a thorough swishing in all its nooks and crannies, she squatted down and crept beneath it, totally obscured from view.

Successfully tucked in her place, she almost burst out laughing. Her stomach nerves were zinging. They did that when she hid, happened every time. Some kind of giddy reaction to hiding. Or being found. She wasn't sure which. But this was her favorite game. Discovering unfindable spots was her specialty. At home, the not so obvious places were always dependable: under her desk with the chair pushed in tight and the seat stacked with books—that was a good one. Obvious places worked well too: climbing a tree or lying on the shed roof, watching the seeker seeking from above. She had recently made an interesting discovery. People rarely looked up.

Crouching under the fern, imagining getting found—it stirred her insides. Since Paige had just quit counting and couldn't possibly be close by yet, Nellie thought it safe to release some jumpy excitement. She uncapped that giggle. Nothing to do now but sit on her heels and wait out the win.

A minute passed, then another, and another. She leaned forward on her hands, taking the weight off her knees, and peeked out trying to see the path. A plethora of ferns blocked her view. All she saw was a sea of green lace. Her ears would have to listen for the warning signals, relying on her eyes was out. And so far, her ears were picking up nothing. No one was coming.

She sat still a moment longer—until her thighs started burning. She fidgeted to find a new position, one that sent relief to her cramped legs. It occurred to her that she might be there for awhile so she went ahead and sat, careful not to disturb any leaves. (She didn't want the movement giving her away to a sneak attack.) Once she got comfortable, she listened again making sure that no one was walking down the path. Convinced that nobody was, she stretched her legs and rubbed at the numbness in her quads.

Sitting on the comfy carpet of pine needles and leaves, she could see short distances beneath the plants. A whole new world of damp earth and insects surrounded her. She automatically scanned for snake skins and other dangling undesirables. She saw nothing but wildflowers and mushrooms growing up through the mulch. As the minutes passed, she decided that she enjoyed the peacefulness. Strange as it was to be alone in the woods under a fern, it had a certain charm. And the air—it smelled incredible, like the fragrance of wisteria.

Voices ended her daydreaming. Instinctively she brought her legs in and turned her ear toward the path. This could be it. Surely Paige had found the girls by now. But the voices were coming from the wrong direction—coming from the archery field. As they grew louder, Nellie caught snippets of conversation, punctuated with laughter. It was the counselors headed in for dinner, leaving their post after a long day. She could hear them discussing food for a party. There was a rumor that went on late at night. All very hush-hush. It was borderline against the rules. But it explained why they were always so adamant about bedtime. It just made Nellie want a counselor job even more. Fun ruled 24/7 if you knew where to look.

Exhaling the breath she'd been holding, she twisted around seeing if she could lean back. Nope. Too many leaves growing in every direction prevented it; she didn't want to break one. She shifted off her tailbone and sat cross-legged. She could barely hear the counselors anymore. A last squeal of laughter was all she got. She sighed.

The waiting part of the game was usually fun—if you

could see what was going on. But the waiting, accompanied by the suspicion that the seeker had quit seeking, wasn't fun at all. Nellie thought it was possible that she'd been left *unfound* as a joke. Her girlfriends could be in the cafeteria eating without her. But then she decided against it. They were way too competitive. Giving up was against their religion. She scanned under the leaves again, looking toward the path for legs that she knew she wouldn't see. What she did see was fading light. The sun was going down.

She cursed, totally perturbed. The fact that she couldn't see the path made her regret going in so far. A tactical blunder. And she really didn't feel like sitting in the dark. She couldn't even hear the sounds of campers anymore, or the whistles being blown to clear the swimming pools. That had all died down. Most everybody was in the dining hall by now.

Branches creaked overhead as a breeze parted the limbs. A firefly—its taillight blazing—flittered by. Nellie peered under the ferns for any sign of her girls, hoping to hear their voices. All she heard was silence. That did it. She'd had enough. It was quittin-time.

Getting up, she felt the centipede's legs creeping along her hand before she saw it. Reacting on instinct, she shook it off. Its clingy feet kept it from detaching. Preparing to flick the stinging bug and send it flying, she stopped herself when she saw what it really was. This caterpillar was extremely large. A vivid green stripe traveled the length of its tubular body. Blue tufts and black spines grew from its bristly back. A single antenna—flared at the tip with a flourish of fine gold hairs—sloped from the crown of its smooth bronze head. It probed the top of her hand, tickling her skin.

Relieved to discover the harmless insect, she brought it to her face. Her very reflection was mirrored in its dark eyes. They tracked and held her movement. She cocked her head. It cocked its head. She blinked. It blinked. She blinked again. It blinked again. Her mouth dropped open. Its mouth dropped open. And when it spoke, her adrenaline seizure caused a whiteout in her brain cells and she nearly passed out.

"Alooooon yooooou?"

Her eyes fixed on a circular row of incisors jutting from its mouth. From there she'd heard the wordlike whistles. As she gaped—resisting the impulse to smash it flat—its feathery legs continued moving up her wrist. She pushed her arm out as far from her body as she could, shaking it savagely. The caterpillar did not fall off. She swept her arm through the dirt. It still didn't budge. Instead, the bug reared up revealing its leathery underside of undulating legs and prolegs. Dipping its head and twisting its body, the hooked crotchets of its tail section stayed gripped to Nellie's skin.

"Weeeeeee." The sound was tinny. "Toooo faaaasss. Caaarfuu."

She quit thrashing to stare. As she did, it rearranged its segmented torso back down on her arm, shaking off debris so rapidly that all Nellie saw was a blur of gold. Dirt from its antenna sprinkled her skin. With its head up, it inched along emitting audible clicking noises. Ones that she recognized. Ones that she used with her own dogs! Amazed, she steadied her arm and brought the caterpillar closer, touching the tip of her tongue to the roof of her mouth, imitating the caterpillar's kissing clicks. It responded without hesitation kissy-clicking back. Whistley words followed as her two astonished faces shone in its two bulging eyes.

"Yeeeesss. Yeeeesss."

With her heart beginning to race and her hand shaking like a leaf, she forcefully blew on the caterpillar, trying to drive the bug off. It squirmed but did not fall.

"You're freaking me out. Stop with the talking." It was a ludicrous statement, that much she knew. Of course the caterpillar hadn't talked. Those weren't words, just insect sounds. "Here we go again," she whispered, thinking she was back to being mental—back to imagining nutty things. The heat hauled off and got me again, she thought. She realized then that ferns probably trapped heat like saunas. So determined to stay hidden, she hadn't noticed. Not until her brain went soft for the second time in two days and the signs of dehydration were back. "You better start taking care of yourself, Nellie," she berated herself.

Closing her eyes, she shook her head vehemently, expecting life would be back to normal when she opened them. Expecting to stand up and jog to the cafeteria. Expecting to take the caterpillar and show it to the girls, get it to do its kissy, clicky, whistley noises. Expecting none of what happened when the caterpillar spoke again.

"Sheeeee weeeeeeeeeeeets"

Nellie brought her arm up, tipping her face out of harm's way and speaking through clenched teeth. "Did you seriously just say, 'She wheats'?" She watched its mouth—daring it to move, daring it to make another sound. The caterpillar bared its boney teethlets.

"Yeeeesss. Sheeeee weeeeeeeeeeeeets." Curling its spine-less back and exposing an indigo underbelly, its head began vibrating.

The inside of Nellie's mouth went thick. She felt disoriented. "She wheats," she repeated. "Who's...*she*? What's wheats?" She prayed it wouldn't answer.

"Yeeees" It hissed. "Sheeeee waits. I come for yooooou." This time the vowels and consonants were deliberate.

Stunned, she stared at its mouth as the caterpillar's spinneret opened and a needley spine to emerged. It arched its body before sinking the stinger deep into Nellie's flesh—trading poison for blood. The absolute shock of it wobbled her knees. She started to run on legs that didn't respond. A log sent her sprawling into the splits, crashing over a fern before her next step. Paralyzing from a fast-working toxin, she discovered that she could not get up. All she could do was rake her fingernails down her skin, digging off the bug and hurling it.

"Nellie!"

Dragging her braids through the dirt, she lifted her head in the direction of the voice. "Nellie, we give up! Where are you, ya stinker?"

"Gwen." She tried to yell but a ragged croak came out. With great difficulty, she propped to her elbows and searched for the caterpillar. She saw it curled on its side by a fern, looking quite dead. She waited to see if it moved, pretty sure she'd killed it. As she watched—pupation began.

The mouth hole widened and split apart, letting ooze bubble out. The substance quickly crystallized into the maxilla and mandible of a shiny black beak while its bulgy eyes clouded over. Even more surreal, the abdomen steadily engorged until the body was stretched thin. It burst, leaving a massive torso of blue-black feathers writhing on the ground and the smell of burning hair in the air. Within seconds, scaly arms tipped with razor-sharp talons tore through its chest and the fatty haunches on its lower extremity started pulsing. With a splattering pop, jointed legs flopped out. Grunting and hissing, the headless atrocity righted itself, hopping and flattening plants, stumbling blindly as wings smeared with viscous fluid unfurled. Fanning them, its balance improved and a grayish frontal bone began swelling into the shape of a skull, allowing stereoscopic eyes to rotate in every direction. When the eyes locked on Nellie, the wing flapping stopped. The creature extended its sinewy neck, straining and pushing. Suddenly an appendage of coiled vertebrae punctured through its feathery hide, distending into a lizardy tail. The tail whipped violently—slashing the ground like a sling blade—while a forked tongue tested the air. With the metamorphosis complete, the winged monster rose to its full height.

Convulsing from the poison, a screaming Nellie lay fighting to remain conscious. As the thing dove at her, she crawled with her elbows, hauling herself away. Not fast enough. A claw clamped around her waist and flung her to its oily back. But she used the momentum to push—trying to slide off its other side. It didn't work. Invisible ropes lashed her to the raptor's backbone.

Lurching forward, the beast spread its wings and lifted from the ground, hacking ferns with its tail. Nellie screamed. The wind shoved the sound back down her throat. Rapidly gaining height, she pounded its neck, struggling to free herself. But as pine boughs rushed by—slapping her in the face—she could not break free. A branch grazed her throat, hooking her necklace and severing the string. Plastic beads peppered the ground, making the escape she'd botched. Banking right, the bird soared up. Nellie saw the oncoming branch. She tried to protect her head. Then her world went black.

*A claw clamped around her waist and
flung her to its oily back.*

Chapter 11

The search for Nellie had become super annoying and totally tedious—lasting way too long. The girls were fading. What's more, a new activity was begging for attention. All they wanted to do was head to dinner and chow down. It took awhile finding Lee and Gwen. Now with hunger gnawing at her, Paige was getting crabby. After checking around every building, she was all for giving up. She really didn't feel like going into the woods. Problem was, when she was counting she had sort of cheated. The woods were exactly where Nellie headed. Paige had just hoped she'd turned back. Apparently she hadn't. So…seriously over it and needing it to be done, they all three kept at, trudging the grounds.

"I'm so hungry I could eat this." Stopping to rest, Paige snapped off a pine sprig, smelling it like a breadstick. "I'm thinkin she went in. Seems to me we should do the same."

Gwen wasn't so sure. As they stood there deciding, all weary and starved, Gwen squalled her most impatient holler. "Nellie! Nellie, we give up! Where are you, ya stinker?" Almost a full minute of kicking dirt and peeling bark passed with no reply.

"Fine. Let's go in." Gwen agreed to call it quits.

They had just turned for the mess hall when they heard it—Nellie's voice doing something unusual. Screaming. And it wasn't a toying shriek hinting at her spot either. It was a blatant cry for help. Its distress offered no confusion. They knew something very wrong—right that second—was happening to Nellie.

Excessive amounts of adrenal fear shot through their veins as they retraced their steps, backtracking from the rifle range and taking a shortcut to archery. Tearing through the woods—caution outweighed by young girl fury—they suddenly stopped dead. It was Nellie's hiding place; they could tell. They saw the gouged earth and the razed plants.

"What in the world... What happened here?" Paige took in the sight. Her hands went clammy.

"I don't know." Lee sounded nothing like herself, but she swung into action. "Nellie!" They listened tensely. "Nellie!" She yelled again. "Nellie!" Gwen screamed with her. Even the crows didn't answer.

"Somethin besides her was here." Paige sounded warbly.

"Or someone..." said Lee. Every thought switched to the missing little boy.

Calling her name, they beat through the bushes, searching and searching. The area in question was in complete shambles. One entire fern—savagely uprooted—dangled from an overhead branch. Of the many that were squashed, a few were even ripped to shreds. The violent sight nearly sent Gwen into a state of shock, so she almost missed it. But making her way through web cities—trying to avoid massive banana spiders in the face—she happened to look down. Stepping over a mangled milkweed, she noticed an object that she recognized—a plastic sunflower bead. She knelt to pick it up.

"Guys, over here!"

She stayed down checking under the shrubs, turning a 360 on her hands and knees, hoping she was about to gottcha Nellie. Rushing to her side, Lee and Paige saw even more beads. A baby blue one lay cupped in a leaf, another was by some mushrooms, two more were on a demolished fern. Gathering them one by one, the girls remained attentive, praying that Nellie's give-away giggles would end the game. Praying that this was some kind of overblown prank. Praying for Gwen to finally shout, "Found ya!" But when Gwen got up shaking her head, the only sounds they heard were their own heavy breaths.

"This ain't good." Gwen said what they were all thinking. "How'd she get away so fast? Where you think she's at?"

Nobody answered.

They split-up hunting for clues, utterly baffled.

"Nellie!" Gwen yelled.

"Nellie!" Lee yelled.

A night breeze was gathering. Time for finding Nellie was growing short.

"It's getting dark," said Paige, looking around nervously.

Lee and Gwen had noticed too. They just didn't want to admit it. Without saying so out loud, they wished away the game, wished they hadn't played, wished they'd listened to Mrs. B and stuck together. Wished their lives were, right then, all about corny camp songs and volunteering for dishes. Not raided by panic—and the lingering scream of a vanished friend.

A pine cone scale ricocheted off a log. Squirrels in the trees, thought Lee. Another fell, hitting her shoulder. One more clunked her head and stuck in her hair. Lost in thought she reached for it—rolling it in her fingertips and dropping it at her feet. Its transparent color was barely visible against the forest floor. Pink.

Like a blathering ninny, Lee pointed at the ground. "Nellie's! That's Nellie's! Nellie's bead!"

From across the plot, Paige and Gwen looked where she was pointing. They didn't get why finding another bead sent Lee into a frenzy. Or why she'd switched from pointing at the ground to staring straight up. So they looked up too— and saw it. From high in a tree, a bead came falling, falling, falling and plopped at Lee's feet with a modest bounce. They stared at it quizzically. Until their heads snapped up, comprehending.

Before now, they hadn't noticed the enormity of the pine they stood beneath; the giant tree dwarfed them. As its canopy creaked in the wind, Paige was certain that a limb was about to break. She pointed out a splintered branch that looked ready to drop. They stood their ground anyway, searching the shadowy boughs. As they did—falling, falling, falling came another. But this was no bead. A single drop of blood kissed Lee's upturned cheek. She wrenched her shoulder up, wiping the smear with her sleeve. Seeing crimson. Smelling iron.

"Gross," she blurted.

"Nellie?" Gwen was at Lee's side in a flash. "You up there? Nellie girl, this ain't funny!"

In the treetops something stirred. A pained rasp, a throaty moan—Nellie's moan. They heard it over pine needles whooshing. Their fingers started tingling. Though out of sight and out of reach, one fact was certain. High in that tree—implausible as it seemed—they'd finally found Nellie.

"Nellie!" They hollered from below. "Nells, are you OK?" "Come down!" "Is this a joke?" "You win!" The shouts overlapped. She failed to respond. They only heard the gusting wind.

"Talk about way overdoin it!" Paige yelled up, exasperated at Nellie's choice of hiding place. "Guess she figured I'd never find her there," she carped to Lee and Gwen. "How'd she even get up that high?" Paige was trying her best to spot her between the branches.

"She's not answerin," observed Gwen. It made her uneasy. "That's not like her."

"She's hurt." Lee knew from the blood.

"I found ya fair and square! Come down! We wanna eat!" Paige tried again but still got no answer.

Gwen stepped back from the tree, growing more anxious by the second. "Look at this place. Everythin's smashed." That's when she noticed. "And look at this." She bent down. "There's Nell's footprints here. Then there's those..." The chilling prints were confined to the center. None led in. None led out. "Those belong to an animal." Gwen studied the shape. "Somethin was here y'all... I can feel it."

"Maybe she climbed that tree to get away," said Lee, checking behind her.

"We'll never reach her in the dark." Gwen was forming a

plan. "One of us gotta run to the cabin and bring back the flashlights." Lee was yards gone before Gwen said another word.

Alone with Gwen, Paige knelt down inspecting the prints. Her color immediately drained. Needing to get a grip on her nerves, she strode to the trunk and bellowed up, "Nellie! What on earth are ya doin!"

"Stop yellin," ordered Gwen in a hoarse whisper.

"Why?"

"She didn't answer us. If she could've she would've. Now you're just broadcastin we're here. That might be a mistake if...if..." She scanned the darkening woods and didn't finish the sentence. She sensed they were being watched, sensed they needed to move with stealth. With eyes the size of ping-pong balls, Paige nodded that she understood. The two quit talking.

Alert for the slightest noise, Paige walked among the ferns tracking down the last of the Nellie beads and tucking them in her pocket. As she gathered those, Gwen figured out which plant had been Nellie's hiding place. It was easy to pick out the trampled giant. Nellie's footprints were all around it—along with a multitude of the three-prong tracks. Gwen ran her fingers through the depressions. She could tell by the pin-prick holes that whatever it was had deadly claws.

Gwen stood up, reassessing the colossal evergreen. Encroaching Spanish moss—like an army of ghosts—hung from the surrounding trees. Twiggy limbs covered in the stuff blocked parts of her view. Pushing a clump aside, her hand touched a wisp of hairs. She ran her fingers down the long blue strands and signaled Paige over. They were absolutely Nellie's—Atomic Turquoise. Leaving them there, Gwen moved to the base of the tree and tested her weight on its lowest bough. Paige watched the woods for Lee's return—watched the sun sinking lower and the sky turning violet and the fireflies start blinking.

Trepidation filled Gwen's brain. She tried making sense of the puzzling events. She wasn't sure how serious their situation really was. She didn't know if Nellie was bad hurt or just stuck or worse. She knew she was working on supersonic overdrive, thinking up horrible things on account of that kid from Stingray. That disappearance set everybody's teeth on edge. But there was one good part. Those definitely weren't gator prints. Still, she didn't know if they should get word to Mrs. B and the police. Didn't know if she should run for Kate. Didn't know how scared she should be. What she did know—that Nellie was in trouble, that Nellie was in the top of this tree, that Nellie's friends would kick butt to get her down—kept her stationed right there.

Beams of hope cut through the forest. Lee was fast. But night was faster. Darkness had come. And it wasn't a starlit dark either. It was a deep in the woods, cloud-covered dark. The incessant buzzing of blood-thirsty mosquitoes just made things worse. Thank goodness for Lee's speedy return. Now they could start.

Running up to join the girls, Lee put her hands on her knees, panting to catch her breath. She'd yet to say a word or hand out lights when she felt the prickly crawler making its way up her ankle. She never hurt bugs. That was uncool. But she was so agitated—so pumped from the run and the adrenaline—that before she could think to brush it off, three hard-cased flashlights swinging in from opposite directions struck it perfectly. Well, not perfect for the caterpillar. Especially since Lee's amped-up swatting moves cost her her balance. The battered bug landed beneath her hopping foot. A half second later, they all heard a loud pop when that same foot mashed its head in. Caterpillar entrails seeped out and fluid began pooling under Lee's tennis shoe. The rubber sole caused a chain reaction. Black smoke poofed from the surprisingly large puddle and went straight up her nose. Acrid fumes made her stagger and gag as she stamped and stamped to stub out the shoe. When the smoke ignited in a blue flash, scorching the fine hairs on her face, Lee screamed. Sputtering like the dying embers of a firework, blue sparks sizzled across the ground in an electrified current before all evidence vanished. The girls stood statue still—stunned and agape.

"Um...y'all?" Paige backed up quickly. "What was that!"

"I can taste it." Lee dropped the lights and started wiping singed nose hairs out of her blue-grunged nostrils. "It burned my face!" She was coughing up phlegm.

Rage flooded Gwen. Losing it momentarily, she yelled to the treetops, "What the *hell* is goin on!" Angry now, she collected the lights and shoved one at Paige.

"You burnt bad?" Positioning her double wattage—one tucked under her arm, the other in her fist—Gwen used the beams to inspect Lee's face. Holding her firmly by the chin, Gwen checked Lee's eyes and nose for injuries—including rising blisters—and immediately got coughed on. Aside from a partially hairless eyebrow and lots of soot, Lee appeared unharmed.

"I'll live." Lee cleared her throat and spit a macho hocker. Snatching a flashlight, she stomped around Gwen and put the light to better use, aiming it at the tree.

"Nellie, we comin! Hang tight, girl!" Gwen didn't care who heard now. She took Paige by the hand and fell in step with Lee, lighting up the armpits of the branches.

Moving toward the tree, something rushed past them so fast that all they saw was a blur. They froze. Sweeping their lights through the deepening dark, they turned just in time to catch the last quiver of a fern. All three beams instantly hammered the spot. The thing tried crouching out of sight, but there was no escaping the illumination. They saw him. The man's scraggly hair hung in hanks around his dirty face. He closed his eyes and raised a hand against the glare, snarling viciously. The girls flat-out screamed.

Lee would have gotten away. She didn't even see the root that tripped her up. She fell hard on her chest, knocking the wind from her lungs. Facedown in a heap, she lay gasping for that first intake of air. Paige and Gwen were equally as unlucky. Spinning fast, they collided skull on skull with a solid crack and took each other out. Both went down. Before they could get up, he flew out of the bushes.

Soaring up with enormous wings, he dive-bombed them. Circling back, he dove again. Gwen and Paige went rigid with terror, too astounded to scream. Lee had managed to flop over—keeping him in her eye line—but she was still worthless, still just trying to breathe. He came at them a third time, but then he pulled up short and hovered in midair. Eerily lit by the dropped lights, he examined their faces. He was pleased by their fear. It could save them. For the lone

one, he was too late. She was surely done. Now came three more scurrying like rats to a baited trap. He was furious. Again he launched himself at them, feigning an attack. To his complete fury, they were too stupefied to get up and run.

He changed tactics. Staying aloft, he gestured for them to remain on the ground. The feathered antennae on his head twitched nervously as he questioned them in a whisper. "You follow the long-haired girl?" He edged nearer for an answer. From that close, the grief in his eyes was palpable. And his urgent tone—it wasn't threatening. It was strangely consoling.

Though the girls weren't about to let their guard down—that would be dangerous—his affect on them was instantly calming. Like an aura sucking up their fear. Sitting to face him, a dazed Gwen tried to speak. "You... You saw Nellie?"

All he did was nod.

"Gwen, what are ya doin? Don't tell it anythin." Paige was visibly shaking.

"Hold on, Paige." Gwen looked at Lee, making sure she wasn't about to charge him or do anything crazy. But Lee was still working out how to breathe.

Gwen took her chances. "We're her friends," she answered. She had to stop and swallow several times. "We were lookin for her when we heard screamin. We think she's up that tree. We think she's hurt." Tenderly checking her own head, Gwen felt through her hair and examined her fingertips for bleeding. With no blood in sight, she started getting up—trying to decide if she was hallucinating.

If it wasn't for a shabby loin cloth and various satchels strapped to his chest, Gwen would be staring up at a practically naked, full-grown man. Then there were those mottled, tawny wings—pumping away—growing right out of his back. It was unreal. He looked like some homeless actor playing a fairy. Like they'd stumbled onto a movie set. Except that they hadn't. There were no cameras. No film crew. And he was actually flying. No wires were holding him up; she'd already checked. And she'd checked his feet. He had man feet and man hands—ten toes, ten fingers. The nails were grimy but they weren't spiked. The prints she'd seen next to Nellie's didn't come from him. She didn't know what was going on. He was either a real miracle or a real demon. She wasn't hallucinating. It was an extraordinary situation.

He kept his distance hovering. He wasn't trusting. Not anymore. Encountering and actually speaking to any human—especially a child—was an unwelcome turn of events he'd never anticipated. He was aware that it could turn out badly. But even the Protector would agree—he couldn't just leave. Not now. Not when he was so close. And not when these girls were in such danger.

With a single thrust, his wings rippled and he fluttered up, darting within the lower branches of the pine. The green eyespots on his forewings made him look like a huge predatory owl. "She should never have come out here alone." They almost didn't hear his heartache. But they did. And all three physically felt a vibration in their chests.

Lingering—sensing the air—he made his decision and flew back to them. "Were you so stupid as to climb," he demanded.

They stared at him, completely dumbfounded.

"Were you going up?" He repeated with a temper.

"Yeah… We was about to," stammered Gwen.

"No! It's too late!"

"Wait a minute. What's too late? What's going on?" Lee had gotten enough air in her to come back to life. The total impossibility of some winged dude hiding in a bush and jumping out to scare them was beyond absurd. She wasn't about to turn her back on Nellie and follow his orders—no matter how real he seemed. Especially how real he seemed.

"You're wasting my time. That girl is gone. Now you only sacrifice yourselves. " He flew up beginning his retreat.

"Wait!" Lee wasn't sure why she stopped him. A gut feeling warned her not to let him get away. "What are you talkin about, gone?"

"Your girl was captured."

The whimper rattling around inside Paige dribbled out.

"Then we gonna get her back!" Gwen stepped forward and picked up her flashlight—just in case she needed something to defend herself with. She prayed that Lee and Paige would do the same. She still had no idea what was going on. And it wasn't like there was time to take a vote. She had to make a move and see how it played out. But he was no fool. He continued hovering well out of reach.

"You can't help her," he fumed. "Now go!" He beat his wings threateningly and swooped over them.

Nellie's moan floated down like a feather. That brought Lee and Paige to their feet. The man turned and soared upward, listening for proof that the captured one was still living. Grabbing their flashlights, the girls ran to the base of the tree. He heard their crashing footsteps and dove.

"No! Get out of here!"

"Try and make us." Lee reached for her first handhold.

"Stop!" He was livid, speaking quickly. "That caterpillar on your leg. Didn't you see it was toxic? If you hadn't killed it before it spoke, you'd be—"

"Spoke? I don't think so, buddy." Lee swung her legs up, effortlessly pulling her whole body onto a limb. "Caterpillars don't talk."

"And men only fly in dreams?" His question wiped the ugly expression off her face. "You can't help that girl."

"You wrong about that," Gwen fired back. "We goin up this tree cause that's where Nellie is. I ain't dreamin it." Gwen shone her light on a limb and grabbed on.

"I just bit my nail to the quick and it's bleedin for real. That means I'm not dreamin, right Gwen," asked Paige from below, talking super fast.

Anchoring her feet against the trunk, Gwen pulled herself level with Lee. "You think you dreamin, Lee?" She squatted on a branch, looking up through the limbs.

"I know I'm not. And I know bugs can't talk either," Lee glared at the man. But that whole exploding caterpillar incident was mystifying. The insides of her nostrils were still on fire. "And FYI," she replied sharply, reaching for a higher branch, "I only killed it on accident."

"That accident saved you." He clung to the trunk like a moth. "You killed it before it changed. Before the claws and wings appeared. Before it carried you away like that girl."

"Claws?" Paige gulped. "Like those?" She was standing on a pair of prominent prints. That made her start climbing.

"They are her beasts," he said. "Her kidnappers."

"What? What beast? Whose kidnappers?" Gwen's voice was high-pitched with new jabs of disbelief.

"The witch who hunts these woods. When she struck last night, when she took that boy, I thought she'd move on. But she wasn't finished here yet."

"A witch got that boy?" Lee thought she'd heard it all but the weirdness kept coming. If it hadn't been for the way he returned her glare, she wouldn't have believed a word he said. But his expression was even more belligerent than hers. Her arm hairs prickled.

"She's pure evil. She sends caterpillars to catch her prey."

"How can a caterpillar do that," quavered Paige, afraid to go further up but more afraid to go back down.

"It's not just a caterpillar!" He scoffed. "Its true form is a monstrous lizard with wings. It could easily carry all three of you. You can't fight it. You can't get away. Once it transforms, it can't be stopped."

"Daddy's shotgun and some barbeque sauce could stop it." Gwen was dead serious. She had a coldblooded look in her eye, wishing she had that gun.

Sneering, he dropped to her branch and loomed over her. "Luck is all that keeps you breathing. And that has run out. When she sees you, she'll kill all of you. I'm going alone."

"You just tell me where she at, I beat her face in." The hostility in Gwen made him smile.

All of the sudden, Lee grabbed a fistful of his chest straps. Toe to toe, she was ready to fight—ready to knock him flat with an uppercut to the jaw. "How do we know it wasn't you!" She was so pissed that blotchy red hives were breaking out all over her neck.

Placing his hand over hers, he forcibly pried her loose. "Punch me. Go ahead. See how far that gets you," he laughed in her face. He cast her hand aside, waiting for her to swing—though her courage was tempting him to reconsider.

Lee raised her fist and stepped toward him. "Get out of my way or I will." They locked eyes—daring each other—but he didn't move. Lowering her arm, she pushed by him roughly and reached higher, pulling herself up. "And stay out of it," she spat.

"You need to go back. You're risking your lives," he warned.

When Lee and Gwen continued climbing, he realized he had no choice. He was out of time. "Stop! Stop and listen to me. *Listen!*" He was insistent. "If you're coming with me, we have to stick together!"

That made Gwen stop and look down. "You don't know nothin about girls, do ya, Mister?" She stared at him hard. "Stickin together is what we do. And we don't need your permission to do it." Glancing around him, she checked Paige's progress, making sure that she was still coming. "You doin good, Paige." Then Gwen reached higher.

He watched them climb, waiting for the slow one to catch up. It was his torment that they would not stop. He had done all he could do to make them turn back. The terrifying sight of him was designed to bring them to their knees and keep them there—until they ran screaming for the safety of their cabin. But it was not to be. They were head-strong. The element of surprise had failed. The shock of seeing him didn't make them run. His ferocity didn't change their minds. He could do nothing now but allow them to fight at his side. The girl was their friend. He vaguely remembered how that felt. This would be a deadly eve.

"What are you?" Paige was the one who had the nerve to ask.

The mothman flew down in a rhythmic hum, doubling back as Paige recoiled against the trunk. Whispering close in her ear—so close that she smelled his lemon-rind breath— he answered, "I am Mother Nature's army sent for the crucial mission. I am an assassin."

Chapter 12

"Paige, you gotta hurry up," groaned Lee. She was dying to get to the top, so afraid that Nellie would come falling like one of her beads, crashing through the tree. At the first sound of breaking branches, Lee was ready to make the catch. She secretly wished that Paige would just stay put. If it wasn't for her nothin-burger pace, Lee would've already sprung catlike to the treetop.

"What if I wait here," begged Paige, wanting to.

"Do it. We'll put the hurt on that—"

"No! We stay together!" He ordered.

Lee's exasperated sigh was deliberately aimed at him. That and a dirty look. It was idiotic dragging Paige along when climbing was clearly not her thing. They needed to focus on getting to Nellie as fast as humanly possible, not coaxing Paige to get the lead out. Even Paige knew that.

"He's right," said Gwen. "We gotta stay together. End of story."

Gwen stopped to check Paige's progress. Paige was about five body lengths below her, four lower than Lee. It dawned on Gwen that she'd never seen Paige climb the rock wall. Then she remembered why. "I don't do heights," Paige had bragged. "Unless it's on the back of my favorite mare." Gwen cringed remembering, watching Paige inching up the tree. It was hard but she forced herself to wait, forced herself not to chew Paige out. Paige was doing her best. Snarking at the girl wouldn't make her any faster.

"Hurry up," griped Lee, agonizing over the situation.

Lee's irritation did nothing to rev Paige's engine. Paige was too nervous to think, too flustered to move fast. She could hardly move at all. The act of scaling a tree gave her vertigo. If that wasn't bad enough, climbing to fight a real-live witch made her want to vomit. Her entire body was rebelling. Her arms felt about as useful as otter flappers, she couldn't feel her feet, and the tears she was trying to hide were proving calamitous. She had to constantly wipe her eyes before grabbing branches. One bad choice already snapped in half and nearly sent her falling. And carrying the flashlight was making the whole ordeal even riskier. Add fear to the mix and she was clumsy, indecisive and painfully slow. The polar opposite of Lee and Gwen.

When a stressed-out Paige finally caught up, Gwen and Lee didn't hesitate. They began climbing again.

From his perch above, he called down quietly, "Drop your lights. She'll see us coming."

Switching them off, Lee and Gwen did what he said. Paige had to be told twice. Difficult as it was to hold, she didn't want to relinquish her only weapon. But he wasn't asking, so she dropped it. They all heard the glass cover crack when it landed on a rock.

Blanketed in a cave of black, blindness enveloped them. Again they were forced to halt while their eyes adjusted to the dark. They couldn't have made out their fingers up their noses and he knew it. His expression changed. This was his chance—while they couldn't see. While they were sitting ducks. Silent as a cloud, he unsheathed a hidden dagger and left his perch, swooping past each girl and then gliding back. Though their eyes didn't detect him and their ears heard nothing, they did feel the sting of flayed skin meeting humid air. Rubbing a prick on the back of their hands, their fingers discovered the sticky wet of beading blood.

"Somethin just got me," whispered Gwen.

"Me too."

"Me three."

"Shush."

They blamed the mosquitoes. They had no idea what he'd done.

He moved again, undisguised this time. They felt him hop down and settle on a closer branch. They still couldn't make him out—couldn't see his blade deliver three infinitesimal slivers of girl flesh to his mouth. It took only an instant for their DNA to enter his bloodstream.

Protectively huddled next to them, he shut his nocturnal eyes and let his head droop. Waves of energy throbbed in his chest and up his neck, pulsing through his eye sockets and thudding in his ears. Trying hard to see him, the girls faced where they thought he was sitting. As they did, their own eyes became heavy. Their heartbeats slowed and relaxation rolled through their forearms. They were aware of a low-grade buzzing. Until the buzzing changed to static, like a transistor radio being tuned. Just as it gained volume, it reverberated into silence. What remained was a vivid connection between the mothman and the girls. They could actually see his thoughts—see his life experiences—playing like movies inside their heads. Without speaking a single word, he filled their minds with his knowledge of *Her*. It shattered their innocence. And their hot-headed bravado.

"She appears as pale perfection—welcoming and glorious, dressed in a gown of white. Fair hair shimmers with jewels and is crowned by wisteria while greetings flow from her lips, chasing away mistrust. To be in her presence and breathe her bouquet—it is heavenly. But it is a trick. Her crown of blossoms is a weapon. The fragrant poison brings on a vulnerable peacefulness. No child suspects that cruelty thuds in her chest. When her catch stands within reach, a golden tassel is offered. 'It has the power to grant a wish.' So she tells them. But it is her wish. Not theirs. And her wish is death. When youthful warmth touches the cursed tassel, the consequences are fatal. Life is stolen. Sometimes she approaches on foot. Sometimes she sends the caterpillar beast. The result is always the same. She draws them in and offers the golden bait, tempting them with their heart's desire. Once touched, they can't let go. Dying at her feet, their bodies crumble and turn into hunks of moss. These woods are overgrown with sorrow. Look around. Carnage hangs everywhere."

As his thoughts described the witch and her powers, the girls saw everything unfolding in their minds. The horrific scenes made Paige shudder. "The Spanish moss is dead kids..." She thought the thought and held on tighter to the tree. Lee and Gwen took it all in. Lee was totally overwhelmed. And, skeptical of whether to believe him.

"I'm not a liar. It's true."

"Prove it," thought Lee.

"If you don't believe me, stay down here." He started to stand, to fly up without them. Gwen reached out and grabbed his arm.

"Lee," she begged her friend with her thoughts, "there's no time for this. We can't gamble Nellie's life away while he's convincin you. Think about it. He's real. If he's real, all this could be real. We have to let him show us everythin he knows. I think he's tellin the truth." Gwen heard Lee's quick breaths and saw her next thought. The one that defied him to show her more, give her a reason to trust him. Gwen felt Lee trying to calm down. Good, she thought. Just relax. Just hear him out. Gwen's next question was for him. "And you been after that witch for how—"

He answered Gwen's thought before she finished thinking it. "I've only seen her once. But I've tracked her my whole life. She doesn't know I'm coming. This will be my first chance at a kill—"

"Your first chance? How bad do you suck?" The thought just came. Lee couldn't stop it. Not that she would have tried.

"Her body only forms when she strikes. Afterward, she evaporates into mist. Her range covers hundreds of thousands of miles. But following her is easy. I know what to look for. She hangs her victims in the trees. Did you think that sound was the wind? If you listen closely, you can hear their despair."

"You mean to tell us all those dead kids is still a little alive?" As Gwen looked down on tree after tree covered in

Spanish moss, she heard the subtlest sound of moaning. It gave her the total heebie-jeebies.

"I wouldn't call that living." His thought was harsh, almost cutting. "I've been in these woods for weeks, waiting for her. But even as I scouted, she struck. Tonight will be different. Tonight I'll kill her."

"*You mean we'll kill her,*" was Lee's thought.

"Only death can stop her. And if your girl touches that tassel, she'll be next. As long as I can see her, I can catch her. When we reach the top, get to your girl as fast as you can and start down. Whatever happens, don't let the tassel touch you. If it makes contact with your skin, you die. Leave the witch to me. Once I've got her, I'll take the body and drop it in the ocean. The sharks can rip her open. But if I...if I fail..." His thought skipped like it was stuck, but the girls saw it anyway, a flickering image in slow-motion: five clumps of Spanish moss—falling, falling, falling from the tree.

"Failure ain't an option," thought Gwen. It took every ounce of willpower for her to keep calm, not barrel straight up the tree. She wanted to grab that witch by the throat and dig her eyes out.

He saw the thought and smiled strangely. "No. Silent and deliberate. When we reach the top, *She* is mine." His lust for vengeance was starkly intimidating. It left no doubt in the girls' minds—even Lee's—that when he laid his hands on Nellie's kidnapper—or his wings, or his teeth, or whatever brutality he had in store—he would be merciless.

Slipping a tin from one of the many pouches strapped to his side, he screwed off the lid and dipped his finger in a sticky brown paste. A sharp smell reached the girls before his thoughts could explain. Their nostrils flared as they flattened their noses with their hands.

Holding out a globbed finger, his thought ordered them, "Rub this under your nose. It will protect you from her scent."

The rancid stench made Gwen's throat tightened and Lee's tongue ping with saliva. Paige's eyes were absolutely terror stricken. Her stomach started churning.

"It's putrid, I know. It has to be to keep you safe."

"What is it," thought Lee, obviously disgusted.

"A mixture of Eucalyptus and opossum dung. It makes your eyes water but that won't last long. Shut them and don't wipe it off."

Shaking her head furious-fast, Paige threw up her hands, stopping him. She gathered her thoughts so they came out clear. "I'm not wimpin out on y'all. Really, I'm not. But if that gets on me, I'll swell-up. I'm allergic to Eucalyptus oil. I put some on my wrists once, aromatherapy stuff. Mother had to rush me to the emergency room before my throat closed. I couldn't breathe. They had to give me a shot." She looked distraught.

The mothman couldn't believe it. His thoughts stopped completely as he grew visibly perturbed. Finally he thought, "Then we have no choice. You have to wait here by yourself in total silence." It was a command. "No matter what you hear above. If we're attacked and the worst happens, don't make a sound or you'll be next. Wait. Wait until she leaves. Once she's gone, climb down and run as fast as you can. Whatever you do, don't stop. And never come back." He shrugged, listless. "That's the best I can offer. Say your goodbyes." He tried to make the thought comforting, but the girls understood the danger—and understood that Paige was now an unprotected target.

Looking at her brave friends, Paige held out her hands and they all squeezed goodbye. Reality was sinking in. If the mothman was right, they would be lucky to survive.

With the hard decisions made, he leaned forward without asking and smeared the salve under Lee's nose and Gwen's nose. The smell was atrocious. Their eyes started stinging. Grimacing, they shut their eyes and waited for the burning to stop.

Rubbing salve inside his own nostrils, the mothman threw his head back in familiar repugnance. He did not shut his eyes as he carefully screwed the lid back on and put the tin away. "Beware the caterpillars," was his last thought as he looked them in the eye—one by one—before lifting from the branch and flying out of sight.

Paige watched anxiously as Lee and Gwen began climbing. She kept watching until she couldn't see the bottoms of their shoes anymore. Hunkered against the trunk, she straddled two branches attempting to blend-in with the tree. Alone now, her head was on auto-pilot looking side to side and up and down. She was trying hard not to jump at every noise.

Gwen and Lee moved quickly up the sturdy limbs, finding safe places to grip and secure footing. They scaled fifty feet in no time. Fifty feet more and faint moonlight began seeping through the branches. Out of nowhere, the mothman was hovering in front of them, motioning for them to stop. Signaling up, he cupped a hand to his ear and pointed to the treetop. All three could make out the sound of female voices.

One of them they recognized.

Chapter 13

She was concentrating, reassuring this pig-tailed brunette. Before the savory boy the previous night, it had been far too long. Admittedly, lurking above this sweet prey alone on the footbridge had been a thrill. Such a child would make an excellent addition. When the girl escaped and dashed for her friends, the disappointment was trifling. In truth, the timing was wrong. But what fun the torment had been. Now the deed was done. The girl did not get away twice for *She* deployed a caterpillar. It was marvelous—watching the insect. It spoke and the startled child reacted. Even spoke back. Wonderful entertainment! Now that very girl sat within easy reach.

Alas, there had been the inevitable delay. Whenever *She* enlisted the services of her caterpillars, there arose the possibility that the child would arrive in a catatonic stupor. The transformation—with its theatrics of bursting body parts—had that effect. The spectacle struck fear into her own being the first time *She* witnessed it. The explosion of blue-black feathers and tyrannical hissing was terrifying. It could easily produce a heart attack in a fragile victim. *She* was fortunate it had not yet occurred. One day it would. The young behaved notoriously melodramatically—proven so on several occasions. Though tiring, dealing with their pitiful outbursts was necessary. *She* always soothed the bellyachers. And this cheeky urchin—with her mild concussion—would be no different. Still, every time the girl demanded, "Who are you? Am I dead?" *She* had to bite her lip not to swoon with laughter.

Eager to move things along, *She* had worked masterfully convincing the girl of luck beyond compare. "Receiving a once-in-a-lifetime gift is a notable occasion. Only exceptional children, the deserved worthiest, are granted the honor of beholding me." Deceit slid from her tongue. "You are special. You are chosen. Make a wish. Anything you like." *She* spoke with the perfect balance of sincerity and enthusiasm. *She* had centuries of practice.

But this treat was proving difficult. Further mucking the matters, her insufferable friends would not stop squealing like piglets below. Thankfully, they departed before the girl fully woke-up. *She* welcomed the quietude, knowing they were gone. Only a litany of monotonous questions interrupted the proceedings now. The girl was challenging. But *She* delivered a flawless performance, concealing her distain and ridding the worrywart of doubt. On occasion these matters took selfish advantage of her patience. Happily, there was no need to rush. No need to slap the tassel against her jabbering jaw and get on with it. That would rob her of her favorite part—that split-second when expressions changed from blissful concentration, whispering wishes, to the horror of dying. A memorable moment. Consistently comical!

Slowly, this one was beginning to trust. The caterpillar toxin was potent and the wisteria was dulling her fears. The child was losing her wary attitude. And none too soon. *She* longed to be done with the pest and bind her to the cloak.

As for Nellie, after regaining consciousness and finding herself in the top of a tree, she immediately scanned for the bird but saw no sign of it. Then the shock of shocks—discovering herself face to face with an angel. She prodded her own neck, searching for a pulse. Blood was pumping under her skin, but she blurted the question anyway, "Am I dead?" Assured by the angel that she was very much alive, she sat stock-still, determined not to fall from the tree and break her neck. Even with a throbbing head, she could tell they were seriously high and that the sun had set.

The wooziness made it hard to think, hard to figure out which mindboggling question to ask first. She remembered being carried off by the bird. Nothing else. At least the verdict was in on Tou-tou. He wasn't completely bonkers. But who in their right mind would have ever believed his cockamamie story if they hadn't seen it for themselves? It was too unreal to fathom—being birdnapped.

Nellie tried remembering what he told her, particularly the part about the bird's master. But it was all so hazy. But wasn't it something bad? Or had he gotten that part wrong? He must have because there it was. There *she* was to be exact. The most ethereal woman imaginable was leaning over Nellie, nursing the gash on her head. Smelling like blossoms in springtime, the woman was holding a clump of moss and swabbing Nellie's bleeding scalp, ordering her to sit still. Nellie noticed that her fingertips were black. That was freaky. But she didn't dare ask why. She didn't want to come off completely uncouth in the presence of a goddess or an angel or whatever she was.

Especially since the woman was completely upset, sighing over Nellie like a worried mother. Nellie saw actual tears. The goddess kept apologizing for the bird and was furious about Nellie's head. She claimed that her winged assistant was youthful with a tendency toward overexcitement. She took full responsibility for its lack of training and promised swift, corrective action. Sometimes the juveniles did not take the smartest flight path. Just the quickest. Crashing into a limb must have been excruciating. Could Nellie please forgive her? The goddess had even begged.

She promised that the bird was sent solely for transportation—so that Nellie could collect her fabulous gift. She felt it was asking too much to make Nellie climb the tree and come to her. Too exhausting and hazardous. She would not allow it. And why would she? Nellie was unaware she was waiting in the treetops in the first place. A flying helper was the most logical way to deliver the message and offer a ride. The goddess took the blame for everything, insisting several times—with her prettiest smile—that she was so very, very sorry for frightening Nellie and particularly distressed by the accident.

"But why are we...in a tree," mumbled Nellie, feeling out-of-it.

"I simply cannot tolerate spies. Ours is a private matter."

After a mouthload of more questions, Nellie began appreciating her unusual circumstance. The confusion in her head was still thick, but she stopped being scared. In fact, the opposite started happening. She felt peaceful. After pinching a tender spot on her arm—proving that she wasn't imagining things and definitely not dead—she sat up straighter. It was like a dream come true. "And hey...miracles happen..." Nellie even said it out loud.

"Yes, my child. One certainly hopes they do," the goddess agreed.

"Gosh..." whispered Nellie. "Nothing like this...ever happens to me. I...I don't even win...school raffles." She instantly regretted saying that. It made her sound so boring loserish. "Another...question," she asked weakly, trying not to slur her words. "Is it...do I...get the wish...even if I'm...not from around here?" Her head was swimming, but she forced herself to ask it. The goddess probably wondered why she didn't have a southern accent. She'd hate to get her heart set on a wish and then find out she wasn't eligible. That would be a buzzkill.

"Oh?" The goddess arched her brow.

"I'm from...California. I'm just here for...camp." She enunciated slowly and tried not to move her head too much.

"Far from your family, are you?" When the goddess's smile widened, Nellie knew it was OK.

"Yep." Nellie grinned, thinking of home.

"Tis the highest honor to meet such an accomplished world traveler," *She* answered, bowing her wisteria-crowned head. *She* set the bloody moss aside—impaling it on a limb. "I strive to seek out commendable recipients for my reward.

I confess, a young lady of your background is unique." *She* reached into her luxurious hair, withdrawing a beautiful golden tassel—its silken cords gathered in twisted tendrils. As the goddess stroked them, they played through her fingers like liquid gold. Nellie wanted to do the same. "I am certain your wish will be well-deserved." *She* was admiring Nellie, gently pushing away an errant bang and tucking it behind Nellie's ear with her black fingertips. "That is better," *She* said. "I could not see your exquisite eyes."

Nellie blushed. The attention made her self-conscious. The compliment part was pretty great, but the "well-deserved" part made her paranoid that her wish would be dumb. She racked her brain for something impressive. Ideas swirled by, but she couldn't concentrate. She started sweating. Her heart kept slowing down and speeding up—beating off rhythm. The blow to her head must have been serious. Even so, this was no time for an epic fail. Not in front of a goddess. She thought harder and studied her kneecaps.

"Where'd the bird go…anyway? Does it…fly off until you…whistle or something?" Nellie stalled for time, acting like the bird was extremely important.

"No, no. It is here." The goddess ran her tassel over a small leather pouch strapped to her waist. "Would you like to see it?" *She* unwound a string of twine and unclasped the top. Stuffed inside, Nellie saw the velvety bodies of squirming caterpillars. "My very large bird has returned to its portable egg."

"Whoa… Those…turn into birds? That's…crazy." There was an awkward pause before she added, "Totally wacked."

Something about those caterpillars was familiar. "Where I come from...that...that would be majorly unbelievable. Nobody would...believe you. My big sis...she...she's gonna go ballistic when I..." Nellie trailed off.

"Then you must make your wish quickly so you can tell everyone."

"Oh...uh... How do I... How do I do it again?" It embarrassed Nellie—asking the woman to repeat it. But she was so spacey that she had to. With her head still spinning, she was drawing a blank, couldn't remember the exact wish-making steps. She could barely remember her own name. Though the goddess seemed fine about it, Nellie could tell she was running out of patience. Probably had somewhere to go—fairy friends waiting on her or something. Nellie just needed to make triple sure she didn't screw it up. It was pretty obvious, with a sweet deal like this one there'd be no second chances.

Standing like a regal queen, the goddess held the tassel by its looped cord, dangling it in front of Nellie's face. This time Nellie couldn't resist. She reached to give the ends a swipe. It must have been against the rules. Before she could touch it, the goddess jerked it away.

"Let me hear your wish first, my sweet." It sounded like a terse reprimand.

"I'm...sorry. I mean... That...that wasn't...official. I just... I just wanted to...to feel it. It looks so...slithery." Now Nellie was the one apologizing.

"One wish. One touch," the goddess stated firmly. *She* brought the tassel from behind her back and set it swinging again with a twitch of her wrist. "We would not want you returning to camp empty-handed." A tight smile stretched across her lips.

"That would've…counted? Even though… Even though I…didn't make my wish?" Nellie fought sounding groggy.

The goddess nodded. Her smile disappeared.

"Oh, man…" Nellie smacked her forehead, trying to be funny. "Should I…say thank you…now? Or…later?" She hoped her super deep delivery would make the goddess laugh. When that didn't happen, Nellie took a nervous breath. "Thank… You…" She tried to look appreciative. Not intoxicated. "I think…I got it. Tell me if… Tell me if I'm right. First…decide…a wish. Then…say it out loud. Then hold the tassel?"

"That will do. Rise."

Using the branches to balance, Nellie stood up. The dizziness tripled. She rested her head on her arm, waiting for it to pass. It didn't. She made herself get on with it anyway. The goddess was tapping her foot—watching.

"Like a teacher waitin on the slow kid," thought Nellie.

She avoided eye-contact by studying treetops. *Think. Think.* Then she examined the tree trunk. As her eyes followed an ant trail, the perfect wish flashed-bulbed in her head. She lifted her hands in celebration. Bad idea. She started swaying. She grabbed back on, steadying herself. And changing her mind. That wish was lame. She looked at her toes. Then at a pine cone. Then back at bark. Nothing was coming. Her brain was shooting blanks.

"See…the problem is…" she began hesitantly, "it's not that I can't…think of stuff. I can. I just… I…I can't decide. Like…should it be for me? Or…can it be…for my family?"

Nellie sighed. "Can it just be cash?" She went ahead and asked, knowing it was totally tacky.

Exasperation peaked. *Her* sternness caused Nellie to flinch. "Child, it can be whatever you want! No matter how small or grandiose, it is yours alone to select!"

Nellie apologized again. "Sorry... I...I just feel kind of... spacey and..." Nellie didn't finish. Too many times making excuses and saying sorry was bound to have the goddess regretting picking her. She knew the clock was ticking.

Almost a minute later, Nellie shamefully admitted the next hold-up. "Please...don't be mad...but...that's just it. I'm...thinking of things. Really. I...I am. It's just hard picking the right...one...one."

"Then I would suggest you close your eyes and clear your mind. The most extravagant wish filling your head is the one you should choose. Do not second guess your heart's desire, my sweet. It will be the perfect choice."

"I can do that." Nellie tried sounding positive. "So I... grab the tassel and...say the wish? No, wait! I mean...the other way around. Say the wish and...then grab the tassel." Nellie corrected herself. This was her last chance to make sure she had the right wish-making order.

"Once you speak it, hold on tightly. Let the warmth of your fingers flow into the tassel." Nellie was so relieved. The goddess was using her gracious voice again. It sounded beautiful.

"Cool," giggled Nellie, shutting her eyes. She let her body relax while she thought her choices through.

Leaning in closer, *She* watched Nellie's eyeballs flitting back and forth behind closed lids. As Nellie's hand left the branch—fingers spreading, reaching for the tassel—she opened her mouth and softly spoke, "I wish for..."

Deep in concentration, Nellie's hand hung in the air as she paused to get the wording right. If she'd opened her eyes and looked at the goddess, she would have willingly leapt from the tree. The woman's face was marred by murder. *Her obsession was boiling over, erupting from every pore. She knew the craving was leading Nellie. The girl would never open her eyes now. The imbecile was focused on greed. Her villainy would remain a secret without witnesses.*

But *She* was wrong.

Obscured by pine needles, the mothman hovered watching the killer. Before he could dive, Lee and Gwen heaved their bodies into view only feet from Nellie— rescuers without a second to waste. When they saw their friend with her heart still beating, they screamed like banshees.

"No, Nellie! No!"

The woman's eyes shifted, instantly recognizing them. Her contorted features rearranged themselves and flushed with astonishment. "Hello," *She* gushed.

Nellie's eyes opened and her head whipped around. Seeing her girls was a shocker—the intensity of their shrieks was jarring. But strangest of all, under their noses they were both greased with mustaches. Though her feet were balanced on crisscrossing branches and her hand was gripping tight, the sudden surprise sent her slipping. She lost her footing. She tried saving herself—her arms went frantic. The goddess made no attempt to help. Instead, *She* lifted from her branch and floated, ignoring Nellie's screams. Holding the tassel in her outstretched hand, *She* drifted toward Gwen and Lee, looking like an animal before it bites.

Not a stem was ruffled as the mothman dove. But now he had to save the girl. As Nellie tripped over her own feet—falling headfirst from the tree—something airborne caught her and shoved her in a nook. She thought the bird was back. Shielding herself and ducking, she peeked between the branches as a man with wings flew at her face. All she could do was throw her hands out screaming. There was nowhere to go; she was trapped. But he backed off and flew away, leaving stink in his wake. She covered her nose to block his revolting smell and felt the slime on her lip. Her eyes started burning. Her hand came away covered with reeking mucous—and a cut.

Nellie's brain started buzzing. Images appeared, like movies in her head. Like someone's dreams. But not hers. Not hers. Still, something was familiar. Someone was familiar. The flying man. The scenes were his. His thoughts. His words. Talking to her. Ordering her. Hide else you'll die! I've come for the witch. *Hide! Hide!* Then her girls were there, in the woods. Calling her name. Searching with flashlights. Huddled in a tree. Talking to him. Trusting him. Climbing. Leaving Paige below. The scenes changed. Mist whirled and spun, forming a woman in white. Holding out a golden tassel. Smiling at a boy in overalls. And a little girl in black. And one in a pink pinafore. The boy from Stingray too. Child after child. Closing their eyes and reaching. And dying. There were no bodies. Only moss dripping from her spiky fingers. Then she was gone.

Like a punch in the gut, Nellie understood the truth.

Clinging to the tree for dear life, she leaned out, looking up.

She flew at them. But they came armed. Lee timed it perfectly. Her busted-off branch connected with a shoulder blade and sent the witch spinning. *She* flew at them again— grabbing for Lee's hair—but Lee defied death and leapt, landing on a lower limb. *She* would have followed, but Gwen attacked from the right. With her feet wedged firmly and her back mashed against the trunk, Gwen swung her stick and kept on swinging. The first wallop connected with pelvis. The second smashed ribs. The pouch *She* wore spilt open and caterpillars spilled out. *She* tried catching them, but Gwen's blows kept coming. Rather than screaming in pain, *She* bristled with laughter and spun away, levitating amid the branches. With one hand swishing the tassel and the other clutching her pouch, *She* studied the girls—deciding which to push from the tree first.

"Shame," *She* said. "Two pretty sweets, wasted. You shall find the fall a thrill but the landing devastating." *She* wore a look of utter boredom. As if this brawl were child's play. *She* never saw it coming. Never knew he was behind her. *She* was profoundly enraged when one arm clamped around her neck and the other cinched into her waist. Caught like a wolf in a steel trap, now *She* howled. He wrestled her to him violently, pressing his teeth against her cheek. Lee and Gwen thought he was going to bite her ear off. When he spoke, his voice was filled with hate.

"I watched you kill him."

She tried to turn—tried to see his face. He was hovering with her, dragging her backward. "Would you like to hear my wish?" He was heroic. "I wish to kill you."

"Oh, merciful knight!" They all heard her cry out.

"I am not your knight!"

Her begging stopped when he crushed her windpipe. The pain made her gurgle. An arm flew up and the tassel nearly grazed his face. He forced the arm down, repositioning his hold and tightening his grip on her wrists, completely immobilizing her hands. But her legs kept kicking, sending the hem of her skirts in continuous arcs. They were welded together in midair when he spoke again.

"I am your executioner."

Not another word came. Gruesomely, regurgitated saliva flowed from his tongue as he licked her exposed neck, slathering her skin and adhering a stream of sticky silk. As the filament surged from his mouth, he began twirling and twirling her, encasing her head in an airtight cast. When her face was no longer visible, he steadily worked down, weaving the fibers around her chest before moving to her waist and binding her arms at her back. The tassel—entombed in her curled, black fingers—was just where he intended. He continued spinning her and spinning her, tightening the girth at her hands and tying her legs with a thousand yards of silken threads until only her feet stuck out—a fleshy lure for the fishies. As *She* suffocated in her coffin, he shifted the weight in his arms and wrapped his powerful legs around the bottom, securing the load. Turning purposefully, he pumped his wings and rose higher and higher, soaring. He circled once—chirping shrill staccato calls over the treetops—and then he was gone.

He didn't even say goodbye.

Chapter 14

Lee and Gwen watched until his silhouette disappeared in the clouds. After silent farewells, they looked down to see the mustachioed face of Nellie leaning from a branch, watching too.

"Hey, stranger," croaked Lee, determined not to weep.

"Hey, yourself," answered Nellie.

"That was a little too close for comfort, Missy." Gwen's eyes were welling-up.

"Just like in the movies...where the girl gets rescued in the nick of time. Thanks doesn't quite cut it...does it?"

"Sounds great to us," sniffled Lee. "Least we get to hear your obnoxious voice and know you're still alive. Can't ask for more than that."

"You guys saved my life." Nellie's eyes were blinking fast, staving off tears.

"Wasn't only us," Gwen reminded her.

"I know." Nellie wiped her lashes, trying not to full-on blubber. "Where'd you find Superman anyway?"

"Sneakin around under the bushes when we was lookin for you. It was quite the shock." Tears got the best of Gwen. She started mopping hers.

"I bet," laughed Nellie, her waterworks overflowing too. "These woods are full of fierce surprises."

"Lucky for you, the guy was carryin a serious grudge."

"Lee," sighed Nellie, drying her eyes, "luck doesn't begin to explain it."

"I never saw nothin like it," blurted Gwen, getting worked-up all over again. "He's the biggest badass ever! That witch didn't know what hit her!" Her hand was pressed over her heart. "And...and what happened now? She got ya up here on caterpillar-bird?"

"I'm not...sure..." Nellie thought for a moment, fighting to remember. "I think those caterpillars aren't just caterpillars. I think they turn into birds. And I mean like... flying monsters."

"Yeah! You gotta kill 'em before they talk! Before they can change," exclaimed Gwen. "Lee found out by accident."

"Really? You saw one too? I'm not nuts?"

"Major really. One was crawlin up my ankle and I kinda squashed it. Sparks shot everywhere."

"No way..."

"Way," nodded Lee. "I didn't mean to kill it. But man if I hadn't..." She drew two fingers across her throat. "We'd all be bird stew."

"I remember it grabbing me. I...I don't remember much else. Except passing out. When I woke-up...she was there.

I thought I was dead. But then…she told me to make a wish."

"A death wish," said Lee, flicking her own escapee tear.

"I can't believe…she almost got me. If you guys hadn't shown up…like…exactly when you did… Guess that'd be it. No star on the Hollywood Walk of Fame for Nellie Landers. Talk about a bummer."

Once again, Lee and Gwen were astounded by Nellie's never-ending pluck, even in the face of death. They wanted to grab her and squeeze her, feel the proof that she was alive. Ever so cautiously, they started down to her.

"What was your wish gonna be? A lifetime goldcard at Chick-fil-A," teased Lee, choking back emotion.

"Lady LeeLee, you know my girl's a Krispy Kremer through and through. If she gonna make a big-time foodie wish, it's gonna be for somethin gooey and chewy soaked in sugar."

They were halfway to Nellie when they heard the splintering snap. Lee and Gwen watched as her limb cracked. There was no warning. No time to scream. Falling, falling, falling—Nellie crashed through the tree, grabbing empty air. Before Gwen and Lee even processed what had happened, she was gone. Hoping for a miracle but dreading the truth, they raced gravity to the bottom.

Paige heard the racket and started yelling up, *"It's OK! It's OK! Nellie's OK!"*

"She's OK?" They bellowed back. They didn't believe it.

"She's in one piece if that's what ya mean. Y'all gotta see this. Wasn't the smartest way down but she pulled it off."

Dropping dangerous fast through the tree, Lee and Gwen slowed as they neared Paige, searching her face for an explanation.

"Right there. Look. She's right there." Paige pointed.

Twenty feet lower, there was Nellie—snagged on a jagged stub and hanging by one of her braids—holding the overhead branches like they were monkey bars.

"*Help.*" Her scratchy voice jumpstarted their hearts. They scrambled down, unhooking her hair while Paige talked a mile a minute.

"She was headed right for me. Woulda flattened me like a pancake if I hadn't been ready. I braced myself and kinda caught her. Slowed her up a ton. But then we slipped. I can't believe that puny stick stopped her. You shoulda seen her swing. She almost made a complete rotation!" Paige described the moment in glorious detail. "Ya gotta headache, hon?" She cupped Nellie's cheeks.

"I swear, Nellie! You're the one that's part cat," shrieked Lee. "Stop goin through your nine lives so fast!" She was picking pine needles out of Nellie's hair. "You know how close that just came to your juggler vein?"

"Quit!" Nellie smacked their hands away. "I'm fine."

"You promise," asked Gwen, checking Nellie's neck. A plump welt was rising next to the vein.

"I promise." She'd barely answered before getting the tightest three-armed bear hug of her entire life. Holding onto the tree with one hand and clutching girls with the other, they buried their heads in each other's hair, praising Paige and counting their blessings.

"What happened up there?!" Paige finally asked, ending the hug-a-thon. It's a wonder she understood any of it. The three started talking at once, leaving nothing out. Time stood still as they described the battle to save Nellie and the mothman's inconceivable attack on the witch.

"And he just flew away to the ocean?"

"He's takin her where it's deep. Droppin that nasty sack in some snappin teeth."

"Ya think we'll ever see him again?"

"No tellin," said Gwen. "Who knows where he came from. Now that he's done what he aimed to do, who knows where he'll go."

"I hope he knows how grateful I am..." Nellie was looking up through the treetops.

"I'm not so sure he'd care," scoffed Lee. "Didn't get the feelin he liked associatin with people. Kinda had his own agenda."

"Circumstances was pretty high stress," Gwen pointed out.

"Guys..." Nellie whispered, becoming suddenly morose. "We have to tell Mrs. B. She has to know...the truth."

"She'll never believe us," balked Lee. "She'll think we're full of—"

"We have to make her believe us," urged Nellie. "We have to."

"That's stupid pointless. She'll think we're mental." But strident as Lee sounded, she knew Nellie was right.

"But why, Nell? It's over." Paige smiled. "You're safe."

"I'm safe but..." It broke Nellie's heart to tell them. Especially Paige. Paige had had so much faith. But Paige needed to know. They all needed to know. Nellie took a deep breath. "She killed that boy from Stingray, Paige. I saw it. The man... He showed me."

Paige's face fell. Her lips started quivering. Nellie stayed strong. "Someone has to tell his family."

"He's really dead?" Tears began rolling down Paige's cheeks. *"No, no, no, no, no, no..."*

"He showed you?" Gwen asked. "You saw stuff?"

Nellie was solemn. "It was weird. Like...after he caught me...after we touched...I could see his thoughts. I could see...his past. I knew he wanted me to hide...but...he never said it. I just...knew. And I knew he was after her. A witch. He...he put it in my head that she was a witch. And you guys too. I saw you looking for me. And talking to him. And then...I saw her. But like...from a long time ago. I saw her with kids... A lot of kids. I saw what happens." Nellie's eyes were downcast, fixed on clump after clump of Spanish moss. Her voice cracked. "That boy from last night. I know what she did to him."

"You saw her with the Stingray boy? You sure, Nells?"

"I'm sure."

An agonizing moment passed before a crestfallen Nellie spoke again. "You guys know what she does...to kids?"

Gwen nodded. "He showed us too."

Gouging at her eyes with her shirt, spreading soot across her face, Lee turned away and started down. "Let's get out of here." She couldn't stomach hearing another word.

The girls followed in silence, descending to the base of the tree and dropping to solid ground. They couldn't wait to run from the place. Spotting their flashlights, they hurried to retrieve them. Lee was almost touching hers when she saw the caterpillar on the switch. Her hand jerked to a stop. Plugging her ears, she unleashed a guttural scream.

"A caterpillar! A caterpillar! Cover your ears!"

The alarm caused the bug to rear. Its gold antenna splayed out just as Lee's shoe did the pulverizing. It popped. It pooled. It puffed blue smoke. Sparks lit the area. That's when they saw. Caterpillars were everywhere. They started yelling—plugging their ears so they couldn't hear the talking. Moving quick and methodical, avoiding the pungent fumes, they squashed caterpillars in the dirt, mashed them into logs and skewered them to the tree trunks. The woods glowed like the fourth of July. When every last caterpillar was ground to a pulp, they abandoned the flashlights and ran— still screaming, fingers still deeply inserted. They hardly noticed the fireflies. Only a few at first—then dozens, then hundreds, then thousands—lighting a path to safety as the mothman instructed.

Fleeing at a sprint, the sight of cabins only made them run faster. Hands dropped from ears, but they didn't slow down until reaching the mess hall. They shoved the doors open and were greeted by singing. And smells of pot roast.

"The four of you are late!" A passing counselor shouted over the harmonizing. Seeing their faces made her stop dead. "Really? Were ya rollin in the dirt?" She crinkled her nose at their bad smell, waving a hand in front of her face. "And what are you supposed to be," she asked Lee. "A raccoon? Whew! Y'all gonna win the stinky badge. Go wash-up please and make it snappy. Everybody else already ate and—"

"We *need* to talk to Mrs. B!" Nellie cut her off. "Have you seen her?"

"Excuse me?" The girl looked irritated. "Y'all smell seriously funky. Go clean-up first." When they didn't move, the girl got snippy. "Don't make me say it three times. I ain't playin. Go on now!" After giving them a disapproving once-over, she turned on her heel and haughtily strode away.

They were not deterred. They scanned the room for Mrs. B. *"There she is!"* Gwen spotted her. Elbowing through the crowd, they slowly started making their way toward the head table. Before reaching it, Mrs. B's second-in-command approached and leaned down talking animatedly in the camp director's ear. Mrs. B's chair actually flipped over backward when she leapt up hustling for the cafeteria office. A phone call was waiting.

The girls stopped in their tracks. *"Now what do we do,"* wailed Paige.

"Find Tou-tou," ordered Nellie.

"Are y'all just hardheaded?" The counselor appeared again.

"We have to talk to Tou-tou *right now.*" Lee's body language clearly told the girl to back-off.

The six-foot counselor didn't back-off. "Are you *sassin* me, young lady? Because that would be a mistake. And anyway, Tou-tou's not here yet. He's takin care of a problem in the art center. Washin machine on the fritz or somethin. Bathroom is that-a-way!"

This time she physically turned them around and personally herded them to the ladies room, even held the door. They didn't want to go, but with the pushy girl breathing down their necks they had to. Once inside, they were immediately appalled. Standing in front of the mirror, Lee, Gwen and Nellie got a first look at their smarmy faces. Paige was too wired to let them gawk for long and getting rid of the foul gunk was way overdo. After scrubbing their nails and noses, they left the bathroom and headed straight for Mrs. B.

But telling would have to wait. The office door was shut. Mrs. B was still on the phone.

Looking around for what to do next, they were spotted by their counselors and waved over to join their cabin table. Seeing no way out of it, they went and sat down, blaming their tardiness on dock duty—retying hooks and putting fishing polls away. "That was mighty helpful of y'all," was shouted over the singing. With nobody questioning their story, the girls reluctantly reached for plates and started getting dinner. Plenty of food was left in the serving bowls, so they dished out spoonfuls of pot roast over dirty rice. After devouring everything in the bowls, they saw a mountain of chocolate cake crumbling at the end of the table. They wasted no time diving in and finishing it off. Amazingly, it was the best meal they ever tasted.

Pushing her plate away but keeping her eyes lowered, Gwen asked, "Should we tell Kate?" The idea had crossed their minds. The four looked down the table at their head counselor, but Kate looked worse than ever—worse than in the morning.

"No," muttered Nellie, suddenly protective of the older girl. One look at Kate told Nellie that the news would do her in. Before she could explain, the mess hall speakers came to life and the song about a hole in a bucket petered out. From a stage in the front of the room, the microphone did what it always did when someone was about to use it. Pitchy reverb was practically a camp tradition. They looked up and saw Mrs. B.

"Evenin, ladies," she said, tapping on the mouthpiece. "Is this thingy on? Can everybody hear me?"

Hundreds of whooping hoots answered her back, "Yes we can!"

"Dynamite! Y'all better listen up cause nobody's gonna wanna miss this!" Her smile was so huge that the whole room could see her molars. "I have just now hung up the phone with Camp Stingray. They had a little somethin-somethin to pass along." Her smile got even bigger. "The youngster who gave us such a fright last night... Well...that young man has *returned! Safe and sound!"*

The walls shook from the uproar. It was so chaotic that nobody noticed the reaction of Nellie and the girls. Gwen was latched onto Nellie's hand, tugging her whole arm, and Lee and Paige were shouting across the table. But words couldn't be heard over the pandemonium. It took extensive arm waving from Mrs. B and repeated requests of "Quiet down!" before the hall was anywhere back to normal.

"Told y'all it was great news!" Mrs. B was shouting. "Turns out he went to take care of business and got himself lost in the woods! He came strollin into camp five minutes ago! I'm told he's hungry and dehydrated, but other than that, he's fine as a fiddle! *Praise the Lord!"*

When round two of celebrating died down, a lone soprano voice sang out from the corner of the cafeteria.

Before the second line of her heartfelt hymn was sung, the entire cafeteria had joined in and tears were balancing on Nellie's bottom eyelashes again. By the end of the song, not a person was seated. Every girl was standing—on benches, on chairs, even barefooted on the plank tables with the leftovers.

"Let's be reminded one more time ladies, please use the buddy system! We've got lots of fun planned in our remainin three weeks and I expect you all to make the most of it!" The rhythmic foot pounding let Mrs. B know that her girls were in full agreement.

"Y'all make me so happy my heart's gonna *bust!*" Mrs. B had to bellow to be heard, even using the microphone. "*Alrighty! Seats!*" Everyone sat. "Since Scary Story Night falls on such a happy occasion, we're tellin a doosey!" She patted the leather-bound book tucked under her arm. "If anybody here is a great big scaredy-cat..." She paused, surveying the room. "You better bug out now!"

"Tell it!" Someone yelled.

"Okie-dokie! I will, I will! Just don't say I didn't warn ya!" She opened the book to its mark. "Now, does everybody know the deal with these woods?"

"They're full of chiggers and mosquitoes," a counselor hollered.

"True enough! I mean the *other* thing about these woods! The *scary* thing." She said it all spooky. "I'll give y'all a hint. Tou-tou dug up a fascinatin story at the town library today. Seems there's a witchy-witch pokin around out there. Evidently, she has a taste for youngins, 'specially my campers." She eyed the room, milking her evil grin.

Most everyone laughed, but Nellie and the girls sat bolt-upright mouthing questions at each other. Nellie could feel Gwen's fingernails digging in her arm again. Staring at Mrs. B with her jaw dropped, Nellie spotted Tou-tou hurrying across the stage. After gesturing an apology to Mrs. B for his late arrival, he joined his colleagues and took a seat in a row of chairs behind the camp director. Nellie thought he must have run all the way from the art center. He was breathing hard, looking a tad frazzled. His shirt was even buttoned wrong. He settled himself in a chair and folded his hands neatly in his lap. Wondering what he really knew, Nellie found herself getting up.

"I know that story!" Nellie yelled, looking around Mrs. B and catching Tou-tou's eye.

"All four of us know it," shouted Lee, getting up too. "And witches don't stand a chance against a gang of Camp Seamisters!"

"Yeah," warbled Paige, leaning on Lee.

"She means Camp Seamistresses, ma'am," corrected Gwen, standing beside Nellie. "But she's right! Bad stuff happens to anybody tries messin with us!"

"And…and we ought to know," added Nellie, unsure of what to say next—with everyone *staring* at them.

But the cafeteria exploded in cheers.

"Oh, *you* ought to know?" Mrs. B's voice boomed into the mic. "Is that so?"

"That's…so," answered Nellie. She was trying to figure out Tou-tou's expression. It definitely wasn't a smile.

"Well, Nellie Landers, if you know all about it, we'd be honored if you'd come on up and tell it!" Mrs. B was gesturing with the book, holding it open. "Can I please get a shout-out for our resident actress, direct from Hollywood! Let's get this gal on up here for some storytellin!" Once she urged the crowd to help her out, the whole room of campers took to chanting.

"Nellie! Nellie! Nellie!"

"Now you done it," Gwen shouted over them. "You better go!"

Nellie didn't move; she wasn't about to go up. But the chanting didn't stop. It escalated. As it continued, Nellie grudgingly put the fork she'd been holding on her plate and licked icing off her lips. With a heart beating out of her chest, she smoothed her bangs as best she could and started walking toward the stage.

"Stop!"

Their screech raised the roof. The hall went silent. Gwen, Lee and Paige untangled their legs from the benches and practically tackled Nellie.

"Girls, is there a problem?" Mrs. B was frowning.

Waving off her question, the three sounded like certified liars. "No, ma'am." "We're good." "She *needs* us!"

Mrs. B didn't press it. "Come on up, then. Anytime we can be wowed by the four of y'all, it's a real treat!" The reference to the dance got a big laugh.

It gave Gwen the chance to tell Nellie the truth. "You ain't givin us the slip again tonight." She took her friend by the arm.

"We're stickin to you like dog hair," whispered Paige, linking elbows.

"So get used to it." Lee grabbed a fistful of Nellie's shirt.

Walking between the tables—stepping on each other's heels—they mounted the pull-out stairs and crossed the stage. Before handing the book over to Nellie, Mrs. B gave the girls a proper Seamist introduction.

"Ladies and gentlemen, for tonight's very special readin of our scary story, I'd like to present...*The Four Stoogettes!* Take it away, girls!"

Thunderous applause filled the cafeteria as Mrs. B took a seat next to Tou-tou and the girls arranged themselves around the mic. Gwen, Lee and Paige planned on remaining physically attached to Nellie for the duration of the night— elbow to elbow, skin to skin, inseparably together. Once the jostling was done to everyone's satisfaction, Nellie flipped the book open and began to read.

PART II

Chapter 15

The Wishing Trick

"Once upon a time—in a land of rolling hills, crowned by stardust mountains, guarding cliff-perched castles—there lived a handsome prince."

Another cheer ripped through the dining hall as the room of rowdy girls jumped on the invitation to imagine a cutie-pie. Carrying on ridiculously boy-starved, campers started pounding tables and clanking glasses. Nellie had to stop reading. Kate—in a complete mood swing and thoroughly appreciating the uproar—stood on a bench to yell. "Very funny, y'all. *Behave!*" It took a minute before the high-spirited ones worked out their sillies. Once they calmed down, Nellie continued.

"His bravery and strength were guided by an honorable, loving heart."

Somebody whistled a catcall and a few others joined in, but the room quieted down before Kate got back up.

"From his father's hilltop castle, the prince could view his playground of orchard-rich valleys cut with fish-gorged rivers. His was a jovial family, complete with four young brothers and three fair sisters. Days were spent on scholarly achievement with a healthy dose of sport and mischief. The elderly king and his truelove, the queen, cherished their children. Keys to happy futures jingled for them all. Sadly, one fateful day, the prince made a disastrous error.

For many a year the noble lad held a fondness for a neighboring princess. Formally introduced as tots, blissful summer days were spent playing tag on the manicured palace grounds. The two courts enjoyed a cordial relationship for the kings were allies. Under their wise leadership, all citizens prospered. As the prince and princess became the dearest of friends, they too appeared destined to prosper at each other's side. When the innocence of childhood marched onward, giving way to maturity, traditional arrangements of marriage were discussed. The royal families rejoiced. The union of the prince to the princess would certainly strengthen their flourishing kingdoms.

The wedding day was glorious. A rising sun delivered the bluest of skies, accentuated by wisps of white. Banners adorned every castle tower as flags flew bearing both families' crest. Additionally, the finest artist in the land had been summoned for a commission. A courtyard alcove was draped with an exceptionally large canvas by her hand—a formal portrait of the elegant bride and her fine groom.

Perfection was displayed throughout the palace. Tulips by the thousands greeted every guest. Wreaths of alpine spruce hung from the many arches. Wisteria vines, bursting with fragrant blossoms, bedecked handrails and spilled from

A courtyard alcove was draped with an exceptionally large canvas by her hand—a formal portrait of the elegant bride and her fine groom.

window boxes. The oaken entryways glowed as never before. The doors were waxed, the brass polished, and the cobblestone lanes—swept and scrubbed with foaming buckets of water—were pristine underfoot. Even the spiders took down their webbing in honor of the eminent couple.

In the kitchen, cooks scurried to and fro, sending tantalizing aromas hither and yon, enticing every appetite. Sausage and mutton crowded the warming stones, oxen turned on spits, soups and stews bubbled in copper cauldrons, potatoes roasted over open flames, corn steamed in husks, meat pies lined every shelf, and loaves of seeded bread cooled near vats of fresh churned butter. Even the Queen's private honey pots were carried from the cellars and unsealed. Absolutely every inch of the kitchen nurtured delectable dishes.

The Hall of Tapestries—chosen for the reception—began filling with desserts as well. Silver trays, heavy with syrupy cinnamon cakes, were placed on the claw-footed tables as pyramids of brandied plums were arranged as centerpieces. Alongside fig and custard pastries, slices of dried lemons and oranges glistened with sun-baked maple crystals. Guests in possession of teeth were eager to indulge in that palace delicacy—the crunchy tidbits were rumored to be scrumptious. Nonetheless, premature nibbling of sweets was strongly discouraged. A stern and portly kitchen maid stood sentry, fending off the sticky-fingered thieves of the castle. The children. She was armed with a sour expression and a switch.

As the great room bustled with activity, a modest orchestra took up position in the balcony. After the tuning of instruments, a minuet could be heard. The jaunty melody swelled and diminished whilst musicians practiced. Below the minstrels, jesters stood atop a raised platform in colorful tunics and striped leggings. Reciting poetry—punctuated by somersaults—they rehearsed with bells on their caps. Soon a loving marriage would receive the divine blessing and the celebration would begin. Everyone wore a contented smile.

Dressing in the lavishly furnished bower, the Princess Ellianna was as busy as a bee. Heavenly scents perfumed the air as ladies-in-waiting wound flowers in her hair. She was a vision of loveliness in her bodice of embroidered silk. It perfectly fit her willowy frame. The neckline, trimmed with milky opals, revealed her flawless skin. Diaphanous sleeves encrusted with pearls and amethysts tapered to her wrists. The gown, rustling softly, boasted layer upon layer of creamy white skirts. She lifted them demurely when the satin heels with rosebud beading—a gift from the village cobbler—were brought forth and slid on with ease. At last, a sheer veil was secured by a diamond tiara. It trailed extravagantly, requiring seven bridesmaids to hold it fluttering above the floor.

As the bells began to chime, Ellianna smiled. She gazed at her bare hand knowing that his ring of wedded love would soon and forever grace her finger. Her heart raced with jubilation as a tear of gratitude threatened to dampen her cheek. She blinked it away with a cheerful breath and took up her bouquet. With the Queen Mother and her giddy handmaidens by her side, the bridal party wound its way through castle corridors, bound for the house of worship.

In his chambers, Prince Ronan was equally ecstatic. Dressing for this long-awaited day, he reflected on the many attributes of his sweetheart. He was a charismatic fellow, full of a thundering zest for life. Though daring and venturesome, he refused to court the vast selection of eligible princesses paraded before him. He had loved Ellianna at first sight. Her compassionate heart and competitive zeal matched his own. On bended knee with head bowed, he nightly prayed that she should be his wife.

This quest became his fountain of vitality for Ellianna frolicked like a boy and often held the victor's crown. She was a self-taught archer—her arrows alarmingly accurate. Not only could they pierce the fruit of distant apple trees, she could launch them into unsuspecting walnuts. More impressive still, Ellianna was the best rider he had ever known. The flanks of her steed responded to the slightest pressure from her heels. He marveled at the bond between horse and girl. To his delight, she insisted on jumping pasture fences rather than guiding her mare around them. He followed her lead. He followed her everywhere.

Donning his wedding finery among friends and courtiers, the prince's eye lingered on a gift from his intended—a chessboard with playing pieces of carved jade. He loved the game. His well planned maneuvers, culminating in bold advances, compelled his fellow lords to hasty surrender. As Ellianna watched the nightly sieges unfold in the grand library, she found the intricacies of the contest fascinating and developed a keen interest in strategies of warfare. The day she bested the prince—suppressing his charge and vanquishing his king—was a memorable one. He had been elated by the defeat. Not only did she prove a clever student, she was soon his most challenging competitor. If his army revealed a weakness, she invariably spotted it—seizing the advantage. Hence, Ronan learned never to underestimate Ellianna.

Lacing his leather boots, the memories brought a smile to his chiseled face. A woman blessed with the intuition to master the battlefield would surely excel in navigating the challenges of motherhood. Their future home would flourish with her brilliance at the helm.

Escorted from the palace by his youthful entourage, the prince stood amongst the overflowing crowds, waiting for the wedding to begin. Majestic in his brocade attire, he gave one last tug to his tailored waistcoat. Trumpeters—noting his arrival—blasted enthusiastic greetings. It prompted the sumptuously-robed clergy within the cathedral to turn and face the doors. Ronan bounded up the steps, three at a time, passionate to claim his beloved before their sacred eyes. He yearned for the sealed kiss. Entering the threshold, he strode to the altar acknowledging his family and the hundreds of honored guests. When his bride appeared in the gilded doorway—dazzling beyond compare, glowing with devotion—his heart swelled with rapture.

Flower girls began the procession. Down the aisle, stepping lightly over sprinkled edelweiss, the princess came to him. Together at last, Ronan and Ellianna knelt before the priest with their hands discreetly touching, patiently enduring the eternal sermon. When the rings of everlasting love encircled their fingers and the oration drew to a close, the monumental question was formally posed. Joyfully, the couple spoke aloud the sentimental words that joined them as one—forever and ever.

"I am yours and you are mine."

Hats were flung heavenward as the groom kissed the bride. Rising gaily, the newlyweds led a procession of royalty and revelers from the church to the reception. The spectacle of jesters, jugglers and the corps of musicians were quick to strike up the merriment. Toasts to a fruitful marriage began at once—both gratifying and endless. Occasionally, inspired by excessive amounts of mead, drunken well wishers delivered comically bawdy speeches. But the desire for peace, good fortune, and a palace of healthy babies was the dominant proclamation. The celebrated couple partook of drink, welcoming countless goblets raised in their honor and enjoying unrelenting attention.

With momentum whirling about them—feasting and dancing with their guests—they sought one another from across the crowded room. When their eyes met, an escape was confirmed. After reuniting in a clandestine corner and sharing a lingering kiss, they secretly fled the hall.

Ronan and Ellianna dashed for the stables. As they went, her sheer veil lifted from her head like a swan taking flight. Trapped in its folds, the tiara rolled down a slope as her flaxen locks slipped from jeweled pins and tumbled down her back. The wisteria remained intact. Kicking off her pumps, she felt the warmth of the grassy hillside underfoot. Ronan, running beside her, had unfastened his tunic and was pulling at its confining sleeves. Freeing himself, he flung the garment over his head, revealing a rumpled underblouse. It billowed loosely from his shoulders as he kept pace with his bride, ignited by fulfillment.

Reaching the stables, they gave a steady push on the barn doors. The sheltered dimness allowed the stalls to remain pleasantly temperate. The invigorating smell of green hay and virile horses met them. To their surprise the hostler was approaching, leading two steeds across the straw-covered flooring. He stopped the muscular animals before his master and bowed deeply.

"My lord. My lady." He addressed them with dignified respect. "I have taken the liberty of saddling ye horses. I suspected a visit. A brisk ride surely be the tonic for digesting marital frivolity." He winked and extended the reins.

The prince let forth his marvelous laugh and gave his faithful man a hearty clasp. "My friend, you alone know our true hunger. You have presented the best wedding gift we could desire."

The princess stepped forward bestowing a kiss to the bearded man's cheek. She took up the reins, climbed the slats of a stall, and settled atop her mare's wide back. Nudging the animal, she charged the open doors and bolted into daylight. In her dusty wake, the prince mounted swiftly. He knew she would not wait. Pumping his heels against the flanks of his rearing stallion, the males took off in speedy pursuit.

They rode at breakneck speed—dodging the sting of wind-whipped hair—exhilarated by the getaway. They had no inkling their departure had been dually noted. The royal parents were not duped. Observing from the watchman's tower, their proud eyes followed their children. Once the newlyweds had ridden from sight, the kings and queens descended the winding staircases to rejoin their guests. Conversing, recounting the abundant blessings of the day, they never fathomed that to be the last of their son and daughter they would ever see.

Ellianna and Ronan galloped until the horses snorted with exhaustion. Nearing the wood's edge, they slowed to a trot and left the meadow. The ride had all four panting and shade was inviting. They chose a shortcut through a stand of Scots pine and took a narrow trail that led to the heart of a tranquil forest. Riding knee to knee, the couple flirted with words of love.

"My lady, what is a novice husband to think, watching his bride galloping away on their wedding day? You, my love, are difficult to catch." He remained out of breath.

"My lord, you hath fully made captive of me long ago. Just as the barn cat chases its own tail, it is futile to chase me for my heart is with you always."

"Then here sits an enviable man possessing two hearts beating in his chest. My stamina will be advantageous. I shall nevermore suffer defeat." He was brimming with boyish charm. "Generous woman, you are a feather in my cap."

"A mere feather? Doth thou compare me to a hen? If that is so, you may be pecked."

"Ah! You have fallen into my trap! I accept the punishment and demand you place the peck upon my lips without delay!" With eyes closed and lips puckered, his whole body slouched toward hers.

The invitation was irresistible. She leaned from her saddle and kissed him tenderly on the lips and the tip of his nose. Righting herself with modesty, she laughed as he criticized her punishment as far too lax. Rather than kissing him again, she urged her mare onward—deeper into the woods.

"Answer this, my darling," she called over her shoulder. "Doth thou advise I rein my mare to a sluggish lope, allowing your stallion to keep up?"

"Chivalry commands you go first. How else may I judge your equitation and the speed with which you outrun the wind?" His grin was devilish as he admired her backside. "Though if you are proposing a challenge, then I am obliged to accept. A champion shall be determined upon our return to the castle. A sunset race to the paddock. Will that please my winsome wife?"

"Indubitably! And what spoils for my victory, sire?" She asked coquettishly.

"Au contraire, lass," he countered. "What spoils for my victory?"

Ellianna smiled and named her trophy. "My triumph will require a bowl of hot dogs and a large Coke."

"What the..."

Everyone heard the girl in the front row. Nellie looked up. "Kidding," she deadpanned into the mic. She really did want that Coke. Her throat was dry from all the reading.

"I thought this was supposed to be scary," a camper hollered. "Sure you marked the right page?"

"It's comin. Keep goin, Nellie," instructed Mrs. B from her chair. Nellie noticed that Tou-tou was lost in space— paying *zero* attention. The man was staring at the ceiling, anxiously chewing his mint. She looked back down and thumbed pages. There was way more to go. Time for a break. Motioning to Paige, she switched places at the microphone and handed the book over. Paige picked up where Nellie left off.

"'Ellianna laughed and named her trophy. "My triumph will require a bowl of sun-ripened raspberries and a second race on the morrow. And a third on the next, and a fourth on the next, and a fifth on the—"

Interrupting, the prince reached to touch her cheek, outlining her face with the tips of his fingers. "Your wish is granted. I only live to see you smile."

"And doth my husband expect smiles often?"

"I shall check for them hourly."

Taking his hand in hers, she sighed, "The everlasting demands of marriage... I fear I shall be forced into gaiety the rest of my days."

"I pray those days be infinite," Ronan whispered, gently squeezing her hand.

"They will, my love," she replied, pulling him close. "For in your eyes I see eternity." She kissed his mouth and added coyly, "And a wealth of frisky children."

Beaming, he bellowed to the swaying birches. "This woman is a gift! Our children shall be born of perfection!"

As a picturesque grove opened before them, Ronan slipped his boots from the stirrups and stood upon his horse. Holding nothing but the reins, he jumped a fallen log and entered the grove—standing atop his mount. Ellianna clapped adoringly whilst he navigated his stallion to an elm tree and halted, leaning his back against the trunk.

"Tis true, Ronan. We shall raise a glorious family." Inspired by his acrobatics, the princess too had risen and was standing on her horse, trotting within the grove. Her bare feet balanced on her supple saddle as she guided her mare in a figure eight. Once again the prince noted, she was as talented as he. His heart could do nothing but soar.

"Ours will be an empire! More than one palace can hold," he boasted. "Hear now my first decree." He held his hands in front of his mouth, pretending to blast the notes of a trumpeter before a royal announcement. "The castle floors shall hereby be polished by tiny scampering feet!"

The princess put her horse into an elegant bow, stepping gracefully from its back. Dipping her head as low the mare's, the females curtsied simultaneously, "Sire, as you wish."

Ronan laughed with abundant gusto—anticipating their night, imagining their future. Ellianna dropped her reins and began a leisurely spin, swirling out her skirts and enjoying their silky weight. She paused as the heavy fabric wound its way around her hips. Once it twisted tightly, she twirled again in the opposite direction, beginning her ballet anew.

"Young minds need scrupulous instruction, Ronan. I shall assist the tutors with their education. In sport, as well. I feel confident their arrows will intimidate the orchard trees." She continued spinning and stopping and reversing, affectionately picturing it.

"Dearest wife, you see the future clearly. Our battalion will toddle aiming first at enemy fruits. Under your tutelage, they will advance and excel. Once proficient, we shall root-out loafing ne'er-do-wells and scour these very woods, hunting down the sharp-toothed troll and chucking its squalid offspring in cook's slop pot for the hounds." As he stood upon his steed envisioning his family of miniature warriors, he bent his knees and acrobatically flipped from his mount. Landing effortlessly, he took several leaps and found himself balanced on an unsteady log. Without hesitation, he leapt again, extending his hands to the limb of an old oak. Grabbing hold, he swung up and over, arranging himself sitting on a branch. Now free to wander, his stallion lumbered away with her mare, grazing on fragrant grasses.

The princess stopped pirouetting and plopped to the ground. With skirts deflating about her, Ellianna's heart pounded with ridiculous excitement. "Shall we don matching suits of armor?" Though intending to raise kindhearted children, she gazed at her husband with tolerant humor and blew a kiss from her palm. He proceeded to catch it, cupping it like a fragile treasure before bringing it to his lips.

"More," he pleaded. "I am famished."

Rising to her knees, she obediently blew dozens more. In return, he thrilled her by catching kisses and devouring them, pretending several times to topple from the tree.

Gladdened by his hearty appetite, the princess teased, "If his Royal Highness continues feasting on kisses, he shall become plump."

The prince objected strenuously. "Your love is nutritious! It enhances my figure!"

Ellianna giggled. Spying a cluster of flowers, she turned from him to pick a handful of daises. Rhythmically plucking the petals one by one, she recited, "He loves me. He loves me not. He loves me. He loves me not." Each and every time she called, "He loves me not." Ronan would shout, "He loves me!" His corrections drowned her words. It was a touching last moment.

Beguiled by the sight of his petal-picking bride, Ronan did not see the tendons of grey moss slithering toward his wrist. He thought to kneel beside Ellianna and return to her lips every sweet kiss she had flung his way. He pushed from the limb, meaning to jump down. His descent was cut short before his feet touched earth. Swinging back and forth like a puppet on a string, he discovered that his left hand was mysteriously lashed to the tree. The smile on his face lingered despite the pain in his wrenched shoulder socket.

With his body slowing, he reached to rip away the wiry strips. Alas, he could neither loosen nor unwind them. Worse still and to his sudden alarm, he felt the aggressive stuff enclosing his free hand. He tried to draw it back and retrieve the short blade sheathed in his boot. He could not. His fingers were instantly shackled to the limb. As the spellbound moss snaked down both arms, his eyes flew open wide and he called to her.

"Ellianna, I am captured!"

Assuming he spoke of love, Ellianna continued decapitating daisies. She did not look to her husband as she concurred, "Ah, Ronan, I am captured too." Laying back fully, reclining on the spongy green, she rested the bouquet of beheaded stems against her breast. Her last plucked petal confirmed the good news. He loved her. She closed her weary eyes.

The prince tried to shout but the coarse bromeliad quickly filled his mouth. It streaked through his hair and crisscrossed his shoulders, tightening around his torso. With tragic foreboding, Ronan recognized the telltale signs of black magic. The plant was unnatural in its dedication to invade him. As it squeezed down his body, he knew it was hopeless. Ronan ceased struggling and bequeathed his final moment to gazing at Ellianna. Awash in the radiance of his truelove, she lay framed by daisy petals. It was breathtaking. Savoring the romantic sight, he refused to shut his eyes even whilst the deadly strands consumed them, blighting out his face. In heartbreaking seconds, the worthy prince was reduced to mossy chunks of ragged nothingness.

When Ronan failed to respond with words of adoration, the princess furrowed her perfect brows. Before she could speak, the squawk of ravens startled her nerves as a hundred wings erupted overhead, spooking the horses. The steeds jumped from their crop of green flora—cantering further away, farther out of sight. The forest fell still.

Ellianna opened her eyes. "Ronan, why do the birds caw so?"

There was no reply.

Sensing herself inexplicably alone, her chest squeezed with a disquieting feeling. She sat up craning her slender neck, looking to where he sat. "Ronan?"

She scanned the surrounding trees, but he was nowhere in sight. "You toy with me, my dearest. Come out, come out, wherever you are. Find you, I will. You cannot be far." The rhyme made her titter. The solitude made her sigh.

Acquiescent, she rose to what she thought was his flirtatious game. Smoothing her skirts with another languid twirl and tottering to a dizzy stop, she hiccupped a giggle and shifted purposely—listening for him. Only the bravest black birds lingered as she began seeking. Their beady eyes watched the tragedy unfold.

She checked first behind the oak Ronan had climbed, sure she would tag him there. She did not. "I shall find you," she sang out playfully. "'Tis a fact, an attentive wife can hear her husband's beating heart."

Stepping around the new formed moss—hearing no heart—she meandered to the far side of the grove, spying a curtain of draping limbs. Its branches masked a hidden nook. Ellianna smiled knowingly and arched a brow. Discovering Ronan was certain. Lifting her rustling skirts, she tiptoed for the niche and stopped before the camouflaged opening. She tried to push aside a bough. It barely budged. Careful not to snag her delicate sleeves, she took a wider stance and reached in deep—deeper than she could see—taking firm hold of a knobbly branch. Breathing in a mighty breath, preparing to push the limb and peek inside, there occurred the unexpected. Her heart faltered when the branch came to life around her fingers and clamped onto her hands.

She wrenched back gasping, thinking it the hiding prince. "Ronan, you give me a fright!" To her dismay, she could not pull away. Something in the bush had seized her and was not letting go. From the dark it mimicked, "Ronan, you give me a fright! Ronan, you give me a fright!" Noxious fumes accompanied a malicious voice.

Ellianna screamed for Ronan, yanking hard with surging strength. Again she failed to break the grip. Amidst a sudden thrashing, a grizzled troll sprang from the bush, forcing her back with assaulting shoves. Fearing she would trip over her own skirts, the princess moved her legs quickly, attempting not to fall. All the while, the goblin raged in her face.

"I am captured! I am captured!" He kept a crippling lock on her hands. "He loves me! He loves me not!" He spun her as if waltzing and raised his singsong pitch. "He loves me! He loves me not!"

With her hands savagely constrained, she tried striking out with her legs. Alas, her voluminous skirts pillowed the kicks. She tried twisting free. He was too strong.

"Ronan!" She yelled, nearing hysteria.

Snapping her head forward and chipping her tooth, the madman jerked her to a stop in the middle of the clearing and held fast—glaring and jutting his jaw. She saw drool molding on his peeling lips and recognized insanity.

"Me fine lady," the troll leered with grand formality. "Ye need not badger ye husband. He not be answerin. He never be answerin again." His jowls jiggled as he snickered, "Gone he is! Sucked up by me fluffs of moss!" Tightening his grip on her hands, he whirled her to face the ruins of Ronan.

Petrified with confusion, she saw only the tassel that adorned his boot. Nothing else was recognizable. No lock of hair. No hint of skin. No arm. No leg. No life. His perfection of flesh and bone—only a memory. Her body shuddered.

Again she tried wrenching free of the fiend. He remained riveted on her, taking pleasure in her desolation. Then, proving his contempt with absolute cruelty before releasing her, he crushed the knuckles of her every finger. Completely aghast, she doubled over from the onslaught of pain and stumbled sideways.

When he did not charge her again, she lunged for the moss, frantic to prove her eyes mistaken. Reaching within its mass, her broken fingers searched the bulk but found no resistance—as if she wrestled a mane of horsehair. There was no man to extract. Renewing her efforts, she clawed wildly, immune to the excruciating ache, determined to find Ronan inside.

"Ronan, Ronan, how can this be?" She touched the tassel with swelling fingers. Terror was beginning to waste her. Nausea was stealing her wits. Breathing fear, she forced herself to survey her wounded hands. Lightheadedness swept in when she discovered that her wedding ring was missing.

"Ronan, Ronan, how can this be?" The deranged gnome crooned her words, performing a jerky jig. "How can this be? How can this be?" He danced about the clearing, shrieking out his taunts. "How Ronan? How?"

She swung around to face him. "Why have you done this," she demanded with authority.

Scuttling behind her faster than she could turn, the troll withdrew a burned stick from his bloodstained trousers and viciously poked her spine. "Why have ye done this? Why have ye done this?" Spittle escorted his shouts. She tried to dodge the stabs, but he was too quick. He rounded on her, delivering a last dig to her sternum before aiming the stick at the prince. The branch commenced to quiver as he recited words of magic.

"No!" Before she could grapple the moss, the prince's grave rose beyond reach.

"No!" The troll flapped his arms dramatically, ranting and raving, stomping like a spoiled child. "No! No! No!"

Beginning to sob, Ellianna pleaded, "What harm have we caused you?"

"What harm have we caused ye? What harm have we caused ye?" Parroting her words, he thrashed inside various bushes, yanking out all size oddities. When he had finished, thirteen soiled bodies stood sniffing at her—growling and baring sharp baby teeth.

"Introduce ye selves," he barked at his children. None did.

"Me keen ears heard ye plans of a slaughter." Advancing swiftly, he made his way back to her. "Ye dare to feed the fruits of me loins to ye dogs! What manner father be I to allow that? I protect me babes!" He wagged a stubby finger in her face. "Ye must pay fer such murderous babble. The princeling boy, he done made amends. Ain't nothin left of him!" He gestured to the branch, guffawing loudly. "But ye..." He could hardly speak for wheezing with depravity. "Ye penance be special."

At first he did not see his one-eyed son slinking closer to the princess, mesmerized by the sheen of her gown. When the boy reached a filthy hand, meaning to touch the alluring fabric, the father struck like a serpent. The stick he wielded changed into a club as he bashed the child, shattering its forearm. The thing howled and tried to run, but the father grabbed it by its neck hair and hurled it to his feet. Raising a thick leg, the troll repeatedly stomped its little chest. The princess heard a series of crisp pops. Within seconds, the child ceased jerking and lay peacefully. Its panicked siblings whimpered as the father raised the bat—eyeing his remaining children like a demon. One by one, they dropped to the ground and groveled in the dirt. Their cowering caused him to belly laugh. Briefly.

Without warning—he struck again. This time his morphing wand scalped the head of bowlegged girl. Collapsing to her stomach, she dug furiously in the soft earth with her jagged nails. Before the fatal stab came, she held high a squirming grub in her crusty palm. Her brothers and sisters acted on instinct, clamoring to steal it. The father was too fast. He snatched it up first.

Pinching the muddy worm for firmness, examining its abdomen this way and that, he stuffed it in his mouth and chomped with decaying teeth. Bilious juices spurted between his lips and down his beard. Chuckling, he licked his gummy fingers and darted his coated tongue of mashed intestines under each yellowed nail. Once sated, he extended a slimy hand to the girl who found the meaty treat, offering to help her stand. Her hairless skull hit a tree before she realized she'd been thrown. As she stuck to the trunk like panting sap, her siblings hunkered down—covering their heads. The sight of their trembling bodies made him merry.

When his attention returned to Ellianna, his disposition was exceedingly jovial. He smiled broadly, gesturing proudly at his brood with outstretched arms. Kneeling down, he took hold of a favored son and bounced him on his knee. Slowly his eyes changed. A psychotic look glazed his irises. "Eh, quit yer snivelin. There be more where thems come from." He wiped the child's nose gruffly. "The Missus, she be sucklin a passel of teethin nibblers with a bun in the oven," he boasted to the princess. "Hark me words, poppet…" he cooed at the boy, mussing his hair fondly. "No one harms me childrens." He did not raise his voice as he glowered at Ellianna. "No one but me."

Quaking, Ellianna attempted to speak. Her mouth was as dry as smoke. "We meant no child harm." She could scarcely be heard.

"We meant...no child...harm. We meant...no child... harm." He repeated her words like the village idiot. "Rubbish! Liar!" Foaming at the mouth, he leapt up dumping the toddler on its head. "Well, I does! I means harm! I means to harm ye and all ye pasty childrens!"

"But..." she quavered, trembling, "we...we were only married this day. We have...no children."

Astounded and blinking rapidly, he pranced backward staring at her white gown. "Only married this day? No childrens?" His mouth went slack, letting saliva trickle out. "Only married this day..." he muttered pitifully. "No childrens?" At last understanding, he placed both hands firmly on his hips. "Bah ha!" He roared and tossed back his head. "Me sees it now!" He shoved his stick between the folds of her dress, admiring its opulence like an appreciative seamstress. Crossing his arms, he posed with surprising sophistication—looking her up and down, up and down.

"No childrens of ye own? Hmmm..." He stroked his germy beard and looked into the treetops. Whilst deliberating, his nail lingered on a piece of meat caught in the hairs. Picking at it, he extracted the chunk and positioned the dried crud between his front teeth—chewing and thinking, chewing and thinking. At length, he spoke his mind.

"Then others will do." He flicked his hand and cast a spell, this time elongating the wand to crack like a whip. Striding to the prince, he whacked the boot tassel with the crooked pole, cutting it loose. As it fell, the flared out strands brushed the ear of a nearby child. The boy instantly disintegrated—laid to rest as a heap of moss. Enraged by his son's stupidity, the troll sent the mossy mound flying with the butt of his wand.

"Ye careless dunce!" He shrieked, punching the air with furious vigor. Such a death would make it impossible to salt and smoke the boy for jerky. At the height of his indignation, the troll poked the golden tassel with his whippy switch and ordered the princess, "Pick it up!"

She stared dumbstruck, afraid to touch it. "What evil is that?" She did not move.

"What evil is that? What evil is that?" He wedged the rod beneath its golden center, angling for balance, and draped the heavy tassel over the bending tip. Swinging it up, he hissed with scornful friendliness, "Take it. Why it be all ye have left of the feller." Puckering his lips and making salacious kissing noises, he jabbed the tassel at Ellianna's face.

She slunk back, refusing. "I shant touch that morbid witchery." She was near to expiring—asphyxiating on the pungent tang of doom.

"I shant touch that morbid witchery," he ridiculed. "I shant touch that morbid witchery." With anger intensifying, he launched himself at pockmarked teen, purposely whacking the tassel against the girl's pimply forehead. With no time to react, she fell dead with outstretched arms—like a snow angel of moss.

"Take that, wee thief! I see ye sneakin fer me!" Peals of abuse rang through the forest as he kicked dirt over the felled bundle.

Piqued by the effects of the executions, the lunatic ran about his surviving children—stopping to adjust his sagging britches—before advancing on the next. The tassel swung wildly as he zeroed in on a mangy boy. Before the father could annihilate the son, the princess cried out, "Stop!"

He did not stop. Sashaying spryly, he held the tassel aloft, impishly dropping it an unsafe distance above the boy. Teasing casts kept the child stiffly rooted. Relishing its pangs of fear, the troll stepped closer, dangling the deadly threads inches from the child's flat head. When the victim could take it no longer, a fetid stench riled every nostril. The shivering pup squalled and squatted, grabbing its dampening hind-quarters before bolting for cover—diving into the thorny brambles. The father exploded with laughter as its brothers and sisters chased it away, nipping at its heels.

"Stop!" She implored once more. The force of the word cut raw her throat. "What do you want of me?"

"Stop! Stop!" He caterwauled to the trees like a jilted maiden. "What do ye want of me! What do ye want of me!" Hobbling with gimpy steps, swaying left and then right, he aimed the tassel directly at her, positioning it well ahead of his approach.

Despair emptied her lungs. She closed her eyes and said her final prayer, welcoming the moment when she would join her dead husband. As he rammed the tassel into her disfigured hands, her head fell back with a terminal sigh. Alas, her serene face felt the spew of his shouts and she recoiled. Bewildered, she opened her eyes—still standing.

"Death is not ye fate, me flouncy bride!" He bawled. "Ye will not fall to the tassel as others do! Ye have a debt to pay!"

A cold sensation numbed her fingertips. Spite prowled within her chest—recasting her bones and seeking out her soul. She felt evil lodging inside her breast. Her neck stiffened as the troll grinned wickedly, watching his magic changing her. He leaned in close and caught her scent. The perfume of her wisteria-crowned hair was still fragrant. He took a long snort and bestowed a sinister compliment.

"Ah, yes..." He cackled merrily. "They will like ye. They will surely like ye."

"Who will like me?"

"Who will like me? Who will like me?" The question annoyed him. "Are ye daft? All will! Childrens be quick to mind a fair-haired enchantress. They not fear ye play a trick. Offer thems a wish. Anything they fancy. Make thems put they skinny fingers to the golden tassel. Then watch thems die." He was gloating.

"I could never do that," she told him bravely.

He stepped upon a log at her feet, bringing himself to her height. His mouth was so near that his breath warmed her face. Her throat constricted. She tried not to retch. "I could never do that. I could never do that." Pouting like a sensitive oaf, he clasped his hands together before uttering, "Ye have no choice."

He hopped down cracking his whip. "Fetch me brown pouch!" A balding boy ran for their hidey-hole and returned with a small leather sack. Seizing it, the father yanked open the flap. Ellianna saw a horde of caterpillars inside. Pulling one out, the troll brought a wriggling body to his teeth as if to bite down. Noting her revulsion, he dropped the hand to his side, laughing.

"Nay! These taint fer eatin! Just devilin ye. These be precious. These be snatchers." He stepped upon the log once more and waved the insect beneath her nose. The air around her simmered. Ellianna sensed its vileness. She knew with clarity that the maggot brought anguish.

"Tis a black-winged menace dwellin in this tender wiggler. Never has ye seen the likes of it. The reincarnation from vermin to beast be a glorious enterprise. From meager flesh swells a gargoyle. Its wingspan be greater than three stout lads put head to toe. It shadows the land and takes to the sky with childrens in its clutches. Unless it eats thems first!" He cackled wholeheartedly, displaying a mouthful of festering boils. "Treat thems well or else!" He shook the caterpillar in her face and stabbed a finger in her throat, underscoring the threat.

"As fer ye, say goodbye to flesh and bone. Into mist ye shall form and join the winds of this earth. Only when ye spies a fetching rascal will ye take shape." Simpering, he caressed her pale hair—touching his whip to the wisteria. "Go fer wee ones. That be my advice. Loners be easy to catch when ye toss down a tempter. Curiosity draws them near fer the caterpillar has a talent. It be ever so talkative." He chortled. "Once a youngling hear that magic, the change comes quick. Easy pickins."

He said no more but watched her closely, patiently waiting for praise. When none came, he grunted and returned the caterpillar to its nest, carefully securing the top. Reaching his stocky arms around her slender waist, he worked the pouch straps snugly at her back. His infested hair touched her bodice. She seized her chance. Raising her arm to gain power, she clobbered his temple with the treacherous tassel.

Taken by surprise, he lost his footing and fell from the log, rolling over and over and over. He came to rest face down with his arms and legs askew, moaning and matted in leaves. Embellishing the hoax, he flopped over twitching. Muffled titters made his belly shake. They grew in volume until he spat out a chew of debris and bounded up—running full force at Ellianna. Lowering his shoulder just before impact, he collided with the softness of her womb, catapulting her to the ground.

"Good cleverins," he thundered over her, pounding his chest. Dander and dust clouded the air. "I live!" He leapt up jubilant—kicking his heels together—proving his good health. "That be a grave shock fer ye! Me sees it in ye face! Try again," he encouraged. "Perchance me require two doses of ye abomination." He pawed the tassel with his nasty toes, grinding at the cords. When that failed to obliterate him, he rubbed the ends between his calloused fingers, tangling the lengths. In time, he grew tired of the ruse and stood up yawning and scratching his groin. "Ye bring out me playful side, lass. But I have news. The tassel holds no power over me."

Aware of his contemptible words, she would not meet his eyes. Elllianna was floundering in the vastness of defeat. In a pathetic ploy, she endeavored to throw the tassel deep into the bushes. To her misery and loathing, it stuck fast to her mangled hands.

Amused, he squatted by her side, petting the top of her head like a stray dog. "Cheer up, hag. No need to be glumped. Ye be merry soon enough. Collect ye mossy numskulls and make a cloak of thems. Wrap thems round ye vaporous bones like the arms of thine dead husband. Now that be a happy thought." His eyes twinkled with attentiveness as he peered into her tear-streaked face.

Ellianna could feel herself no longer. She knew that she was altered and that time was running out. With each lethargic breath came a greater hatred of the living—particularly children. Controlled and calculating, she met his gaze. "Will that bring him back to me?" She regarded the troll with a thoughtful frown.

"Will that bring him back to me? Will that bring him back to me?" Repeating her question, he eagerly shook his head yes, yes—confirming her fervent hope. Then, coming within an inch of her downcast mouth, he blew one word into her parted lips.

"Never."

Ellianna's sorrowful eyes lifted to gaze at the shroud of Ronan. A butterfly landed on his lifeless remains. It fanned its orange wings but did not linger. Sensing a predator, it darted away. She watched it go in the softening light of the saddest evening, agonizing that Ronan would never emerge from his deathtrap like a monarch from a chrysalis. Grieving over his demise, she felt her ravaged heart breaking into pieces and dropping to her gut.

"Cocooned and killed, I release you." She raised a maimed hand and blew a farewell kiss to her forever beloved.

Predictably copying, the troll gestured flamboyantly with his magic rod. "Cocooned and killed, I release ye!" He gyrated side to side like a demented jester, thrusting out his veined belly and blowing kisses at the prince with his wart-covered hands. Unable to restrain himself any longer, his unbridled rage goaded him. He liberated a smoldering vengeance on the princess—viciously lashing her. "Cocooned and killed, I release ye! Cocooned and killed, I release ye!" With each mocking shout, his blows cut deeper, scarring her neck with the crippling sear of his whipping stick. The stings knocked her flat. Finished.

"Fools, ye were!" He screamed scornfully, kicking her sides. "Fools to ride through me woods, disparagin me own with ye wicked tongues!"

He paused to crack his whip. The rapid motion caused the wand to shorten. Filing the tip with his gnashing teeth—biting and tugging it out swiftly—he checked the point with his bulbous thumb. Assured of its sharpness, he speared the tassel from Ellianna's hand and wove it into her hair for safekeeping. Once done, he wedged the hilt beneath her chin and jerked her head up so that she could see into his black-hearted eyes.

"Fer that mistake, ye will spend thine everlastin eternity sufferin me wrath and fillin woods with ye insipid breed. Let them greedy snots hang from the trees. Whole forests will strangle on me tassel moss! Now be gone, ye pathetic witch!"

Ejected from the ground by her jawbone, Ellianna was propelled into the air. She lurched out a blackening hand but was robbed a passing touch of her beloved prince. The brute force of the troll skyrocketed her beyond the treetops, into the heights of a solitary dusk. Hurdling toward the heavens, she heard the cannibal below—running berserk—demanding a dinner of his tastiest tot. The mayhem echoed like a pack of wolves as his children ran for their lives, yipping and barking. Their terror forced an eerie laugh from Ellianna's throat—until their hopeless screams faded away.

Soon she was so high that only icy wind could be heard. She feared that she would plummet through the clouds at any moment, but she did not descend. Her body had turned nebulous and misty, effortlessly riding the gloaming sky. As she went, a new compulsion gnawed and needled her. Enslaved by its control, Ellianna flew west—rabid for little children. She cared not whether they were boys or girls. With the illicit caterpillars strapped to her waist, her mournful purgatory would net them all.

In the days that followed, she flew over open water, determined never again to cross paths with the fiend. When she discovered a land rich with oaks, she knew she had found a home. Oaks—forevermore—would remind her of Ronan. In that sheltered place, she honed her skills and learned to stalk. By week's end, she made a first kill. The troll was correct. Standing before a lost girl in the woods, her body returned. The child was captivated by her beauty and glad of the encounter. Eager to make a wish. There was no question of the outcome. The girl perished within seconds— the first of her mossy family tree.

Purely by accident, she put her caterpillars to use. One fell out. As she watched the exchange from the top of a sycamore, she grew petrified. Then enthralled. That her companions transformed into such terrifying creatures was intoxicating. She acknowledged their prowess with renewed awe. Together their results were remarkable. So remarkable that she was forced to move on. There remained not a vacant limb from which to hang her cloaks.

As months turned to years and years rolled by in decades, she rode the winds—searching. Drawn to climates near the sea, she scoured the coasts performing her deeds on the defenseless sons and daughters of the lowlands. Tassel moss flourished. On her hundredth birthday, she saw her reflection in the waters of a lake. Ellianna was old but had aged little. Five hundred years later, she appears magnificent and womanly, lovely to behold yet fatal to intercept when she appears—which is often.

So beware of her charms if you brave the woods alone. Take heed! For the witch flies still, yearning for death and fixated on the hunt. Fueled by a widow's passion, Ellianna presents the golden tassel on her black and broken fingertips, offering the wishing trick to the luckless unwary. Forests weep as her massacre swallows them whole and mossy children fall victim at her feet. Paying her debt. At this very hour, the soulless bride haunts these very woods, cursing the troll and snaring the lonely, ever pining for the loss of her dearly departed—her truelove stolen away—and ever vigilant for the intrepid one.

"THE END"

Nellie and the girls said it together.

Enslaved by its control, Ellianna flew west—rabid for little children.

Chapter 16

Lee—who'd taken over for Gwen, who'd taken over for Paige—slapped the book shut. The unexpected pop made campers jump. "And any of you thinkin she's still out there grabbin kids and stringin up moss, we're here to tell you... *Not!*" Lee looked at her friends.

"That's right, y'all!" Gwen leaned into the mic. "Us four and a flyin renegade just kicked her butt to Timbuktu!"

Shouts broke out. The absurdity of Gwen and her gang taking on a fairytale princess turned kidnapping witch got everybody mouthing off.

Like a cop with a walky-talky, Lee droned, "That's right people. The witch has left the building. Her b.s. is officially out of commission. The forest is now safe. Over."

Half the room went wild, loving Lee's butch bluster. The other half booed. She just laughed. With a perfect toss, she frisbeed the book at Tou-tou, expecting he'd be enjoying the ruckus as much as anybody—pleased that she wasn't making any little kids cry. But when he caught the book, he looked angry. So angry that if Lee hadn't known better, she'd have sworn he was mad at her. Like she'd done something wrong. It crossed her mind that maybe he thought she was making fun of his story. She made a mental note to set him straight later. For now, she huddled with her girls in a teetering embrace. Mrs. B had to step around them for her closing remarks at the microphone.

"Nice teamwork, ladies," she said, nodding their way and clapping. "How about we give the Stoogettes another round of applause! Why am I not surprised to hear they hang out with renegades and witches. I'm sure I speak for everyone when I say we're real, real glad to know y'all are watchin out for us. We'll sleep like babies now." She gave the girls her sunny smile. "Alrighty, let's wrap it up. It's late. Head on back to your cabins. Tomorrow's another big day. Lights out in fifteen minutes. Nighty, night!"

Tired campers rose from tables and filed out the double doors, into the warm night. Walking down the path, Nellie tried to shake the doldrums that had settled over her and the girls. "So...you think that's how it went down? Like she was this totally cool princess until that troll got her?"

"If that's true...it's the most awful thing I've ever heard..." Paige sounded downright gloomily.

"Ya think he knew?" Gwen asked.

"Who? Tou-tou?" Nellie said it without thinking.

"Oh yeah!" Paige exclaimed. "Tou-tou brought that story. Talk about a coincidence. Kinda creepy, don't ya think?"

Nellie shut-up. The girls didn't know the exact details of her earlier conversation with Tou-tou and she wasn't about to go throwing suspicion on the man. He couldn't have possibly known what was going on in the woods—that the bird was back. He would have told her, would have had Camp Seamist and Camp Stingray locked down for safety. Remembering his encounter must have gotten him riled-up all over again, sent him searching for clues and finding the book. Paige was probably right. It was just a really bizarre coincidence.

"I meant the mothman," clarified Gwen. "I wonder if he knew what happened to her?"

"Well if he did, he sure wasn't tellin us. Or thinkin it for us to know," said Lee. "But it doesn't matter what happened to her. It doesn't matter if she was nice once or not. She wasn't nice now. She had to be stopped."

"What about the troll?" Nellie asked.

"What about him?"

"You think he's out there?"

"The story said she flew west to get here. I remember reading that part," answered Lee.

"So that troll ain't from around here. He'd be back where she came from." By Gwen's reasoning, that made perfect sense.

Nellie thought about it. "If you go by the story, this is where she ended up. This is the lowcountry, right?

"Sure is," confirmed Gwen. "We in the middle of it."

"But Spanish moss is up and down the east coast," added Paige.

"There's this cemetery where I live called Bonaventure. It's crawlin with moss."

"That's Georgia, right?" Nellie asked Lee.

"Savannah. But I tell you what. When my softball team went to Argentina for Junior Worlds, I saw it there too, all around the motel."

Gwen whistled. "She been busy."

"If she flew west to get here..." Nellie stopped to think. "What's the next continent to the east? Europe?" She knew that much basic geography from school.

Paige nodded. "And it said she flew over water. That must have been the Atlantic."

"French, I bet." That was Nellie's guess. "She probably came from France."

"Maybe..." Lee mulled it over. "Or Spain or Switzerland. Even Norway. She could've been Russian. She could've been from a bunch of places."

"You got a good listen, Nells. Did she have a accent?" Gwen asked.

"Something different...but...I couldn't place it..."

"Just as long as that troll ain't here. That's all I care about." Gwen kept her eyes on the woods. The girls did too. But the hideous grunt could have been watching from the trees, standing in plain sight with his hands on his hips. They'd have never seen him in the shadows. It made them speed up.

"If she's been at it for centuries, she could've circled the globe lots of times by now. We should research all the places that have Spanish moss because if Tou-tou's story isn't the whole story, like if some part got left out, it'd be hard to pinpoint where it started. The prince's grave could be right next to archery. There's nothing but oaks there. And tons of moss." Nellie was hopeful that the dangers really were over. But they couldn't be too careful—knowing everything they knew.

"And that's all...*kids?*" Gwen shivered. She couldn't bring herself to say dead kids. "Holy Moly..."

"Please stop. Y'all are freakin me out," whispered Paige.

"Guys, come on." Lee was having none of it. "First of all, I guaran-damn-tee ya there's no trolls here. You ever heard of castles in the Carolinas?" She had a point. "And even if there were, which there weren't, he would've died a long time ago." She seemed sure.

"How do you know how long trolls live? Or what happened to his kids? The princess and those caterpillars were sure as crud still alive and that's a fact." It's not like Paige wanted it to be true. It just could be.

"Why be worried about his kids," snorted Lee. "He probably ate 'em."

"Shut-up! You're gonna make me puke." Paige nailed Lee for her perverse sense of humor—until she realized that Lee wasn't kidding.

"That's sick," grimaced Gwen.

"Snakes, alligators and trolls? I'm officially done going in these woods."

"Don't forget witches and mothmen, Nells." Gwen completed the list.

"Y'all are bein paranoid. That mothman would've warned us about trolls," said Lee. "The only bad thing around here was her. Thanks to him, she's a goner."

"What's second of all?" Nellie asked.

"Huh?"

"You said 'First of all'. What's second of all?"

"Oh..." Lee hesitated. "I don't know. I just... I say at this point...we don't tell anybody anythin. Not about the mothman. Not about the witch. And definitely not about the moss bein...kids. It's too...horrible. Too depressin." She looked ashen. "It's finished. Nobody's gonna get hurt ever again. And it's not like they'd believe us. They'd just think we were startin rumors cause we needed attention and—"

"You know what though?" Nellie interrupted. She stopped talking while a group of campers passed by them. When they were out of earshot, she continued quietly. "That boy from Stingray *was* dead. I saw him touch the tassel. I totally saw him die. But now he's back alive again. *How?*" Nellie quit walking. "I think something else must have happened."

"Ya mean like when the mothman... When he... When he..." Paige couldn't say it.

"When he killed her." Lee had no problem finishing the sentence.

"Yeah..." Paige paused, sighing heavily. "I guess he did it." She looked dejected.

"I know he did it! You didn't see him when he grabbed her. Nothin but coldhearted payback keepin that guy goin. Once he laid his hands on her, she didn't have no chance." Gwen told it like it was. But even she looked shell-shocked remembering his face.

They stood there deep in thought until Lee broke the silence. "You saw that boy die, Nellie? You're absolutely sure? Cause that could be about the best news ever."

"That's what I was thinking," Nellie said. "Like maybe the tassel spell reversed itself once she died?"

Paige lit up. "That would change so many lives..."

"For the better." Gwen got goose bumps. "Think of it. All those kids... All those parents... Everybody she tricked gettin a do-over..." Gwen was hopping up and down, squeezing Nellie's fingers.

"What if that *is* what happened?" Nellie squeezed back. "That'd be so... incredible."

"Wouldn't it," gasped Gwen.

"All this because we couldn't find Nellie?" Lee looked completely amazed. "Wow."

"But still it's *so* tragic..."

"Here we go again. How's that tragic, Paige?"

"I mean for *her*, Lee. For the *princess*..." Paige looked like she was about to start crying. "Can ya even imagine it? The love of your life killed on your weddin day? Your whole world destroyed? It makes me feel so sad for her..."

"That's cause you weren't in the top of that tree. You gotta believe us, Paige. She *wasn't* a fairytale. She was *real*. And she was tryin to *kill* me and Gwen and Nellie. And if she had, you wouldn't be feelin sorry for her right now cause you'd probably be dead too. Try and remember that." Lee hated getting emotional. She'd had enough crying. The fact that the witch's death possibly brought an end to so much suffering should have given them a reason to celebrate. Lee slapped Paige upside the head, trying to escape her own conflicted feelings. "Snap out of it, ya dopey romantic!"

"Always gotta be the tough girl, don't you, Lee," teased Nellie, coming to Paige's defense. "It's pretty easy to see you don't have a romantic bone in your body." Nellie whacked the back of Lee's head just for yucks. "But I for one thank you for it! And I thank you, Gwen! And I thank you, Paige! And I thank you, Mr. Moth!" Yelling her list to the night sky, Nellie thunked Paige and Gwen upside the head too. "If it wasn't for my friends, I'd be moss bait."

"Awe shucks, girlie. Ya know what they say? That's what friends are for." Gwen put her arm around Nellie's waist, giving her a squeeze and noogie.

"Saved by the bell?" Paige slipped her arm around Nellie. "Pish-posh," she giggled. "That's old school. Saved by your friends, that's what we're talkin about!"

"We'd have never left you out there, Nellie. With or without his help, we'd have found you." Despite her best efforts, Lee's eyes got watery. She figured it was OK. No one could see her tears in the dark. Latching onto Paige's free side, they started down the path, attached at the hips.

"I owe you guys big." Nellie walked with her arms around her friends.

"That's the neat part," chirped Paige. "Cause now ya got your whole life long to keep payin us back."

"Yeah, cause when camp ends, don't think you gettin rid of us, Sweet Cheeks. We all comin back next summer. Pick up where we left off."

"Promise?"

"Big-time promise, Hollywood," nodded Lee. "Mark it on your calendar. And as far as havin a romantical bone in my body, I'll just leave that girlie stuff to you three. Y'all can save it up for the next dance."

"The next dance!" Nellie squealed, remembering handsome Dalton and Trevor the teddy bear. "Can't wait!" She giggled. "Can't imagine what trouble they'll have gotten into by then."

"Or what trouble the four of you will get in while we're there." Lee grinned at Gwen and Nellie—in the know about the stink bomb and pulling for more of the same.

"I tell ya what," announced Gwen emphatically. "If all this is true and we really did just help save all them lives, then we need a *way* better nickname. Stoogettes don't come close to cuttin it!" She punctuated her insight with a robust hip-bump. It pushed Nellie into Paige, and Paige into Lee—forcing Lee off the sidewalk. Lee swung around trying to jump on Paige's back, but Paige took off running right as Gwen and Nellie gave Lee a wedgy. Lee retaliated by tickling anyone in arm's reach. Evading her fingers, they raced down the path, laughing their heads off. They took the rough-housing straight inside, enlisting their whole cabin in a feather-flying pillow fight. Fifteen minutes later—after much needed showers—they drifted off to once-upon-a-time dreams filled with a prince and a princess and a fearless mothman.

It wasn't until the next morning that the discovery was made. "The heck? What happened to your hands?" They were standing at the bathroom mirror brushing their teeth when Kate said, "Please tell me y'all didn't do that on purpose."

Between the index finger and thumb, dried blood was on the right hand of each girl. They stopped brushing to stare, examining themselves in the mirror. The curious cuts—no bigger than a corn kernel—didn't hurt or itch. The girls told Kate they honestly had no idea how they'd gotten them.

They finished getting ready and left the cabin, guessing at the possibilities all the way through the flag-raising ceremony and on the walk to the mess hall. The discussion lasted through breakfast. As they stood on the porch munching the last of their bacon, they still had no concrete explanation for the scrapes and finally grew bored talking about it. Adventures were starting up all around them. Depending on which direction they ran, they could do any number of activities. The breeze was the tie-breaker. And a regatta was slated to start within the hour.

"Four-girl teams with the brains to work together." That's how Mrs. B put it during morning announcements.

"I b'lieve we the poster children for that race," said Gwen, looking across to the sailboats.

"I do b'lieve you right." Nellie agreed, showing off her southerness.

"Last one to the dock's a rotten egg!" Lee jumped the railing and hit the ground running. One second later, Gwen and Nellie shot off the porch. Paige—turning to the door for more bacon—was caught off balance. Refusing to be the rotten egg, she abandoned the pork and took the steps one at a time—like a proper Charleston Deb.

After waiting in line and signing up, they waded out to their assigned Flying Scot and climbed the stern ladder. Lee headed to the foredeck to fasten and set the jib. Paige unstrapped the mainsail, attached the shackle to the head and released the mainsheet. Once that was done, Nellie cranked the halyard winch and hoisted the sail. Casting off from an anchored buoy, Gwen unhooked the mooring clip and stowed the bow line. As they made their way around a sloop and left shallow water, Paige lowered the centerboard while Nellie manned the tiller. With sun in their eyes and a slight breeze, they sailed toward the starting line to join the fleet—tacking throughout the countdown, getting in position—listening for the horn blast that would start the race. Kate and Madison, plus two more from their cabin, came abreast on their starboard side.

"Should we make a bet?" Kate shouted from her boat.

"Bet y'all lose," yelled Lee. Her competitive juices were flowing.

"Fat chance! I got Mad Dog here at the tiller." Mad Dog was Kate's pet name for Madison—on account of her puppy-dog eyes and impulsive personality. "Already warned her what happens if we don't win. Counselors are confiscatin those Krispy Kremes on sight."

"Your brother's coming today!" Nellie got all excited. The thought of sixty glazed originals made her mouth water.

"Told ya I'd call daddy." Madison's head started in bobbing. "Graydon took the day off. He'll be here around noon with the five boxes. Just like I promised."

"Oewww Lonnie! Now there's somethin to race back for," crowed Gwen.

"What do ya think, Maddy?" Paige hollered. "Is Kate gonna fall in love when she lays her eyes on your bro?"

"Bet she will!" Madison hollered back, bobbing double-time.

"That is not the kind of bet I was talkin about!" Kate laughed.

The horn blared and the talking stopped. Twelve Flying Scots trimmed their sails and picked up speed.

"Smart," shouted Lee, fixing her loose-footed jib. She adjusted the jib sheet and it stopped luffing.

"Thanks!" Paige grinned. They high-fived.

"What y'all up to now?"

"Nothin, Gweny," giggled Paige. But she couldn't keep a secret. "Just that if Kate's thinkin about a good-lookin boy showin up, we might actually beat her."

"Beat her like a drum," hooted Lee.

"You guys are the worst!" Nellie chuckled.

"Yeah, we're pros."

"What'd I tell you goobers the other day? Winnin is everythin!" Standing on the bow holding onto nothing, Lee faced the water with her arms flung wide. Nellie thought she looked half *Titanic*, half *Pirates of the Caribbean.*

"Warped is what y'all are!" Gwen shouted over the wind. "Glad we on the same team today!"

"Just 'til we hit land, maties!" Lee scrambled off the bow, into the safety of the cockpit. "Then we pair off and it's back to the firin squad for you two lassies!" She'd gone all pirate.

"Bring it, Peg-leg," challenged Gwen.

"And watch your head. Ready about!" Nellie called before she tacked. The winds were picking up nicely at around 17 knots. "Hard a-lee!"

The boom swung wide and the boat heeled on its side at a 30 degree angle. Lee ducked in the nick of time, joining the girls on the port rail. The four sat thigh to thigh, getting drenched with spray, as they leaned out over the water. By the time they rounded the Windward mark, the mainsail and jib were smooth as ironed shirts. They pulled away from the pack and sped down a clear lane, gaining on Mad Dog's tail. If they kept their sails filled with clean air and didn't mess up and capsize—or foul anybody—they just might give Kate a run for the trophy.

They didn't dump themselves in the river, but they didn't win either. They came in second. As acting Skipper, Nellie said it was a difficult choice but a calculated decision. No way around it. She couldn't risk the doughnuts falling into enemy hands. Teenage girls could be ruthless when it came to dessert. Her gang wouldn't get as much as a whiff before the counselors ordered them to get lost and marched off with the goods. She'd have to suffer in sweet-toothed agony while those donuts were devoured without her. That was not happening.

In the end, it was funny how it worked out. Kate denied that Madison's brother had anything to do with it—but it was obvious that he did. Kate unwound her usual side ponytail and went around with her hair combed and her lip gloss on all day. When Graydon showed up after lunch, striding across the lawn with his tan biceps and his famous green eyes, Kate made sure that she was the one who greeted him at their cabin door. She was the one who took the stack of heavy boxes. She was the one who introduced him to her campers. She was the one who walked him back to his car. And she was the one whose phone number he told Madison to get when he hugged his little sis goodbye. The whole cabin was carrying on about it, whispering and giggling—torturing Kate. With her first bite into warm doughnut deliciousness, even Lee got over coming in second.

When Nellie and the girls visited Tou-tou later that day, everything seemed back to normal. He was his usual charming self in his flowery shirt and gracious attitude, busy helping the throngs of campers coming and going. Lee decided to blow-off the look he'd given her the night before. She didn't bring it up. Nellie, on the other hand, pulled him aside telling him that she had something extremely important to ask him about. In private. It didn't seem odd—since the art cabin was filled with girls—when he shushed her. But she noticed the sternness in his voice and the look in his eye when he told her that now was not the time. He asked if she would please come to the cabin later that evening. He pointedly requested that they all come. He excused himself when she agreed and went to clean up a can of kicked-over paint. Red was spreading across the floor.

They came back after dinner, contemplating telling him everything. Without revealing their bird conversation, Nellie had convinced the girls that maybe they should. Confiding in a trusted adult could be smart, especially since Tou-tou was the one who brought the story. They planned on hearing what he had to say first. Then they'd decide how much—if any—they would divulge to him.

A petite woman wearing a blousy sundress was coming out of the art cabin when they approached. She was a new face. It was from her that they learned, "Monsieur Pitou's not here anymore. Poor man was called away out of the blue. A family emergency, I'm told. We really don't know when he'll be back. It might not be until next session. I'm the fill-in. Can I help you ladies with somethin?"

Nellie couldn't hide her agitation, but the girls covered for her, telling the woman that Nellie was a jewelry junkie with a necklace in need of restringing. The sight of the cabin closing for the night was tough on her beading sensibilities. The woman laughed and urged them to come back and fix the necklace in the morning, bright and early. They did, but Tou-tou hadn't returned. Tou-tou never returned.

In the jam-packed week that followed, the girls were feverishly active and mostly inseparable. They were out on the water every day—sailing, skiing and wakeboarding constantly. They even tried out for the ski team. Gwen was the only one who qualified. Because of her athleticism (and self-proclaimed, "*Afro*-dye-tee thighs of steel!") her slalom sit-spins were the featured trick on the team. As for Nellie, she was excited to finally straddle the banana. She made sure her whole gang did it together. Backward. Predictably, it sent everyone flying but Lee.

On land, they took the off-road jeep excursion with their cabin mates and came back covered in swamp mud. They jump served and bump passed and spiked volleyballs until their wrists turned splotchy. They hula-hooped and tether-balled until they were dizzy. They played doubles at the tennis courts and shot hoops for nickels. The nightly limbo contests gave them sore muscles in places they never even knew they had muscles. Lee, Gwen and Nellie climbed the rock wall daily. After jumping horses, Paige would watch from the bottom in her jodhpurs and spurs, snacking on carrots and timing their races to the top.

At midweek, their cabin—along with four other cabins—boarded the *Sea Skippy* and embarked on a cruise. The entire group was dressed alike in their Seamist shirts and sailor caps. They docked downriver and shopped in a quaint town, ate at its local fishery and spent the night. Back at camp, they made oatmeal facials and laid in the sun with cucumber slices over their eyes—until Paige ate everyone's cucumbers. At Lee's insistence, they joined the softball team and played in the weekend tournaments. Lee was voted MVP. All four hung out with Dalton and Trevor at the next dance. There were no signs of trolls.

Week three had Gwen organizing a cooking class and teaching everyone how to make, "The best barbeque sauce ever!" Paige got special permission to take them horseback riding on the beach. They rode through lapping waves at low tide and counted jellyfish in the surf. They wrote a skit for Talent Night and performed it with their cabin mates; Nellie won Best Actress. The gown Paige made her from recycled newspapers and a rain tarp won Best Costume. Madison did a stand-up routine of her cleanest, dirtiest jokes. She brought the house down. It helped Cabin 21 snag the Spirit Award. They zip lined and blobbed to their hearts' content. They canoed in the camp lake and fed the turtles. They hung out with Dalton and Trevor again. (Nellie and Dalton almost kissed.) And team GweNell—who finally outshot team LePaige—gleefully administered and videoed the punishment at the last dance. With a slight change. Lee and Paige were allowed to wear shoes with their atrocious dresses. High heels to be exact. Lee did not disappoint. She was epically wobbly.

By week four, the constant splash of saltwater healed the wounds on the girls' hands. The source of the cuts was still in question. They'd stand in a circle holding out their hands, fingers touching, studying the red marks. The identical gouges looked like friendship tattoos.

The afternoon that Gwen, Lee and Paige went to hit a bucket of golf balls turned into an unforgettable day. Nellie had decided to head to the art cabin and take a crack at the potter's wheel. Working her spinning bowl, shaping its edges with grey water dripping between her fingers and thinking about her wish, something jogged her memory. She recalled what happened when she first laid eyes on the man with wings. She remembered throwing her hands out and feeling a sting—right before his thoughts poured in. She stopped smoothing clay and raised her hand, looking closely at her heart-shaped scar. That's when she knew.

It wasn't an accidental scrape or a bug bite. It was a message. The curving symbol of faith, the universal sign of love, the souvenir from that extraordinary experience in the woods—it was a gift from their mothman. A permanent reminder to stay safe and stay together. She could almost hear them all—her parents, her sister, Mrs. B, Tou-tou, and him—whispering, "Stay smart. We're warning you." She smiled to herself, rolling her eyes and shaking her head. Still, she felt grateful for all the people who put up with her and loved her. She knew she would cherish that scar forever and ever.

Without thinking, she raised her hand and kissed the heart. For the next 16 seconds she sat in a frozen trance with her hand in front of her mouth, dripping clay water down her chin. Only because the kid next to her shook her, asking if she was alright, did Nellie lose her connection with him. The young girl watched Nellie making-out with her own hand like a complete fruitcake—frantically kissing the heart again and again. But the images had stopped. All Nellie got was flickers of static. Leaping up, she shut off her wheel, pried her lopsided vase loose and threw it on a shelf—didn't even cover it with a damp paper towel. She ran from the cabin and sprinted to the driving range, shrieking for her girls at the top of her lungs. What she had just seen was going to blow their minds.

Chapter 17

He flew directly toward open water. The Neuse River, with its variations in depth, wouldn't do. Even the Pamlico Sound could prove too shallow. The churning Atlantic was his destination. Its crescendo of roiling waves, its miles of submerged canyons, its Black Tip and Bull Sharks—there yawned her morgue. On favorable winds he flew the despised prisoner over whitecap waters. Holding his wings open, he sailed through the night easily riding the coastal currents.

She never once struggled, never again tried to speak. He had expected tricks, maybe bribes, even in her incapacitated state. He was ready. The only response she would gain would be his resolve to destroy her; he'd prepared himself to be swayed by nothing. Exacting revenge for the loss of his childhood, along with thousands of other childhoods, had become his single rational purpose, his balm of comfort—a pathetic consolation prize for his dismal existence.

For years he had fantasized about this event, picturing countless scenarios and playing them through in his imagination. In truth, shouting her into Hell had been the single source of entertainment for his lonely life, his private one-man show for a deceased audience.

During his nightly performances, he would yell from the treetops, describing her devastation of so many innocent lives until she wallowed in shame at his feet. His rage-fueled tirades left no words unspoken, no argument considered too unworthy—beginning with bragging.

Accusing her of blatant stupidity, he would wing through the trees like a hawk on the hunt, demonstrating his keen instinct for tracking new moss. Without fail, he would anoint each mossy gravesite with his pledge of retribution. On the rare day when contempt bored him, he would rehearse scathing confessions, admitting how he'd hidden in a bush and watched as she ruined his boyhood friend—too young and terrified to help. Most often though, he toyed with tormenting her: describing his brooding youth, his moral decline, his mental meltdowns—eating, sleeping, breathing only for this day. The day his bouts of depression would end. The day he would wipe out evil and its bitter results. The day he would celebrate a murder. *Hers.*

But now that he had her, he said none of those things. Her stillness—her absolute silence—it was unsettling. It kept him on edge. He sensed her plotting a last strike, so he tightened his forearm around her neck and dug his other into her waist. His legs continued immobilizing her. As he flew with the wind, gripping the weight, he wanted to bear down and constrict. He wanted to smash her brittle bones to pieces before dumping the body in the ocean. A sliver of dignity kept him from doing it.

"Her demise must be handled in an efficient manner. That is of utmost importance." The Protector had cautioned him. That same elder would be appearing soon. The plan to rendezvous over the ocean had been put into place weeks ago. When the mothman trilled the alarm—signifying that the witch had been spotted, detained and interned—his kind would have heard the call for miles around. The elder would have taken to the sky immediately. By now he must be close.

"Just a little further," he railed at himself, fighting to control his demons. "Then her fate will be sealed. She'll sink like chum to the bottom of the sea."

But vengeance prevailed. He did squeeze down callously to injure her. He couldn't help it. He wanted to cause debilitating pain. His chest hurt—he actually ached that much to hear her suffer. Despite his barbaric behavior, she did not groan for mercy this time. In fact, she offered no resistance at all. The fight in flight he long anticipated was not to be. It only added to his hatred. He jerked her back in place and flew on struggling to appease his seething resentment.

A figure emerged from the fog and hung in the air. As the mothman drew near, he could see that the wings of the elder showed age but were still quite capable. Their iridescence reflected moonlight and lit the surrounding haze so that he looked suspended in a halo of green glow. His lean body was naked except for a burgundy loin cloth. There was no greeting. The Protector studied the bundle with a solemn expression.

"The witch and tassel are within?" The mothman smelled mint.

"I wrapped until I ran out of silk. She can barely breathe. Her hands are tied at her back. That lump is the tassel. It will go down with her."

"How did you locate her?"

"I left Stingray after they went in for dinner. I had a bad feeling and flew to Seamist just in time to—"

"She formed to attack?"

"The attack was in progress."

"She made another kill?!" The elder became instantly distressed and surged forward, knocking into the witch with his torso. The mothman had to flurry his wings to halt his backward momentum.

"Almost." He answered quickly.

"Almost? Someone *escaped?"*

"A girl. She came seconds from dying. Her friends would have been next. They were in the woods looking for her. They found me first."

Elders were the oldest members of the mothmen clans. Those possessing considerable acumen rose to the status of Protectors. In his few encounters, never had the mothman seen one become physical toward a fellow kinsman. He reassessed the situation, purposely letting himself drift back to a safer distance, unsure of what to expect. He didn't want to be too close. Protectors were authoritative creatures. Decisive and intimidating. And this one was obviously displeased.

"Things got out of hand. The witch had the girl in the treetops. Her friends could hear her moaning. They refused to leave. It called for unprecedented action."

"They are *alive?"* The mothman heard disbelief in the elder's voice.

"They survived. But they'll never be the same. The captured one, a girl named Nellie—"

The elder was on him in an instant. His large black hands encased the sides of the mothman's head. *"Did you say Nellie?!"* His face was riddled with shock. *"The witch had Nellie?!"*

The mothman felt the crushing strength in those hands. But he was loyal, prepared to tell the elder everything, even if his reaction was unpredictable—or worse. "One of the friends only saw me. But the other two climbed the tree. They saw the witch. I couldn't stop them. The Nellie girl, she saw everything. And a caterpillar was used. She knows about the bird."

"She already knew about the bird!" Before the mothman could ask how, the elder took him by the shoulders. "You saved her..." His voice trailed off. He was overwhelmed. A rescue was unheard of.

"It wasn't just me. They saved themselves. The two who climbed fought for their friend."

"They *fought* the witch?!"

The mothman smirked. "They went after her with sticks. I think they broke bones."

The elder was momentarily speechless. Regaining his composure, he replied, "The clan is humbled by your unswerving devotion. You will always have my profound gratitude." He looked into the younger man's face, guessing the mothman's age to be close to ninety. By human standards he looked like a man in the prime of his life—aside from the dark circles under his eyes.

"Your burden will soon lighten, if only you let it. Do not carry misery in your heart another day. It ends tonight. Please, promise me that."

The mothman was at a loss for words. Numb regret—coupled with revenge—was all he had ever known. Days filled with ordinary pastimes would be baffling. "I'll...try." The word sounded hollow in his ears.

"You must." The elder released him. His directness—his penetrating expectation, the optimism in his eyes—it had an uncanny affect. But the moment was brief. The elder dropped his gaze to the witch. He laid one hand over her face and placed his other around the back of her head. Pressing firmly, he determined that she was still breathing. Unlike the mothman, he had no urge to choke the life out of her. Like the mothman, he sentenced her to an immediate and formal death.

"I sanction this just deed and grant you the authority to pass. Fly on. When you feel the current cooling and the air thinning, complete your mission." He unhanded the prisoner just as a gust of wind signaled an approaching storm and clouds began to part. It cut their meeting short. "I will not accompany you. My absence brings questions."

Eager to return, the elder's wings twitched and beat. Despite clear warnings, Nellie's life was almost taken. Lee, Gwen and Paige had been put in jeopardy as well. How they all weren't dead was a miracle. Anger was the last emotion he should be feeling, but that's exactly what he felt. Anger for not sensing the magnitude of danger himself and fury for their reckless behavior. Had they been tricked, it would have been the calamity from which he never recovered. He needed to see with his own eyes that they were safe and breathing. At the appropriate time, he would question them. The mothman required no further assistance. He had proven himself laudable. After all, he was the sole reason the witch was discovered and brought to their attention in the first place. It was permissible that he should dispose of her body on his own terms. So be it.

"We are inspired by your due diligence. It greatly honors your childhood friend. You are destined to fulfill your oath as the conqueror. Alert me when she is dead. I will listen for your trill throughout the night. If you do not call… If I hear nothing…" The elder's face grew stoic at the possibility of some unexpected failure. "If I hear nothing from you by tomorrow night, I will know that she somehow revived. That she regained her abilities. I will assume you did not survive. I give you my word, we will search out your body and take you home for a proper burial."

"I give you my word *She* dies tonight! Not me. Besides, you wouldn't find anything. She prefers moss, remember. Not bodies."

The elder accepted the correction and looked wistfully away. "The clan truly hopes her hour of reckoning will be tonight."

The mothman sneered at the comment. "You tell the clan not to waste their time hoping. I never do. Tell them I *know* she dies tonight."

"They offer sustenance equally, my son—hoping and knowing. The comfort of hope is as nourishing as the advantage of knowing. Together they are nectar that appeases both heart and mind. This I *hope* you will one day *know*."

But even the Protector could not know the astonishing events about to unfold—that he would listen by his window throughout the night and into the next day but hear no trill from this younger kinsman, that he would leave Seamist unexpectedly to gather his warriors and lead the exhaustive search for his body, and, that all they would ever find of the mothman would be his severed wing floating on the water—so he raised a hand and chose his farewell thought carefully. The mothman obediently pressed his forehead against the open palm.

"Find the joy."

The intensity of the message made a crackling sound. Then, just as he had appeared, Tou-tou dropped from sight and was gone in a whoosh.

The mothman did as he was told. He flew on. She scarcely noticed his strangling grip for her listless heart had done the impossible. It was floundering. Now she focused on the caller in her gut, sputtering to find a beat. She was amazed that the ransacked organ could still thud in the bile of her belly. The flopping meant it too sensed the end. The vast circle of her tumultuous life was coming to a close.

One minute later, her captor slowed in midair and stopped.

"Ronan."

It wasn't the blustery wind. He heard it distinctly—just as he let go. Her last word skittered over his eardrums. It didn't sound like a curse so he took no defensive measures. Instead, he cheered her dive. He had intentionally gained substantial altitude, hoping that she would shatter like shards of glass on impact. He counted six full seconds before hearing the bundle hit water. Hovering high overhead, he watched the froth and scanned the radius of her entry, ready to battle her foul soul rising from the murky depths. But the bubbling waned and then ceased entirely. The ocean—floodlit by moonbeams—reflected the mystery of deep water. He saw no trace of escaping air.

From his elevated height, he remained tense, on the lookout. His reoccurring nightmare—that an arm would rise from her saltwater grave and find his throat, pulling him under—kept him charged. As the minutes slogged by, his fear eased. He bravely swooped over the water, darting between the peaks and valleys. His need to scream final damnations down to her worthless carcass brought him lower. He skimmed the surface in a bold flyby at the precise second that she died. His fear of something unforeseeable happening in that crucial instant was justified.

Something did.

Doubling back for a last reconnaissance, he was savagely yanked toward the heavens. Every disc down his spine cracked as he spiraled out of control, reeling through the night with his wings suctioned around his shoulders. The left wing buffeted wildly against the side of his head—streaking his face with powder—before ripping off and vanishing in the turbulence. He did not scream. In his heart of hearts, a violent ending was always anticipated. He wasn't naive. He assumed she possessed powers beyond death. His last conscious thought—before blacking out—was of being a child again, playing in the woods with his very best friend. He was at peace, gladly surrendering life in his quest to slay the witch. He was even smiling.

Upon impact, she had sliced through the water like a sword through downy feathers. She held her breath as the ocean bombarded her casing. Sinking fast and barely alive, the cold-shock clawed her skin and dove for her innards. Shivering began instantaneously. Still, she waited. She needed to be deeper. When she could delay no longer, she sucked in water through her nose and mouth. The layers of silk slowed the liquid. But worse, her fear of drowning caused an unwanted reflex. She gagged—coughing the sea from her lungs. She forced herself to inhale again. Faith gave her the courage to pursue death.

Behind closed eyes, silhouettes formed and faded and formed. Her body sank—rolling and rolling, over and over—to the will of the pressing water. The ocean gushed through her ears as voices from the past played her to sleep—a lullaby for the sunken. Blood slowed. Shivering stopped. Life let her go.

In death she heard him—far away, calling her. She turned to face him—to listen. Dying kept her from moving. Even so, warmth kindled in her expired breast for his voice did not hush.

Light beckoned. A curious lovely fizzed within her belly. There he was again. Clearer. Louder. Calling her name. She tried to open her dead eyes. Her lids quivered. The binding at her face went lax. More light—coraly pinks singed with orange—met her half-opened eyes. Again her name skipped blithely along the shores of Heaven, or Hell. She was not sure which.

"Ellianna."

Ronan's voice passed by on a breeze. Trying to focus, trying to determine what surrounded her—its serenity, its familiar intimacy—she took it all in. Accompanied by oxygen.

She was not rolling anymore. She was fully reclined and drifting backward—floating and drifting and floating. She wanted to stop. She longed to be still. Panoramas of greens swayed above pillars of browns. The colors merged and blurred, making her dizzy. Instinctively, her arms sought to steady herself. They slipped to her waist as the silk bondage continued dissolving. Silvery strands draped from her arms like tattered butterfly wings.

She reached behind blindly, groping for support. She found a brace and grabbed on tight. Her body stopped. Lengthy stalks filled her probing hands. She squeezed them and tugged them and ran them through her fingers, causing her heart to skip a beat. Her hands were nimble. The petrified tips were not throbbing. They moved and curved and clenched without pain. The smile of an angel spread across her lips. Ecstasy coursed through her dead limbs. Her arms, her neck, her shoulder blades and back, down her chest and through her stomach, zinging past her thighs— everything tingled. She bent her knees and extended her legs, wriggling her toes. A splendid sensation massaged her calves and shot through her arches.

A shadow crossed her face. It lingered whilst airy flicks tickled her nose. She tilted her head, smelling sweet musk, as a blush rose on her cheeks. Her sleepy eyes, so languid in death, tried to behold her celestial setting. But the shadow blocked her view. She shifted slightly and shut her eyes. She went completely still when a warming smother pressed down upon her mouth.

"Ellianna, I am captured."

She tasted his ghost. Body heat was even present. Her eyes fluttered open and there he stood—an ethereal Ronan. A thrill filled her corpse when the phantom leaned in close. Imagined warmth flooded her skin as he nuzzled her neck. He pulled back smiling—watching her affectionately—then brushed his lips against hers once more. Ah, heaven! Her soul was free. She reached to embrace his illusion and felt her jeweled sleeves sliding up her arms. Her hands came to rest on his shoulders. A sigh escaped and then a gasp as her pink fingertips danced across his arched brow and his warm cheeks and his stubbled jaw. She drew them back in awe— staring at her wedding ring—before touching her own face and throat, finding youthful skin. Seated on the ground, surrounded by a profusion of daisy petals, her eyes slowly widened.

"Cocooned and killed, I release you," she whispered tentatively to his face.

The sight of Ronan's quizzical expression seized her with red-hot exhilaration. He was so real. Everything was so real. This heavenly awakening bore evidence of the living. She even felt a racing heart. Her heart! As if their inconceivable victory had been realized. As if she had *won*. Her sly trick against the troll, her cunning ploy for salvation—had it succeeded? Three spells were cast on that infamous day. The first stole her truest love. The second stole her chaste soul. But the third spell was her own doing.

"Cocooned and killed, I release you."

Much more than a melancholy farewell to her beloved Ronan, those carefully chosen words were Ellianna's counter attack, smuggled to her on the wings of a butterfly—her strategy of warfare against the spell-wielding troll. The beast, so intent on mocking her, repeated the phrase and waved his magic wand—as she desperately prayed he would do. She had waited centuries to learn if that morbid enchantment held the power to outsmart the cretin. She had hunted for an eternity, seeking out a notorious creature—the only one with the wherewithal to stop her. All the while, possessed by the malignant spell, she tricked the hapless that crossed her path as she sought out those fearsome Mothmen from that secret wood. She knew they existed. The butterfly reminded her.

Naturally, her childhood tutors had schooled her in the study of moths and butterflies. One mercurial teacher—a passionate Lepidopterist—spoke reverently of an elusive clansmen of moths, inhabitants of a faraway land. "A volatile species with uncanny dexterity." The learned instructor often lectured on the breadth of their wingspan, allegedly measuring over seven feet.

"Undoubtedly deadly, undoubtedly deadly," he would mutter from his desk as he calibrated and recalibrated reams of detailed sketches.

Day after wretched day, her search yielded no evidence of such a clan. After centuries of meticulous tracking, she lost her conviction and woefully accepted that her wizened tutor had been mistaken. Mothmen were nothing but an old man's fantasy. Incarcerated wickedness would be her cruel and relentless destiny.

Then she found the mothboy.

The flying imp was naturally cautious. Following him in flight was nearly impossible. So impossible that she failed to locate his hometree or any sign of his menacing moth kinsmen. Ultimately, after lurking in his wood and sighting him with regularity, she painstakingly learned his routine. At a loss to find an adult mothman, she cultivated a new plan. *Enrage the mothboy and topple his world.* That would be her mission.

Stalking him became her obsession. Until it delivered a glimmer of hope—a stunning surprise. It delivered his friend. A human child. She spied on the boys for days, impatient for her chance. When it came—during that fateful fishing excursion—she struck without remorse, making sure that she was seen. Alas, her liberator was merely a scrawny mothboy. She would have no choice but to wait. When the mothboy grew to be a mothman—a formidable adversary—then she would learn if the seeds of retaliation were deeply planted.

Now that day was upon them. The mothman's dogged quest for her, fed by his steadfast revenge, had it freed her at last? For she had not bellowed, "Oh, merciful knight!" as erroneously interpreted. She had wailed, "Oh, merciful night!" in exultant hope that she was about to die—*that her wish would be granted.* She was cocooned. She was killed. Was she truly released?

Ronan's radiant humanity and touchable presence—they were undeniable. Stroking handfuls of his glossy hair, she pulled his body against hers—jugular to jugular—and discovered the miraculous truth. Under his pulse she was reborn.

"Cocooned and killed?" His husky baritone made her shiver. "'Tis a gloomy thought for a wedding night. Rest assured, my love, you shall be cocooned in my embrace." That boyish grin spread across his face.

Cavorting with flirtatious vitality, he slid one hand beneath her skirts and the other against the small of her back, scooping her from the ground and whistling for the horses. She heard the stampede of hooves and felt the vibration of their swift approach.

Pulling her close, Ronan's whispers came softly in her ear, "My embraces shant steal your life, though my kisses shall release you." A robust laugh accompanied his look of seduction. She remained flabbergasted. Spinning to face the advancing animals, he carefully set her standing, then dropped to one knee cupping his hands before her. She placed in one bare foot and stood into his palms. Her mare did not break stride as Ronan timed the mount perfectly. Ellianna landed on its back and took up her reins.

"My husband," she shouted, hearing her young voice once more. "The sun is setting. To the race! To the race!" She knew they must escape the ominous grove quickly.

With legs clinging to heaving flanks, Ellianna turned to her cherished dearest. Her eyes traveled beyond him, beyond his tasseless boot, to the far corner of the glen—to the hidey-hole. She knew it was there. The vilest of things. The troll. She knew it was watching—knew they all were watching. Now they could wait, counting the hours and dreading the day. The day she rode back with an army by her side, and Ronan, defiant to smite the demon father and bury his charred stumps with the maggots. They would reclaim this nature by force and by fury. Oh, yes. She would return.

Flexing her thighs with steady pressure, she relayed her need for the mare's most imperative maneuvers. Ronan wasted no time. With customary agility, he mounted in one leap. Ellianna's eyes misted with tears of joy as both riders sped from danger.

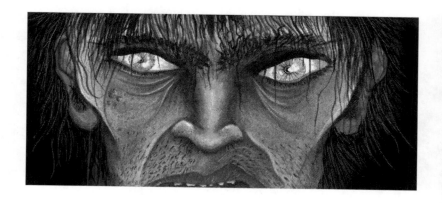

She knew it was watching...

Gaining quickly, Ronan shouted from his stallion, "A word of caution, my lady! Should you best your future king, be assured it is simply that he allowed it!"

Careening single file along the narrow trail, they burst from the forest. Ellianna forged ahead as her mare found dependable footing in the open meadow. Over her shoulder she called, "I am newly educated! Chase victory with heartless abandon, my husband! That you must do! Only then will I concede that your love of me is as great as my eternal love for you." She professed that one sweet confession from the myriad she must tell. Though revealing her harrowing ordeal could wait. That would come. Soon enough. This violet dusk, these twinkling hours of nocturnal sanctuary, this night of nights was for tender devotion.

Closing fast, Ronan replied, "Treasonous words! You well know tis I that loves you most!"

"Nay, sire," she bellowed heated. "Tis I that loves you most!"

"Madame, nay! Tis I!"

"Nay, my lord! Tis I!"

Chunks of earth flew beneath the galloping steeds whilst Ellianna's mare held the lead and Ronan's stallion remained steady at her withers. Try as they may, the males could not outrun the females. Another race would surely be held on the morrow, just as Ellianna predicted. Despite the din of thundering hooves, orchestral music reached their ears. The wedding revelers, merry with feasting and dance, still frolicked within the palace. The royal court was ablaze with candlelight and laughter as the celebration continued under a setting sun.

Beneath the rising moon of a second chance, the prince and princess turned for the stables. Shouts of "Tis I! Tis I! Tis I!" sang from their dueling tongues and echoed over the rolling hillside. Immersed in their first lover's quarrel as husband and wife—friends for life—the newlyweds did not rein in their horses. Joining hands, they galloped knee to knee, ever expectant and fully blissful, rushing back to happily ever after.

Epilogue

Voices sent the chipmunks scurrying back to their dens.

"Did ya find it," hollered a boy. The lonely wait had him pacing.

"Heck, yeah," his friend yelled, swooping into view. His feet touched the ground in a rough landing. Running a few steps, he tripped to one knee but didn't go down entirely; he was too quick-footed for that. And his wings fanned out, slowing him up. Once he was steady on his feet, the wings folded flat down his back—out of sight.

"It was at that old fort, just like I thought." The mothboy whacked a corduroy sack on his leg, patting off dirt. "Stuffed in that rusty cannon." He tossed the treasure bag to his buddy. "Where'd it go?" He didn't see the caterpillar.

"I don't rightly know." The boy sounded surly. "Dang thing just up and disappeared."

"Darn it! Knew I took too long!" The mothboy kicked the blowball of a fluffy dandelion. Parachute seedlings took to the air. "But..." he admitted, "I think I kind of got lost."

"Nah...it's my fault. Think I kinda fell asleep. Only for a minute though, scouts honor! I been searchin, but best I can

figure a bird gobbled it up. Then I sorta got…distracted."
He acted real apologetic, even as he gagged on a giggle.

"What's so funny?" The mothboy asked.

His bud's smile turned guilty. Reaching inside the bib of
his overalls, he pulled out the distraction.

"I found more," he confessed, dropping the corduroy bag
and staring into the eyes of an easy target.

The mothboy shrieked and flew straight up, zipping
within the branches of a pine, turning just in time to catch a
hurled mushroom and chuck it back before his pal started
running. The boy screamed like a girl when it splattered the
top of his head.

"You better run," the mothboy shouted. "You're in for it
now!" From his vantage point, he spied a white-bomb
goldmine. Flying down, he snapped off as many heads as he
could line-up in the crook of his arm. When he peeked
around a tree, ready to fire, he saw no sign of the boy. Ever
so slowly, he crept out into the open.

"Incomin!"

A battle cry came from above. Before the mothboy could
duck, a mushroom hit him square in the stomach, dropping
him to his knees. He grunted as his armload of ammo rolled
away.

With the toe of his shoe wedged in the foothold of a rope
swing, his buddy leapt from a tree and zoomed past
squealing, "Direct hit!"

The boy swung up, up, up—just beneath the limbs—before swinging back and pelting his very best friend with a handful of fatties. The mothboy tucked into a tight ball as mushrooms exploded all around him. Jumping to his feet, he grabbed hold of the rope and pumped his wings, pushing the swing as high as it would go. He flew alongside—circling up and around, back and forth—soaring right next to his rope-swinging pal.

"Look at you," the mothboy yelled, accelerating through a spinning dive. "You're flying!"

"Look at me," his best friend shouted—full of life and laughter, "I'm flyin!"

"We're flying! We're flyin!"

They never did find that caterpillar. Before long, it was forgotten. Neither boy recalled the Lady. Or the loss. Or the resurrection. There were dreams (and the occasional nightmares) but they were not immediately shared. Their boisterous homecoming took place as if nothing had ever happened. So it was with all the children harmed by the troll's spell and flung to the trees. They too found their way home to the loving arms of their mothers and fathers—just in time for dinner.

As for the moss, it clings still—always and forevermore—in remembrance of an illustrious princess. If not for her valiant poise in the face of utter peril, the cursed days were meant to be infinite. The hex was cast for perpetuity. Its undoing unforeseen. But the power of truelove was invincible, proving Ellianna's staunch and ferocious guardian. Neither the miles of separation nor the threat of detection could stop her secret pilgrimages back to Ronan's gravesite—to touch and remember and weep—before vanishing into seamist and continuing the hunt. Her mind and body outfoxed the fiend and reclaimed what was stolen away. Reclaimed her prince and her purpose and her palace of scampering feet. The woods released their prisoners, allowing every interrupted life to thrive once more. The splendor of nature ascended to its revered and glorious place, permitting the moss to billow quietly, a tribute to *truelove* in honor of a princess—Ellianna the Avenger.

And as for the mothboy and his inquisitive friend, those two stamped that lowcountry woodland with the criss-crossing footprints of friendship. Adventures pushed them deeper into the forest where every day was etched with fantastical memories. Once they even rounded a bend and surprised a flat-headed troll digging for grubs. It bounded into the thorny underbrush before they could catch it.

Alert for the exceptional finds of that magical place, they grew more watchful in the woods and stayed together, on the lookout for things enticing and hidden, things concealed in the shadows. Those discoveries made their fingers tingle, filling them with insatiable excitement—one they could pluck from dirt and hold in the palm of their hand, never ever failing to satisfy their hearts' desire.

Mushroom wars and laughter were the priceless gems of their summer days. For the riches of life aren't granted by a wish; happiness requires no enchanted spell. The company of a friend is the pinnacle of wealth, and friendship—the most treasured of possessions—will always remain free for the takers!

 *SPLAT*

About the Author

TASSEL MOSS is Michelle's debut novel. Raised in a family of storytellers and athletes, Michelle is a graduate of the University of Missouri-Columbia, where she played Varsity Golf while earning her BA in Theater. She lives in Southern California with her family—including a terrier mutt, a min-pin imposter and a slithery, green snake.

About the Illustrator

Austin grew up with a paintbrush in one hand and the reins of a horse in the other. Her sculptures and paintings have shown in local galleries, upscale boutiques, and the U.S Capitol Building in Washington, DC. Her collaboration on *TASSEL MOSS* brings imaginative richness and delivers the essential element of any fairytale—intriguing artwork.

13789458R00159

Made in the USA
Charleston, SC
01 August 2012